Photo: Derek Speirs

Frank Connolly is an investigative journalist who has written extensively on current affairs and politics in Ireland over the past thirty years. His journalism contributed to the establishment of two judicial tribunals into planning and police corruption. He has worked with numerous Irish media organisations over the years and has been a regular contributor on radio and television news and current affairs programmes. A graduate of Trinity College Dublin, he has also lectured in journalism and regularly appears at book and cultural festivals and events to promote his work. He is currently Head of Communications at SIPTU. His previous books include *Tom Gilmartin: the Man who brought down a Taoiseach* and *NAMA-Land*, and he is the editor of *The Christy Moore Songbook*.

A CONSPIRACY OF LIES

FRANK CONNOLLY

MERCIER PRESS

MERCIER PRESS
Cork
www.mercierpress.ie

© Frank Connolly, 2019

ISBN: 978 1 78117 662 7

A CIP record for this title is available from the British Library

Printed and bound in the EU.

To Mary for our deep, enduring friendship and love, and for her invaluable guidance through this imaginary journey.

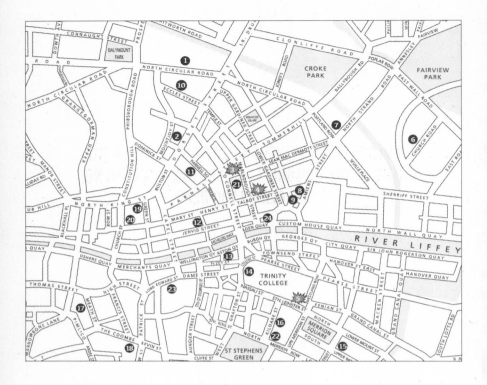

1. Mountjoy Jail
2. Dorset Street
3. Parnell Street car bomb
4. Talbot Street car bomb
5. South Leinster Street car bomb
6. East Wall
7. Humphrey's Pub
8. City Morgue
9. Store Street Garda Station
10. Mater Hospital
11. Granby Row
12. Jervis Street Hospital
13. Palace Bar
14. Trinity College
15. Holles Street Hospital
16. Leinster House
17. The Liberties
18. Fallon's Pub
19. Special Criminal Court
20. The Bridewell Garda Station
21. Gresham Hotel
22. Shelbourne Hotel
23. Dublin Castle
24. Liberty Hall

EVERYONE REMEMBERS WHERE THEY WERE AT THE
TIME OF THE BOMBINGS, EXCEPT THOSE TOO YOUNG,
TOO OLD OR TOO DEAD.

PROLOGUE

It is a warm, early summer's afternoon as three cars move slowly through the streets of Dublin. Each driver knows what to do. Find a good parking spot and disappear. On Parnell Street, a green car pulls up outside a garage just yards from the city's main thoroughfare. Its Northern Irish registration plates stand out. A tall, blond man emerges from the car and walks quickly away. He doesn't lock the door. Pulling a dark cap over his head he mingles with the bustling hordes heading for the train station in the evening rush hour. 'Soon they'll get a taste of what's been coming to them for a long time,' he says to himself. 'I hope the boys get away okay.'

SUMMER 1974

1

JOE

The bells of the church tower ring as I walk through the gates. It's warm out here, bright, noisy, full of people. The cars are lashing up and down the North Circular, heading for all the places people can go when they're not banged up. When it's safe, I cross to Berkeley Road and walk towards the cream-coloured box. I have to call the ma. Two pence in the slot. The house phone rings.

'Hello? Who's that? I can't hear you,' she answers.

I've forgotten how to use the thing. Press button A, for fuck's sake. The phone in the 'Joy's been broken for months.

'It's me, Ma. I'm out. On the street. Early release.'

'Joe, merciful hour. Are you alright? Are you coming home for tea? When did they let you go? And your sister about to drop.'

'I'm fine, Ma. Where is she?'

'Holles Street and due any minute.'

'I'll surprise her before I come home.'

'She'll like that and I'll have some steak for you, love.'

Crossing Dorset Street, I look up at the huge Guinness ad with the couple lying in flowers. I'm tempted to drop in somewhere for a pint, but it's too early. Besides, I can't go into the hospital smelling of gargle. Tricia wouldn't like that with her first baby on its way into the world. I pass the Garden of Remembrance on Parnell Square. Pity she's not in the Rotunda just around the corner. Where all the northsiders are born. I could see her there and still grab a pint or two before heading home.

There's no fucking buses. A few are parked up, empty, but none are moving. The busmen are on strike. Bus stops with no queues, on a Friday! Jesus, I'll just have to leg it to Holles Street.

Crossing into O'Connell Street, I pass Tom Clarke's old tobacco shop under the shadow of Parnell. A kid is pumping petrol into a grey Morris Minor at the garage in Parnell Street. Brown hair, early teens. Cars, double-parked, all shades and sizes, a guard directing traffic, a woman pushing a pram, fucking gorgeous. I spot my da's car pulling up at the garage, his olive-green Hillman. Then a tall, fair-haired man gets out. Mid-forties. Not my da. Northern reg: DIA. Didn't cop that. Anyway, Da's likely on the high stool in Nolans by now. First pint, browning black, and a chaser. Old bollox never came to visit me once. No mercy for the sinner.

I pick up speed down O'Connell Street. *Blazing Saddles* is on in the Savoy, Forte's is packed with people eating ice cream, there's a smell of cooking oil. I'd mill a bag of chips. No, Ma's steak is what I need. The Clery's clock says ten past five. Crowds are heading down Talbot Street for the trains, the paper boy says there's no end to the bus strike.

'Hurdle and Pressed – No buses for Dubs this weekend,' he shouts. Over the bridge. I wonder who's in the Palace Bar as I get the whiff of coffee from Bewley's.

I pass the imposing gates of Trinity College and follow its wall around to Nassau Street. There's a smell of freshly mown grass. Across the street, I notice a bunch of flowers outside a shop. Tricia will like them. I head over. A girl with blonde hair wearing a light yellow coat over a short skirt walks out as I enter the newsagent. She drops her pack of ten Carrolls into a small red handbag. Beautiful. About my age. She returns my gaping look with a shy smile and heads up the street, towards Merrion Square. I pay for the lilacs and tulips wrapped in coloured paper. Outside, I see her up the street, crossing towards the college wall.

Two big cracks erupt like thunder from the city centre.

Another almighty bang, much closer, and a ball of smoke. The ground shakes. I tumble onto the street, dropping the flowers and my kitbag on the footpath as I fall. Then, silence. People are shouting, pointing. Flames and smoke are rising from a car not far down the road. I pick myself up and run. I approach the burning blue car. Beside it is the girl in yellow, her leg almost torn away, her blonde hair covered in blood as she lies on the footpath, still gripping her red handbag. Pure terror in her pleading eyes. I take off my jacket, cover her near-severed leg. I kneel down, taking her hand. She looks at me and screams.

'My leg, please help me, please save me, please call my mammy.'

I gently raise her bloodied head.

'What's your name?' I ask.

'Carol ... My leg, I can't feel it.'

The handbag falls from her hand.

'Carol, you're badly injured. Try to stay awake. The ambulance is near. Can you hear the sirens?' She looks at me, her mouth opens, but no words come out. Her eyes close.

It seems like an age before the men with stretchers carefully lift her into the back of the white van.

'Do you know her?' a white coat asks.

'No. Her name is Carol though.'

'She's still breathing, just about,' he says.

I pick up her red bag and place it beside her on the stretcher. The mutilated body of another woman is lifted carefully from the footpath and put on board. I grab my jacket from the ground and follow the ambulance as it weaves its way slowly through the injured, shocked and helpless. On Lincoln Place it picks up speed and disappears into Westland Row.

As I turn back, a few guards are pushing people away from the bomb site, from the burning wreck, towards the modern office building on Clare Street. I hear the sound of cracking glass from above.

'Get them away from the fucking building before the windows come down,' I shout at one rookie as he and other guards herd the stunned onlookers into danger. He looks up and shouts at people to move away from the building. It's a miracle no one else is killed when the sheets of heavy glass crash to the footpath from four and five storeys above. It's fucking hell. The air is full of smoke and sirens blare across the city. My jacket and shirt are stained with Carol's blood. I don't go to Holles Street, just a few hundred yards down Merrion Square. I can hardly walk straight. I wander back towards town. I wait in line at a phone box to call my ma and tell her I'm all right. I don't tell her I've blood all over my shirt and I won't be going to see Tricia in this state. I hope she's all right, baby and all.

'Get out of there, Son, before the whole place is blown apart. The world's gone mad,' she says.

'I'll be home soon, Ma.'

I put the phone on the hook and break down. I've seen the aftermath of car bombs on the telly before, but I've never seen a dead body on the street. Not to mind holding the hand of a beautiful young woman in terrible pain. My head is reeling and my hands are shaking. I don't know what to do, where to go, or how to get there.

When I woke this morning I was in the safest place in Dublin. Safe if you discount the assortment of thieves, strokers, abusers, dealers and general no-good gangsters that share the corridors and cells of Mountjoy Jail. Not to mention the screws – peculiar and often dangerous specimens with almost as few scruples as the men under their care and control. My home for one year, three months and six days. For hash dealing. Nothing to see but the chimneys of the Mater, the odd pigeon and a soundtrack provided by freight trains, traffic and the odd ice-cream van on a summer evening.

I was stirred from my slumber by the loud hammering on the cell door.

'Heney. Get yourself up and ready. You're out of here today, you lucky bastard,' the Seagull shouted.

'We have to make room for some other scumbags,' was the explanation for my early release. It took a while for the paperwork to be sorted, so it was the afternoon before my cell door opened.

Seagull was at the gate with my release slip just after 4.30 p.m. I resisted the temptation to remind him of the nickname he had earned as a greedy bastard always on the look-out for money in exchange for the smokes, vodka, porn and hash he smuggles in for the unfortunates whose cash has helped fill the beer belly protruding from his size forty-fours. I just smiled as he sneered, 'Free at last, free at last.'

Into this fucking mess. I walk down Nassau Street to find a screen to tell me what the fuck's going on. Windows are cracked and smashed along the street and in the college library. As I round College Green, retracing my earlier steps to freedom, hoards of people are coming in my direction, some bloodied and in tears, all scared. On Westmoreland Street two young guards are telling people not to cross O'Connell Bridge. Some ignore them. I don't. In the Palace punters are crowded around the TV and the evening news. Pictures are coming in of three bomb sites, the dead and injured scattered on the streets and the absolute chaos of a city rocked by the unexpected.

Three car bombs exploded within minutes of each other around half five on Parnell Street, Talbot Street and South Leinster Street, the newsreader tells us. Over twenty dead, more sure to follow, hundreds injured, thousands shocked and terrified. All the bombs were planted on roads leading to the train stations on the day the buses are on strike. The pub is full of people crying, shouting at the TV, skulling pints and looking for answers. I see my mate, Donal, a struggling photo-journalist, camera round his neck, tears in his eyes. Just back from Talbot Street, he says. Blood-stained like myself. In shock.

'I saw a woman's head and someone's arm. There's blood pouring down the gutter outside Guiney's,' he tells me. I describe holding the hand of the beautiful young woman. Her yellow coat and red bag. Her leg hanging off. We hug and hold on. We're both sobbing like babies. Who did this, and why? I'm not long in the place when the images come through from a border town where another car bomb has killed a lot of innocents in a pub. The tears come again. The late edition of the *Press* carries the headline 'No end in sight for bus dispute'. The date on the masthead reads 17 May 1974. The first pint tastes bitter.

2

ANGIE

I'm on the East Wall Road when I hear a massive bang, then another, and a third, farther away. The aul one I'm talking to says it's the Germans back to bomb the North Strand. I laugh. She's nuts. But we can see smoke rising from the city centre, less than a mile away, and the scream of multiple sirens cuts through the normal sounds of the day. There must have been a bad accident, or worse.

I move on, going door to door collecting the pools money for the Central Remedial Clinic. Everyone I talk to is wondering what happened, but no one knows what's going on. I turn into Church Road and the man at the first house has the radio on. I can hear the reporter talking about three bombs exploding in the city centre, on Parnell and Talbot streets and near the Dáil. A dog barks. A lone magpie flutters from a pole.

One minute I'm doing the rounds for the CRC, the next I'm running down the street in a panic, shouting, 'My mam's looking for a pair of shoes for me on Talbot Street,' to no one in particular. I'm heading for the Black Widow's, the sweet shop run by the woman still in mourning for the husband lost at sea God knows where, and the only place nearby with a phone.

As I burst through the door, I shout, 'I need to call my Aunty Joan in Humphrey's. I have to find my mam. She goes there for a drink after the shopping. I need to know she's safe.'

The widow knows me and can see something is wrong. 'Go ahead, love. Do you need change for the phone?' I shake my head and dial the number of the lounge bar, my hand trembling.

My aunty tells me she's in the snug waiting for Mam to join her for a glass of stout on her way from town.

'Maggie's not here yet but I'm sure she's fine, Angie love,' she says. I can hear the worry in her voice and I don't believe her. It's well after six, the shops are closed and Mam's still not there. She should be on her way home to make the tea by now.

I play along anyway. 'Will you tell her to come home as soon as she gets there?'

'Of course, love, why don't you go on home and make sure she's not there already. After all that's happened she may have gone straight there. And if she is, let me know.'

I hang up and run back to our house, but there's no word or sign of her. I fear the worst. My ma always says I'm gifted, or cursed, depending on which way you look at it, with a sixth sense. I've a habit of expecting things to happen before they do. Bad things. The loony cycle, my ma calls it.

My da's in the sitting room watching the TV. He's trying to stay calm, so as not to worry me. I can see he's edgy and afraid, trying to keep his worst fears to himself.

'I'm going into town to find her, Da.'

'I don't see the point of that,' he says. 'Why don't you wait here, Angie, and I'll see if I can track her down? You check the neighbours and I'll go into town.'

We both know she won't be at the neighbours. Margaret Whelan is always home to make the tea, unless she says otherwise well in advance. He's trying to distract me because he doesn't want me to witness the chaos and carnage in the city centre that he's seen on the evening news. I grab my jacket. 'I'm going to town, Da.'

'I don't want her to come back to an empty house,' he mutters. He sees that he won't be able to stop me, though, so he gives in. 'Okay, I'll drive. We'll find her together,' he says, trying to smile, his courage restored.

Before we leave, I put the pools money away in a box in the kitchen. Mam'll kill me if the meagre investments of our already poor neighbours fall into the wrong hands.

We're not the only ones making for town. Streams of people are heading on foot to the city centre in a near-silent procession. The No. 53 isn't running due to the bus strike. Everyone shares the same bleak foreboding as we begin the search for mothers, daughters, sons, husbands and wives, not knowing whether they're dead or alive. Da picks up three of the sorry pilgrims, who pile into the back of our VW.

We go first to the city morgue on Store Street. Many have joined the queue there, hoping to rule out the worst. We do likewise. My da doesn't want me to go in. I insist.

'If you don't find her here try the hospitals. The injured were moved to Jervis Street and the Mater. You'll have to walk. The guards have blocked cars from the city centre,' says the matter-of-fact doorman as we enter. It's a scene of human wreckage and despair, the odour of death and antiseptic in a room where over a score of bodies in various states of disrepair have been laid on slabs hastily assembled to receive the unfortunate victims. We're confronted with the horrific remains of the day's atrocity: mangled body parts, blood-stained sheets and a bewildered team of medics trying to identify which limb goes with which torso. Mam is not among them, thank God, but the heartbreak and pain of the callously bereaved burrow their way into my already frantic mind. I recognise the faces of some who've found their loved ones dead and in pieces. I am close to throwing up and my eyes are glassy, blurred with tears. In contrast to the noise of the sirens, inside it is almost quiet, the only sound the muffled cries and whispered prayers of people as they find mothers, fathers, daughters and sons.

I walk past a table converted to a makeshift bed for the recently deceased, where a corpse is shrouded in dirty white linen. I stop when I hear a slight murmur from under the blood-stained sheet. The sheet twitches. A ray of sun through the window casts a sudden light into the room. My hands fly to my mouth. The body stirs again. It makes a loud, groaning sound.

'Help, it's alive,' I scream.

A woman in white rushes over. Whoever's underneath the sheet is trying to sit up. 'My good Lord,' she gasps. She recovers, lifts the blood-soaked sheet and finds a teenager, the top of his head sheared open, brown hair matted a rusty red, covered in blood, one ear hanging off, one eye open. There is no skin on the other side of his face. Just raw flesh, red, black and blue. His look of absolute agony penetrates my soul.

'This one should not be here,' the medic says, back in control. 'Over here, quickly.' The lad makes a high-pitched sound as he is shifted onto a makeshift stretcher by two shocked mortuary attendants.

I collapse into my father's arms. Five minutes and a splash of water on my face later, I walk outside gripping Da's left hand, weeping floods of tears.

'We'll have to check the hospitals,' he says, recalling the advice of the doorman.

'Where do I start?' I say, dismissing my da's reluctance to let me, or my hand, go.

'You shouldn't be walking around the town on your own. What if the bombers come back?' Da says.

'What if Ma is lying in the rubble somewhere?'

'Okay, I suppose we might find her sooner if we split up,' he says, a look of fear in his eyes, his hand still in mine. 'I'll go to Talbot Street. She said she was going to O'Neill's for your shoes. Then I'll try Jervis Street hospital. You head up to the Mater and then go straight home if you can't find her.'

Both of us are trying to remain calm, at least on the outside. He hugs me again and reluctantly lets me go.

He leaves his car parked by the morgue and we head our separate ways. I'm silently thankful he's gone to Talbot Street. I couldn't face it if we found bits of Mam or her clothes on the road.

The eyes of the boy Lazarus are still in my head as I stumble up the street. The ambulance with him inside races past me, sirens blaring, towards a place for the just-about living from one for the already dead.

In the Mater Hospital the injured are stretched on every surface, doctors and nurses calling out instructions and treating the crying, shocked and bleeding casualties. A girl not much older than me, in a white uniform stained with the residue of the evening's human traffic, asks me my mam's name, her age and what clothes she was wearing. She is calmly trying to match the names she has on a list of the admitted with distressed visitors searching for hope and resolution.

'Margaret Whelan, fifty-one, brown hair, a dark-green coat,' I say amid the scene of confusion and chaos.

'And you are?' the nurse asks.

'Angela, Angie, her daughter …'

She tells me to try and find a chair as it will take a while.

As darkness falls outside, the same nurse approaches me. She takes my arm gently and leads me up a flight of stairs, into a corridor and to Mam, lying on a trolley with white bandages across her eyes, sound asleep. Her handbag is lying across her chest. A page from her children's allowance book with her name and address is taped to her leg.

A young doctor appears and tells me that she was brought here from Talbot Street and she's been treated for injuries to her eyes, the seriousness of which he cannot determine without a specialist's opinion. All he can tell me is that both retinas are damaged. 'She appears otherwise intact,' he continues dispassionately, 'with some cuts and bruising to her head, face, arms, hands and legs. We have to monitor her for any possible internal damage that we have not been able to identify yet. You can see we're completely stretched and there's a long wait for X-ray.'

Anger and relief swell in my head in equal measure. That's my ma he's talking about in such cold terms. I'm thinking about the mental trauma that must go with being suddenly thrown into the air by an explosion only a few yards away as you are innocently walking to a shop to buy a pair of shoes for your daughter.

'She's lucky,' the young doctor continues, interrupting my thoughts as he completes his dry and formal assessment. He rushes off to tend to more urgent cases.

I join a queue for the public phone and call May Delaney, one of our neighbours.

'Tell my da I found her in the Mater. He should be home by now. Her eyes are hurt but otherwise she seems to be okay. They don't have the full picture yet. She's asleep and I haven't been able to talk to her. She's in St Brigid's ward,' I say.

'Oh, thank God. Don't worry, Angie, I'll tell your da, and do give your ma my best when she wakes up,' May says and hangs up.

I'm holding Mam's hand and begging her to get well, to go back to what she was before today. I curse the fact that she went shopping for me, for stupid shoes that I don't need but that she thinks will help me meet a nice fella and settle down. I told her I didn't want the shoes and refused to go looking, so she went to buy them herself. She's always rushing about doing things for other people. I wish she wasn't such a living saint, with her candles and beads, always praying for good things to happen instead of looking after herself. I curse myself for the row I had with her over the swanky shoes and dress she wants me to wear like a fucking peacock in heat for the debs. I told her I've no intention of going, let alone with some twit I don't even know or like. 'I want to go to college,' I shouted, 'not get tied to a kitchen sink.'

'You and your fancy notions,' Mam said. 'English litterture, for feck's sake ... excuse the French, God bless ... and Irish. Who the hell needs Irish nowadays? Well unless you want to become a teacher like Mary down the road, now that's a proper job. Students, up all night, like you'd be with that layabout brother of yours, listening to that hippie music. Blowing in the wind is right, that's about all it's good for.' She stopped, looked at me and melted, as she does. When she continued, her tone was softer.

'Ah well I suppose you're not so bad; at least you do your study and help around the house. But I'm going into town to get you those nice shoes, whether you like it or not.'

Before she left she issued some last words of warning. 'Mind that pool money, love. There are chancers and gangsters out there who wouldn't think twice about robbing a young one. This town has gone to the dogs.' Then she was gone.

As I sit by her side, I cry silently.

When she finally wakes up, my da is sitting on the chair beside her trolley, holding her bruised and bloodied hand.

'Your eyes, Margaret, your beautiful eyes,' he says. 'What have they done to you?'

Barney Whelan bursts into tears.

3
JOE

As the summer months bring their usual cocktail of sun and rain, we've not made much headway in deciding who bombed the living daylights out of the city back in May. By 'we' I mean the young, unemployed and otherwise occupied professionals, students and artists that make up my circle of friends and drinking buddies in the Palace and nearby watering holes. Some of us had a close shave that afternoon. It is a sombre memory, the shock replaced by a mix of sorrow and anger. My unexpected return from forced exile is all but forgotten. Anyway, we all know that I'm not exactly hard chaw criminal material, just a bungling college dropout with decent taste in music and an eye for good-looking women.

Donal has asked me more than once what I'm going to do next. He's one of the few who visited me in jail. Every now and then, after a few pints, he tells me again about the woman's head in Talbot Street and how the stressed-out news editor in the *Press* told him to fuck off when he offered some photos of the bomb site. I remind him about Carol and her yellow coat, her red bag and her cigarettes. Two women were killed on South Leinster Street. Neither is called Carol.

'She must have survived,' I say.

'Too swamped to be looking at amateur snaps, he told me,' Donal complains about the editor. 'And me fresh from the scene with original photos, gruesome stuff, heads, legs, gallons of blood and dozens of shoes scattered along the street. I got a picture of the two-year-old found wandering around after her folks were wiped out.'

'Maybe they were too shocking for the papers,' I say in an effort to console him. 'The images they did publish were gory enough – a whole family blown to bits on Parnell Street, body parts strewn everywhere.'

'There's no rhyme or reason to it all. How can blasting our town apart be a blow for Irish freedom?' he asks again.

'It was hardly the Provos bombing the biggest city in their own country,' I say.

'It doesn't stop them wrecking the second biggest, which they claim to own as well,' comes the response.

'The loyalists are sending us a message to keep our noses out of their little Orange state. That's why one bomb went off just a hundred and fifty yards from the Dáil,' says another barfly.

'Only 'cause the Brits let them,' the barman intervenes.

The May bombs were not followed by official days of mourning. The flags did not fly at half mast as they had after Bloody Sunday. It was left to their own to bury the dead. Days of funerals had followed across the country – many of the victims were from outside the city, some from farther afield. A young girl from Paris, a boy from Casalattico in Italy, unwitting martyrs in a foreign war. The government is blaming the IRA. Whether they did it or not, it's all their fault. Republicans are blaming the Brits and their loyalist friends. In the Palace we are still trying to make sense of it all.

'The UVF and other loyalists said they'd nothing to do with it, though Sammy Smyth from the UDA says we had it coming,' says Donal. The people say 'a plague on all your houses'. Then they choose to forget. Let sleeping dogs lie.

Life is returning to something close to normal since my release. I got the ma's steak, my sister had the baby, the da bought me a pint and said he was sorry he didn't visit me, but he couldn't bear the sight of me behind bars. He even gives me a hug. And he hopes I've learned my lesson. That was it. Through a friend of his in the catering trade I've got a job in a restaurant. It's called 'The Bistro'.

Da's done a lot for me over the years. We were never left wanting, me and my sister. He helped me through college though he didn't earn much as a foreman for the Corpo, and now he's got me work.

'Part-time, but it's a start,' he said. 'The owner is a bit of a gobshite, I'm told, but you need the work, so hold on to it.'

My hard-earned experience in the kitchen of the 'Joy will come in handy, although I wouldn't mention it in my CV. Not that I have a CV. I tell my new boss, Aidan Murphy, that I've worked in several kitchens in well-known establishments at home and abroad, mostly in London, and that's good enough for him. He doesn't expect much, and pays even less. Rent money. Free food. It helps cover the urgent necessities of life, like girls, music and drink, though not necessarily in that order. Not all of the time. At least it gets me out of bed in the morning.

Murphy is the sort of unpredictable guy who likes to keep his staff guessing as to his mood on any particular day. But this summer he has reason to be more manic than usual given that he is undergoing a revenue audit, that his attractive wife, Paula, is determined to spend the few meagre bank savings he thought he had managed to keep from her, and that the May bombings brought business to a halt for several weeks. They also cost him his commis chef, who returned home to the States before he found himself with a missing limb or, worse, in someone else's fight. So Murphy tells me, three weeks into the job.

When he overhears me during a tea break going on about who's responsible for the bombings, the various failures of the government and the police, and other sinister conspiracy theories, he loses it.

'Stick to making the fucking French onion soup instead of bullshitting like Danny the Red,' he tells me. 'You're getting on my wick with all this political crap. And I don't want to hear any more about that trade union stuff either.'

Murphy has a thing about unions. 'I don't mind unions once they know their place, but if I had a choice they'd be run out of town. It's enough to be screwed by the taxman without the fucking commie bastards from Liberty Hall trying to wreck my business,' he complains to his uncaring wife and anyone else in earshot.

What really bothers him, though, is that an extra layer of discretion is required in 'The Bistro' because it attracts a clientele of influential business and political big shots, whose custom can help make, or break, the aspirations of an eager and ambitious restaurateur like himself. During the one fifteen-minute daily break enjoyed by his staff he declares that 'no one is to discuss this bombing thing on the floor of the restaurant. There could be anyone, government ministers, judges, guards, the fucking newspaper people, God forbid, listening to you,' he warns, directing a long and searing gaze in my direction.

It seems that everyone and everything in the city has been shaken by the blasts one way or another. Everyone remembers where they were at the time of the bombings, except those too young, too old or too dead. But no one talks about them much. The instinctive and cautious reaction, as with the boss, is to shut up. Nothing to see here. Maybe that's for the best. I've enough on my plate without losing the only job I can get for speaking out loud concerning things I don't really have much of a clue about.

Besides, I've been in enough trouble, getting involved in things I should have stayed well away from. As an impoverished student I'd supplemented my income with an ill-advised bit of dabbling in the drug trade. I bought a quarter kilo of hash wholesale from Harry Steele, an old schoolmate in Crumlin and a rough diamond from the other side of the tracks. I broke the lump into smaller ten spots, making a not insignificant profit in the college bar at UCD at fairly minimum risk. I never carried more than a few, easy to discard packs of deals at any one time and was careful to avoid any unnecessary confrontations with drunks, idiots or guardians of the law, on campus or otherwise. It was to be my first and last foray into the hash business.

My fatal mistake was to fall victim to complacency, stupidity and greed, mainly the last two. Steelie dropped off a load at my gaff one evening and offered me £20 to keep it 'offside' for a few days. He said it was for 'the lads' – some of the crowd fighting for Ireland when they're not shooting each other. I barely thought twice about it. I never thought at all about the consequences of being caught in possession and charged with supply of a large quantity of Moroccan red concealed in a ceramic water jar.

I also didn't consider the motivation for Steelie's unexpected arrival at my house. It certainly wasn't for the love of any cause, as Steelie is first and foremost a 'me féiner'. His only real passion is motor bikes. He sold me my Honda for a tenner. The nifty fifty gets me around. Steelie's nickname sums him up, really. He has a bit of a name on the streets for hot-wiring Yamaha models, which are all the rage and get a good price on the black market. But times are tough and I should have guessed that he was mixing with the political hard chaws to supplement his crust.

Only the discovery a few days later by the police of a similar load of pottery full of dodgy stuff in Ringsend alerted me to the danger lurking in the coal heap in the garden shed. I quickly dumped the load in the nearby allotment plot of a recently deceased neighbour, whose garden shovel and fork had, helpfully, been abandoned in the wake of his premature departure.

'He won't be needing those where he's going,' commented an early riser as I returned from the moonlit burial of Steelie's ill-gotten gains with the implements.

'I thought I'd tidy up Eddie's plot, God rest him. May as well put his tools away in case someone else needs them,' I replied.

The two heavies who arrived at the front door two nights later were not, as I first feared, from the drug squad or Special Branch. It was worse than that. Ignoring the pleasantries, they bundled me into the living room of our terraced house and proceeded to interrogate me about Steelie, the hash and details of any recent trips I may have taken to Africa, Europe or any other exotic places.

'I haven't a fucking clue what you're talking about,' I protested as I looked down the barrel of a revolver.

'We know Steelie gave you stuff to mind. How do you think

we got here? He was keen to tell us everything after the accident with his left knee. We want to know who arranged the shipment from the 'Dam,' said the man with the gun.

'I told you, I don't know anything about it. He asked me to mind this fucking vase. That's all.'

'Where is it?'

'In the field out the back.'

I did not need to be told who I was dealing with to recognise that I could soon end up in the same queue at the pearly gates as the dead allotment owner. But they were more concerned about the circumstance and arrangement of the delivery than about losing it to the guards.

Lucky for me, at least one of the pair seemed to accept my negligible role in whatever dodgy deal was going down.

'Did Steelie mention anyone else involved at the other end?' the smart one asked.

'No one. I didn't even know it came from Holland until you told me.'

'What the fuck are you doing in the drugs business, anyway?' the same one said.

'I'm not,' I lied. 'Steelie asked me to do him a favour for 20 quid.'

'You're a lucky man. Now go out and get the fucking dope,' said the other as he put his weapon inside his trouser belt and took his eyes off my shaking knees.

'We'll be in touch,' the nicer one said with a smile as his comrade lugged the now-recovered vase, covered with an old blanket from the hot press, into the back of a van parked a couple of doors down.

A few days later, as I sat on a high stool in Nolans, the same one approached me.

'Well, Joe, how's she cutting today?'

'Alright, so far,' I said warily.

'We confirmed your story, but we also know that Steelie was giving you stuff to sell. We could put a stop to your canter, even get you fucked out of the college, or worse. But we're not inclined to do that. Instead, we want you to do us a favour, seeing as you're not afraid of taking a risk, once it's worth it.'

'What kind of favour?'

The man sat closer and explained that the drugs run had been a one-off venture by a former member of theirs living in Holland. He had used a secret route set up by the organisation to import guns and other weapons needed in their campaign for Irish freedom and a workers' republic.

'It's not the hash we're worried about. But the same bloke brought it in using our private courier service and that's not good for us or for him.'

'So why are you telling me?' I asked.

'Because we think you might help us. In return we'll ignore your little dealing operation in UCD. The movement is hard on drugs, but our members in the student union seem to have no problem with you.'

'I wonder why?' I said. A survival mechanism in my brain told me not to add, 'They're my best customers.'

A week later I'm standing at a phone booth near the entrance to the central station in Amsterdam wearing a light-blue jacket and carrying a copy of that day's *Financial Times*. My head is covered with a baseball cap, eyes with dark shades. Wrapped inside the paper is a large wad of English fifty-pound notes – twenty grand's worth. Across the street my new friend and anti-drugs crusader is sitting at a café with a young woman in red.

I've been told to wait for a man with unnaturally blond hair wearing a dark pinstripe suit and carrying a copy of today's *Wall Street Journal* to approach me. He is to ask a prearranged question and I'm to reply with the answer I've learned off by heart.

'Are you Steelie's cousin?'

'No, but I'm going out with his sister,' I say to the blond stranger with a Dublin accent.

I can't unload the *FT* quick enough and point blondie to the woman, now sitting alone in the coffee shop, to deliver his end of the bargain. I'm not told exactly what's going on, but it can only be a drugs deal. I don't want to know.

Steelie had agreed to set up the arrangement in return for a guarantee that his right knee, and probably his brain, would remain intact. I was chosen as I had a clean face, not recognisable to former revolutionaries turned drug pushers from Dublin. I reluctantly agreed to play my part, in return for a promise that my role in the vase episode and the hash-peddling business would not be disclosed to my family, college dean or anyone else in authority. I was also not averse to the offer of two hundred quid plus expenses for making the two-day trip. When it came down to it, though, I had little choice in the matter.

After the brief exchange I didn't wait to see or hear what happened next. I even avoided the temptation to score a nodge in the nearest hash house. I took the next train to the airport.

Back home, I saw the news coverage about an Irishman who had drowned after falling into a canal in the Dutch capital, 'a man previously known to the gardaí with criminal and republican connections and possibly linked to a gang of international drug dealers'.

I sipped my Guinness and decided, there and then, to never dabble in crime or politics, at least those of the risky variety. I'd keep up my small hash-dealing operation in college just to cover the money for pints, but that was it.

Although I remained on nodding terms with the local heavies, my brief role as an international conspirator was consigned to history. I didn't ask what really happened to the man in the 'Dam, and neither did anyone else apparently. I just hoped he didn't have a copy of the *Financial Times* with my prints on it in his house. The whole incident was soon forgotten among the piled-up victims of Ireland's various conflagrations, or so I thought. That is, until I got the early morning knock, had the house searched, was dragged into the Bridewell and shown a copy of my plane ticket from the 'Dam and a neatly transcribed statement from the nice revolutionary who turned out to be an informer for the Branch in his spare time. Or had recently been turned into one. And they found a few ten spots, all wrapped in tinfoil and ready for sale, under the saddle of my Honda 50. I pleaded guilty to possession with intent to supply, got sent down for two years and disappeared into the bowels of the 'Joy for what the judge described as the punishment I deserved for having the 'stupidity of a sorry young man driven by greed'.

Thus my college education and part-time dealing business came to an abrupt end and I embarked on my own journey of discovery in the University of Crime populated by the involuntary inmates in a volcanic melting pot of no-hopers, dangerous lunatics, clever grafters and, in some cases, very skilled and self-educated conmen. My daily concern was physical and mental survival, and to this end I willingly obliged any request from my fellow guests of the nation and our minders to carry out chores, including cooking, cleaning, writing and reading letters for the illiterate, and passing stolen goods. In fact anything short of providing the sexual services that were always in demand at a certain price. That I would not do.

I kept my head down and counted the days. I had no steady girl so only my ma, sister and a few close friends filled the occasional visit slots and kept me in touch with the outside world. My one prized possession was a forbidden short-wave radio which, deep into the night, wired me into another world, a universe of language, sounds and stories, and kept me sane. I got it from Seamus Russell, a cellmate who also left a few books behind when he departed almost as quietly as he arrived in the jail, halfway through my stretch.

Russell was one of dozens of republicans who landed in the jail as the row in the North seeped across the border. Except Russell was not housed with his political mates and did not engage in their loud and determined protests against prison uniforms, work or anything else that made them like the rest of us crims. He was doing time for drunk and disorderly and assault, after hitting a garda on the head with a bottle during a pub fight on Summerhill. Strange though, he didn't seem like a rowdy boozer. He kept his head down, working with me in the kitchen, and was polite, reserved and friendly with sinners and screws alike. Rollies were his only vice and for weeks I used some of my meagre allowance to supplement his supply of skins. He went through a lot of them, especially on Friday nights. That's when he wrote a letter to his faithful girlfriend, who visited every week for thirty minutes on a Saturday. Long letters scrawled in tiny writing on almost half a packet of cigarette papers stuck together, wrapped tightly and sealed in what he called a 'comm'. Passed with a kiss. Concealed communications in tiny print. He told me he didn't want the screws reading his personal stuff.

The night before Russell left the jail, time served, he told me that he knew I was set up rightly by my revolutionary friends over the Amsterdam caper and warned me to keep away from them.

'Not so bright for a college kid. You might pick up some fresh ideas from these,' he said as he placed the books and radio on my bed.

'See you down the road,' he smiled. 'And don't store them in here for a while.'

Twenty-four hours later, three of the head IRA honchos jumped into a stolen helicopter that landed in the prison yard and flew away to freedom, leaving behind a jail full of cheering convicts of all persuasions and none. Mine was the only cell in our wing to be torn apart in the subsequent searches. The Special Branch spent two hours grilling me about 'that bastard Russell', even though I told them I knew little or nothing about him. The men behind the wire in D-wing laughed and sang their way through the beatings.

It turned out that Seamie's girlfriend was also kissing comms with one of the men in the republican quarters. According to the angry screws, she probably hired and hijacked the chopper. Their problem was the police hadn't a clue who the girl was.

Once I'd retrieved them from a hiding spot among the vast array of pots and pans in the kitchen pantry, I consumed the books I'd inherited from the master escape planner. Stories of Irish history, politics and world revolution by household names I'd never given a blind curse about before. The radio provided a nocturnal escape into an exotic world far beyond the stifling confines of my cell and daily routine. That's how I survived my spell inside until my return to normal life with a bang in May.

***

By the end of the summer I've settled into a steady if boring routine. Suits me down to the ground. Most mornings on my way to work I pass the walls of Trinity. My mind returns to the injured woman on the road, the body parts of the young mother and someone else's daughter that were scattered across South Leinster Street just a hundred and fifty yards from parliament. Perhaps it's the history student in me, or the politics of reality I learned the hard way in the 'Joy, or just the plain feeling that I don't know the half of what's going on around me. I used to think that we control our own destiny. Now I'm not so sure. You can be walking down the street one minute, and lifeless or limbless the next. Who decides?

So I try to find out. I read everything I can about that day and use the generous facilities of the National Library to read up on who was killed, hurt and may be guilty. I find it hard to understand how the police investigation into the attacks could be wound up within three months.

According to Donal, when the Irish Home Affairs Minister met his British counterpart at the high security meeting in

Baldonnel in September, not a word was spoken about the bombings. It was all the talk in the newsroom of *The Irish Press*. For whatever reason, there's no appetite in government to take on the bombers or to ask the Brits what they know.

'Keeping their heads down in case the loyalists and their puppet masters in the shadows pay us another visit,' says Donal. Like me, he's still trying to make some sense of that day.

4

ANGIE

I'm staring out the bedroom window at the clothes waving from the line, blues, reds and whites, at Da's blooming flower patch, yellows, greens and purple, at a robin on the branch of our neighbour's small pear tree with a cat ready to pounce. Only a few weeks ago I was a political innocent starting the Leaving Cert. Now I'm trying to grapple with a world where people are blown to bits on their streets. Of course, I've seen it on the TV, scenes from Derry and Belfast and other places just a hundred miles up the road. But that seemed so far away, different people, distant lives. How fucking naive and stupid we all are.

Mam is home and resting, waiting for the appointment with the consultant which will determine the future prospects for her vision. Her eyes are still covered. She's settled down after weeks of pain, pills, tests and daily visits from the doctor. The X-rays didn't show any internal damage to her bones. But her bruises came in all colours and only hot baths and Radox seemed to help. And then there was the crying, day and night. The non-stop bawling and keening which erupted at the least expected moments. It's easing off, thank God. She's coming back to herself.

Since the exams finished I'm at home with her every day. My da hasn't got over the shock of it all and Mam's bad eyes, but he keeps himself busy doing his bread rounds, helping out with the credit union and fussing over her when he's in the house. He's not even fifty-five, but he's aged this past while. Still, he's relieved to have her alive and home, something he keeps repeating like a mantra – it seems to bring him some comfort, so I don't tell him to stop.

My brother Tony came back from London for a weekend to see the damage and couldn't leave fast enough. He doesn't handle trauma very well. When he heard her moaning with the pain and saw her helpless in the home she's ruled all our lives, he disappeared for hours and came back three sheets to the wind. She told him to go back to London.

'Get a decent job, love, and make something of yourself. Sure I'll be fine with Angie to look after me,' she said to help salve his guilt at leaving so soon.

I go downstairs and make her a cup of tea, for the tenth time today. For the twentieth, she asks me about the debs, and the shoes and the dress I'm going to wear. Once again, I say that the nice young barman from Humphrey's is going to bring me. I got shoes that looked like the ones she told me she was trying to buy in O'Neill's that day. She feels the beautiful blue and gold cotton dress I bought with the last children's allowance money she will ever get, now that I've turned eighteen. The tears soak her bandages as she touches every stitch and bow. She is sad she can't see it, but happy to be alive for my big night. I don't let on that me and my friend Terry have other plans for the debs night and they don't include dressing up like Maxi, Dick and Twink. Nicky the barman is happy to let on that he's my date for the occasion, as long as I go to the flicks with him some time. Fair deal. Although I'm going to have to get some photos taken in my debs gear.

Compared to me, Terry's a wild one, always has been. Laughed and joked her way through school, never did a tap and charmed everyone, parents, teachers, nuns and priests, along the way. Butter wouldn't melt in her mouth. Ignored the dress code, the smoking rules, homework, in fact anything required by the heavenly authorities to ensure a Christian girl's proper upbringing. She's going to be a hairdresser, so poetry, history and science mean nothing to her. Now she's engaged in the study of the modern male species and dragging me into her crazy plans. We're chalk and cheese and I can't survive without her. Not these past few months anyway.

***

On a warm day, with the end of summer approaching, I'm sitting in the kitchen with my da. He's finishing his lunch, ham sandwich and a cup of strong tea, listening to the good news and the bad. The good news is I've passed my Leaving with flying colours and have been offered a place to study English literature, history and Irish at Trinity College starting in September. The bad news is that he wants to know exactly what job I'm going to get after all this 'highfalutin' stuff.

'If you tell me you're going to end up in the bank or a hospital as a nurse, something you can hang your hat on, I'll beg, borrow or steal the money for you. Irish and English is fine if you're going to teach it, but look where history got us. Bombing and shooting all over the country and politicians filling their pockets while the poor go hungry and idle, for Christ's sake. I'm not paying for my young one to be hanging around with hippies protesting over this, that and the other, not able to do a hard day's work.'

'But Da, that's what college is about. And you never know, I could end up as a teacher. First I have to learn about the world, try and find my place in it, broaden my sum of knowledge. You're always saying I should read everything I can. Look at your bookshelf. You're always going on about Yeats and O'Casey. What's wrong with me learning about that stuff?'

The look on his face tells me I'm not making much headway. He doesn't see the point in learning unless it's for a definite career with prospects and a pension.

'I'm going back to work, to the job that pays for food on the table and the roof over your head. If you can tell me what decent job you'll get after three or four years of "learning about that stuff", I'll pay your fees. If not, you can sing for your supper, young lady.'

He slams the door as he leaves. Gentle Barney Whelan isn't so soft anymore. He hasn't been the same since Mam's accident. The man who introduced us to galleries and libraries as children, to the Dublin mountains and the Wicklow hills, where he personally knew every branch and bird, is gone. The bombings shook him to the core and seemed to throw his world off its natural axis. Of course it doesn't help that my brother dropped out of college and legged it to London to get stoned or laid, or both, all paid for by the British social welfare system. Dublin was too small for Tony, too parochial and backward, he says, church-ridden and run by well-mannered thugs. Brendan Behan and Oscar Wilde were more his type, good sounds and a squat in London his nirvana.

I'd usually talk to my mam about my worries, but she's recuperating from surgery to her eyes. Her vision is gone completely in one and she can barely see through the other – the doctors are worried she might lose her sight entirely. So the debate about my future plans to be a scholar takes place with my hardened father instead. As he watches my mam stumbling around, trying to regain the control she had long enjoyed over all matters domestic, I can see that he's angry, bitter and helpless with no one to blame. And she won't let him help. Tells him to stop fussing over her. She has to regain her rightful position as the homemaker. She's determined to overcome her injury and, as she tells herself and anyone who asks, there are many who are a lot worse off.

'Look at all the other poor creatures, losing their mammies and children, and people walking around with only one leg to stand on,' she keeps repeating.

Dad is afraid, for her, for me, for everyone. I know this is why he is insisting that I should find safe and secure employment, permanent and pensionable, while I wait for the man who will provide me with security and my own nest, but that's not what I want.

'That's not good enough for me,' I say to the kettle when he's gone. 'I'm in no mood to find Mr Perfect and spend my life cleaning his dishes, making his dinner and washing his clothes. I want more. I'll just have to make my own money and pay for college myself.'

Mam is not one bit happy when I break the news that I won't be accepting the offer of a college place this year. Her earlier reservations about literature and learning have gone out the window with my Leaving results and her condition. All she seems concerned about now is that I'm happy.

'When your father hears about this he'll have a fit. Sure he's proud as punch that his girl has been accepted by Trinity

College, of all places. All he's trying to do is make sure you're not going to waste your best years on parties and protests that block up the streets, disrupting people who are only trying to do an honest day's work. Look at your brother sitting around in a London hovel going nowhere fast. Sure your father's told the lads at work that you've got a college place. What's he going to tell them now, or the neighbours for that matter, forever asking about your future as if theirs depends on it too?'

'I'm going to sign on and look for work and then I'll pay my own way next year. I'm going out of my mind in this house. I'm sorry, Mam, but I need a break from all this.' I cry aloud for the first time in ages and we sob together, bringing all the pain and anxiety of the summer months to the surface of our ruined lives.

'Sure your da's not himself,' Mam says when we pull ourselves together. 'He doesn't show it very much but he's very proud of you. He wants you to achieve what we couldn't have. Don't mind what he says sometimes. He wants you to go to college and be happy. And where would I have been without you these past few months, with Barney wrapping his guilt and fear around him like the sliced pans in the shelves of his van, and Tony across the water.' We share a laugh.

Tony has tried to convince me to join him in his misadventures. Him and thousands of others seeking jobs and freedom in 'the motherland'. 'You should come over, Sis. You'll go bonkers at home with Da doing your head in about your prospects. Life is cool over there. You can have some fun before you go to college,' he said on the last day of his trip over in June.

'Why would I want to sit around in a London squat, stoned out of my tree, worrying where the next hit is going to come from when I'm hoping to go to college and change my life?' I'd replied. 'Besides, I can't leave Mam. She's trying her best to get back to normal, but she loses her balance and has a head that constantly aches unless she lies down. Who's going to look after her while we're living the high life in your crummy little flat in Kilburn or wherever it is?'

As he left to catch the ferry from the North Wall, I told him I'd try to get over for a weekend soon, but there's little hope of that on my tiny savings. Besides, I'm back on track to start college in the autumn.

I don't know if my mam talks him around, or if he is moved by my determination to get a job and pay to do the course I want in college, but over the next few days my da changes, his mood is better and he drops his irrational views about the subjects I've chosen to study. Although he agrees to help me pay for college, I think it's still a good idea to get a job. After all, I can't expect him to pay for everything or to fund the social life I'll have when I get to Trinity.

I spent the weeks before the exam results doing domestic chores and helping Mam learn to renegotiate the geography of our small home. Moving things out of her way and discreetly introducing a regime that makes it easier for a woman blinded in one eye and almost sightless in the other to find what she needs in the core of her existence, the kitchen.

Now, with the help of friendly neighbours and relatives, I take a little time to get out and about to look for part-time work. I hand my somewhat sparse curriculum vitae into shops, restaurants and hotels in the city centre. I go back to collecting the pools, and enjoy the odd night out.

I arrange to meet Terry to celebrate our escape from the slavery of school and exams. We're heading for a music venue near Dorset Street where the sounds, according to Tony at least, are as close as you can get to some of the better venues in London for blues and decent rock and roll. Before I leave the house, Da slips me a fiver to make up for all the fuss and anxiety.

'You're a good girl, Angie. I'm so proud of you. And I'll support you whatever you want to do. Don't ever forget that,' he says, dropping the note in my coat pocket as I put the final touches to my hair at the hall mirror. As close to a declaration of peace as he can make.

The Music Place is not the cleanest, but the sounds from the record player are cool. Sitting in what passes for a lounge, we order two pints of Guinness. This prompts an older man leaning on the bar in front of a half-empty glass, evidently with quite a number of full ones already in him, to wonder what the world is coming to.

'Women drinking pints!' he mutters.

We laugh and Terry makes a face at him.

'Not as many as you, Fatso,' she mouths when he turns his back on us.

When I go to order a second round, there's a familiar face behind the bar. It's the prat of a doctor from the hospital. When he turns to take my order he looks closely at me. I can almost feel his eyes inside my tartan shirt and jeans.

'I know you from somewhere,' he says.

'I met you the day of the bombings, in the hospital, with my mam,' I say.

'I remember now. How's your mother? Jesus, but she had an

awful shock. What's the latest with her eyes? I know it could have been worse but still … what can I get you?'

I'm taken aback. This is the same man who could barely find the time to speak to me that night in the hospital, never mind asking my name or whether I was okay. Now he's a polite and sort of handsome bloke, acting like a normal northsider, not like the jumped-up Christiaan Barnard I came across that awful night.

'She's lost the sight in one eye and we are waiting for news on the other. She has to see the consultant again and there's a bit of a queue in the Eye and Ear. So we don't know yet what the story is, whether it can be saved,' I say.

'If I can do anything, let me know. I'm just a junior doctor, in training,' he says. 'At the very bottom of the medical food chain. I'm more likely to be counting bandages or changing bed pans than deciding the waiting-list priorities. But I'll do what I can to help your mam. Maybe I can find out when she can get an appointment. You'll need to give me some details, though,' he says in a soft voice.

He goes on to explain his behaviour in the Mater the first night we met. Says he was under strict instructions to deal with patients and their relatives as promptly and professionally as possible, given the overwhelming demands placed on nursing and other medical staff.

'I hope I wasn't too brisk with you … sorry I don't remember your name. It was a mad night, terrible.'

That's how I get a half apology and he gets my name, my mam's and our address.

'I'm Brian. The music starts in ten minutes, Angie,' he says with a smile. It turns out he runs the bar upstairs where the live music is.

Tonight's performers are The Red Peters Band, fronted by a hairy man with a ginger beard who sings the blues like a Harlem native. According to the friendly doctor he's a taxman in his spare time.

'It takes all sorts,' he says.

The lead guitarist is giving it loads to great roars and whistles from the fans. He's tripping out on his own music.

When the gig finally ends, we tell 'Doctor Zhivago', as Terry calls him, that we'll be back, and fall out fairly locked, happy and in time for the last bus.

***

The next afternoon, as I arrive back from my job hunt, I run into our local curate, Father Bennett, as he closes our front door. He's a bit of a creeping Jesus, but likeable, and has been good to Mam ever since her accident. A young guy, he's not long back from the missions, and doesn't have the reputation some priests do for delving into the secret places of their young followers that have little to do with God or salvation. Not yet anyway.

I decided long ago that I wanted nothing to do with the Church, given the harsh treatment me and my friends were given by a small number of genuinely psychopathic and cruel nuns at school.

'Hi, Angie. I haven't seen you at Mass lately,' Father Bennett smiles. 'But then I know you are doing God's work and that's what matters. Where would your mother be without you?'

Before I know it he starts on about how great it is that

I'm going to university, the first from the street, possibly even the whole area, to do so, and what joy and high regard it will bestow on the entire family. He's clearly been hearing my mam's confession.

'I'm glad your dad came around. He only wants the best for you, though you might not think it, Angie. He's very proud of you, they both are. Sure you could end up a teacher or even a professor some day and there'd be no looking back then,' he says.

'Thank you, Father,' I say.

Three days later the envelope with the blue Dublin University logo confirming my acceptance arrives in the door. I quickly tear up my mental notebook with the alternative plans I had considered and look forward to a few weeks equipping myself for the college course with book lists, notepads, some new clothes and other items essential for a Fresher. Da helps me with the few quid for all I need. Harmony of sorts is restored to the Whelan household.

But I can't get rid of the thick knot in the pit of my stomach that steadily grows as the day approaches when I have to walk through the intimidating wooden front gates of Trinity as an actual student. I'm beginning to seriously doubt my ability to engage normally with the sophisticated strangers I'm about to encounter.

'They'll all have a good laugh at me,' I tell Terry over a pint.

'Bleedin' snobs the lot of them,' she says. 'Any problems and I'll sort the feckers out.'

SPRING 1975

5

JOE

On my break, I grab one of the newspapers the boss has introduced as a service to customers dropping in for a morning snack.

'The first bistro in Ireland to provide *The Irish Times* and *The Guardian* for our dedicated and educated clientele,' he boasts, 'along with filtered coffee and croissants. Yes croissants, no less. Like fucking Paris,' as he grabs another from the tray.

Peter Ivers, our new head chef, has introduced the more exotic cuisine, which he learned how to make during the six months or year that he served his apprenticeship in France, including how to bake a croissant. I'm lashing butter and jam onto one as I open *The Guardian* for my daily ration of bad news. The world seems to go from one disaster to another.

Ivers is not big on current or international affairs, but at least he's prepared to listen and learn when he isn't barking orders to the kitchen and waiting staff. He takes his job and his position very seriously.

'The Chilean poet Pablo Neruda didn't die of cancer. His family says he was killed by that bastard Pinochet,' I declare from my newsreading perch.

'I'm sorry to hear that. Now could you get a move on? There's a mountain of veggies to get through,' replies the chef.

Business has been helped by a positive review in the *Independent*, which for some reason chose the restaurant as the subject of its first-ever, and exclusive, column dedicated to fine dining. The four out of five stars might well be the result of the copious amounts of French Beaujolais which the boss poured down the lavish palate of the well-endowed food critic and her equally corpulent guest. It helped to wash down the sizeable portion of pepper steak with chips, or French-fried potatoes as it describes them on the menu, for the man, and a baked fish stew with mash and a white wine sauce for her ladyness. We watched Murphy's exercise in pure obsequiousness with a mixture of amusement and embarrassment, but were pleased with ourselves when her review recognised the quality of both the cooking and the service. It also made the boss happy for at least one afternoon and he carefully posted the review at the nearest point to the entrance where it would be visible to the passing public, as well as to his customers. What it also meant was that a table at The Bistro is now one of the most sought-after in town, day or night.

Due to the demand on our time and talents, it has been decided that fresh staff are required and Ivers, with my assistance, has been going through the recent job applications to identify suitable cooks, waiters, dishwashers and other help. After a round of interviews by the boss and his wife, a few positions are filled before Murphy panics at the prospect of surrendering a hefty slice of his profits to meet his substantial and mounting outlays.

'Another cross to bear for people like me,' he complains to all and sundry, 'the only ones keeping the fucking country from bankruptcy.'

One dry but chilly morning in early February, a dark-haired vision walks through the kitchen door wearing the new waitress uniform of black slacks and white blouse. Slim, round face, very long black hair, juicy red lips, fucking beautiful smile, piercing, blue-green eyes.

'Holy shit, Peter,' I say, 'who's that?'

'That's for me to know and you to find out,' he says, before relenting. 'Angela Whelan. Part-time.'

She's some beauty, I think. But she has an air about her. She's not about to engage in any banter with a waster like me.

'Out of your league,' he says, reading my thoughts. 'Trinity student. Knows a bit about arts and culture. Probably doesn't know one end of a carrot from another. And why should she? Only passing through this kip, while we're in it for the long haul. Anyway, you look like you were dragged through a hedge backwards,' the chef adds for good measure. 'And if you don't mind, from now on my name is Pierre.'

Over the next few days and weeks I somehow manage to spend an extra few seconds combing my tangled hair in the morning, shaving the scrawny patch on my chin, and occasionally thinking about the smell and state of the clothes I throw on. Guinness and tobacco. I even have a weekly bath, when the water is hot enough, and spend an hour or two in the new launderette down the road. I've forgotten what it feels like to be fresh and cleaned up.

After I got my first pay packet, I moved out of home and into a bedsit in the Liberties, close to a couple of mates who work in the brewery. It didn't take long. All I own is my bike, records and books, and the few bedclothes my ma could spare. Steaks and spuds, rashers and eggs from The Bistro are my staples, rescued from the clutches of the binman. I'm fed at work and I've enough at home for my days off.

The new bird doesn't talk much, to me at any rate. A polite hello and 'Can you pass me the butter, please?' at morning break, formal exchanges as plates pass from the kitchen to the tables through her delicate but steady hands. 'See you tomorrow,' as she carefully hangs up her apron at shift's end. Inscrutable, intriguing, incredible.

'*Amárach*, Angela,' I stutter.

'Call me Angie, everyone does.'

'I'm Joe,' I say.

'I know.'

By her third week she is adept at taking orders, setting tables, explaining the flavours of the limited selection of Beaujolais and Chardonnays on offer, and generally doing what waitresses are expected to do for the minimum hourly rate. She gets on well with the other staff and the owners. Pierre likes her. I may as well not exist. My attempts at humour go down like a lead balloon.

On a wet Monday afternoon, as we eat our soup and sandwich lunch, I try to start a conversation. I ask her how she likes the job. Then, before she gets a chance to answer, I tell her that it's one of the better places in the town, but there's no union in the shop so staff don't enjoy perks like overtime, holidays and other rewards that some hotel and other workers get.

'The boss says he has no intention of letting "a bunch of commies from Liberty Hall wreck my business,"' I say in my best Dalkey drawl.

I laugh at my take on Murphy's accent and arrogance. She doesn't. I crawl back under my rock.

6

LEINSTER HOUSE

In his office on the fifth floor of Leinster House the Fianna Fáil spokesperson for Home Affairs, Bob Clarke, and his political and public relations adviser, Myles Fenton, are planning their future. It's clear to both that the honeymoon enjoyed by the National Coalition of Fine Gael and Labour is well and truly over. An international oil crisis eight months into office saw to that.

Since then, it's been all downhill for their political opponents, with one disaster after another. The conflict in the North has gone from bad to worse, the IRA is wreaking havoc, death and destruction from Belfast to Birmingham, crime and poverty are on the rise, and Ireland has the highest taxes and inflation in the EEC. And, of course, there were the bombings in Dublin and Monaghan.

'Jesus, after sixteen years of uninterrupted rule, we're only out of office for two and the people are pleading with us to come back,' says Clarke.

'Nothing like a bunch of idiots and intellectuals to make a hames of it,' agrees Fenton.

'You know, if we could only fix things in our own party, we'd be back in power in no time,' says Clarke.

Clarke is an ambitious man. He's just been given a front-bench position and although he would have preferred an economic or foreign affairs role, he'll settle for the Home Affairs brief, for now at least. It's a senior post but delicate, and he has to tread a fine line between republican flag-waving and over-heating the pot of nationalist fervour which could engulf the entire island in a futile and dangerous conflagration.

'My father always warned me that the biggest danger to Fianna Fáil is the greedy bastards who jump on the bandwagon when they realise power means money. But now if you don't encourage them, they'll trample you in their rush to find someone who will,' says Clarke.

'Which means we have to be astute in our dealings, in our strategy,' says Fenton. 'Just because you are in Home Affairs doesn't mean you can't pursue other interests. After all, who knows what might happen in the future. We need to continue to build on the connections we've made in business over the past two years and we should nurture the relationships we have … for the good of the country, of course.'

'You're right, Myles. Between my political nous and your back-room dealings, we've done well, but we can't rest on our laurels. I'll need to make friends and influence all kinds of people if I want to continue climbing up the ladder.'

'Just like you're doing with that young reporter from the Indo? I hear your off-the-record briefings are getting later and later,' laughs Fenton.

'She's a bit of a handful, but once I feed her enough, she's happy to make it worth my while. And Jesus, a man has to get some light relief.'

'Spokesman for Home Affairs. Such irony,' says Fenton.

No less ambitious than his boss, Fenton has carved out a repu-tation as a talented election organiser, with his clever handling of inquisitive and intrusive press people, and close attention to the time and tide of internal party dynamics. With an accent and attitude honed in private boarding school and polished during post-graduate studies in Cambridge, Clarke has found that his advisor also has a useful knack for fostering important and potentially valuable political contacts in London.

'Let's face it, we'll need all the friends we can muster when we do *get back into power. God only knows what we'll be facing, given that the North's getting out of hand and the present crowd has no sense of how to deal with either the Brits or the Provos, not to mind the economy,' says Clarke.*

'Speaking of the North, I'm hoping we can build solid relations with the British embassy people here. I've already made a call to someone I trust in Ballsbridge,' says Fenton.

'That'll be a start, and try to set up the meeting with the Americans as well. Just because I've changed hats from my foreign affairs brief doesn't mean we can't keep in touch. I've heard that the Labour Party is planning to nationalise the oil and gas deposits and the Yanks aren't one bit happy.'

'Another oil crisis. Just what we need to give them a fright,' laughs Fenton.

'It's not funny,' says Clarke. 'I've a serious problem on my hands if that crazy plan goes ahead. We made commitments that we'll be more flexible than the other shower when we get back into office. Promises I can't break, but if this government makes a mess it could be a real problem. There's no point in having riches under the continental shelf if no one can afford to dig them out.'

'I'll get on to it straight away,' Fenton says, rising to leave. 'But we'll need to keep any meetings away from this place. You can't take a piss without someone noticing. Have you ever been to The Bistro?'

7

ANGIE

The job is handy, close to the college and pays me enough to cover my weekly costs with a few quid left over for Mam. It's certainly better than the barmaid's job I was doing at weekends in Humphrey's. I couldn't bear the lingering smell of smoke, stout and strong whiskey on me all week. The owners and staff in the restaurant are nice, though Joe, the commis chef, seems a bit full of himself. Not long after I started he began making a childish and not very funny play on my name every time I arrived in to work on my bicycle.

'So how's Angie Wheelin' today?'

Him and his nifty fifty Honda. Thinks he's Easy Rider. When I didn't laugh, or even smile, he soon gave up.

Most of the customers are friendly, though a few are ignorant and pompous. They represent the most privileged of Dublin's business and political elite. I learn not to be intimidated by those who believe that hot, freshly made food should be served up almost before the order is written down. Or those who get louder and more arrogant in direct proportion to the number of bottles of wine they've consumed. I have my limits, though. I won't indulge, even for a second, any man who thinks he's entitled to touch my arse when I pass his table or lean over to collect dirty plates and glasses.

The boss reluctantly concedes that I was right to bawl out one plump solicitor who groped me during my first week. He's not so sure, however, that 'accidentally' spilling a cold cup of coffee over his silk shirt was a justified response to his rude and misogynistic behaviour.

It was not the first time that the loudmouthed arsehole had done it. This time I reacted without even thinking of the consequences. My fierce reaction was the talk of the floor and kitchen for a day or two. Little did they know how terrified I was of the repercussions. I was lucky the boss's wife saw what happened and agreed that the lout's behaviour was unacceptable. She even had a laugh about it.

***

It's Friday afternoon in late spring and the restaurant is full of slow lunchers finishing off the business week in style. Two middle-aged men are engrossed in what seems, from their expressions, to be a not too friendly conversation. Even when I'm up close I can't hear what they're saying as they're talking in hushed tones. Anyway, it's not appropriate for a waitress to eavesdrop on her customers.

They've finished their meal, but they're not showing any signs of leaving. The discussion continues over a second bottle of wine ordered by the one with a noticeably upper-class English accent. The second man I've seen before in The Bistro, and I know from the other girls that he's some kind of advisor to the politicians who frequent the place. As a regular, he's on first-name terms with the boss. Paula Murphy also knows him, but she doesn't seem too pleased with the man. When he came in, they barely nodded to each other, and she keeps her distance from the table.

The advisor becomes visibly agitated when the guy with the marbles in his mouth pulls out a fountain pen and starts to scrawl something on the piece of red tissue paper that passes for our napkins. He pushes the paper across to the advisor, who looks shocked.

As I pass them to retrieve another customer's coat from the cloakroom in the back, I hear the Englishman say, 'That's something else for you and your man to chew on. We know everything about him and his little games, so make sure he gets the message. I expect I'll be hearing from you shortly.'

He gulps down the rest of his wine and stands. 'You'll deal with the bill, Fenton, won't you?' Without waiting for a reply he turns to leave.

The man called Fenton remains seated, glaring at him as he walks away. An unfinished glass of red wine sits on the table in front of him, almost the same colour as his cheeks. He looks at the wine, then orders a Scotch. I leave the bill on the table with the glass of whisky. He covers it with three tenners. He's not in great shape as he struggles to get up from the table. I help him put on his coat and he stumbles as he tries to retrieve some change from his trouser pocket. Some of it drops on the floor which he gathers up clumsily and presses into my hand. The crumpled napkin, which fell out of his pocket with the coins, is left lying on the ground. He ignores it.

'Can I call you a taxi?' I say, as I help to steady him.

'No, thanks, I'm only going up the road. You're a sweet girl, you know, and friendly. Not like some others I could mention in here,' he says looking around the now near-empty restaurant, before swaying uncertainly towards the door. I watch him go, then turn to clear up the debris of the two-hour lunch. I pick up the dirty napkin from the floor, throw it on top of the pile of dishes, glasses, cups, saucers and overflowing ashtray, and carry the heaped tray into the kitchen.

I'm about to empty the rubbish into the bin when I feel Joe watching me. As I turn, he looks away as if he is trying to avoid me catching him at it. I haven't spoken much to him, but we've been friendly enough since he got over his weak attempts to make jokes at my expense and he seems to take a genuine interest in me. Besides, he's cute in a boyish kind of way, with a nice smile.

I cut him some slack. I tell him what I've just witnessed at the restaurant table. 'Two guys were having a row in there.'

'Who?'

'You know your man who hangs around with the big politicians?' I reply.

'Fenton? He comes here quite a bit. Fancies himself as a political know-all. He's a handler for Fianna Fáil.'

'Him and some English guy. The English guy wrote something on this napkin that seemed to rattle him.'

'What does it say?'

'I don't know, I didn't want the boss catching me looking at a customer's private business.'

Curiosity gets the better of Joe. He retrieves the napkin gingerly from the pile of dirty dishes and uncrumples it. Clearly written are six lines:

Bob Clarke,
100k,
Bank of Bermuda deps,
to Bond Street,
London to Dublin,
Canada oil and gas.

Joe lets out a low whistle. 'If I'm not mistaken, this looks like a reference to deposits of money travelling between Bermuda, London and Dublin.'

'How do you know?'

'It's the only conclusion that anyone with basic intelligence would gather from the information scrawled here.'

I ignore the implied insult and say, 'The advisor man was not one bit happy about what the other bloke said to him before he stormed off.'

'Whatever it's about, it seems that bastard Bob Clarke is up to his neck in it,' he says.

'Who's he?' I ask.

'A top man in Fianna Fáil. Ambitious fucker. Him and Fenton are as thick as thieves when they're in here, which they are, a lot. Trust me, you won't like him.'

The door opens and the boss's wife walks in. She doesn't notice Joe slipping the napkin into the pocket of his not-so-white apron rather than the bin, where it belongs. She looks at us and wonders aloud whether anyone is 'actually working in this place anymore?' As she leaves, Joe gives me a wink. We've shared a secret, but I haven't a clue what its significance is. All I know is that my new friend has a grasp of things way above my pay grade. It seems he's not just a pretty face. And I don't think he meant to insult me.

8

ANGIE

Over the last few weeks, I've settled into a steady regime at The Bistro. I've even got used to Joe Heney. I've started to enjoy the brief coffee breaks when he imparts some of the news he has gleaned from the morning papers, and his analysis of it, which takes somewhat longer. I realise that what I initially took for arrogance is simply confidence. He likes sharing the fragments of knowledge he picks up on any particular day in the hope of inspiring some intelligent conversation that might satisfy his insatiable curiosity about places, events and people, especially people. It helps that he's lean, good-looking and has a sense of humour, even if it takes a while to get used to. He's got long hair, good teeth and deep-blue eyes. We even occasionally talk about the red napkin and what it was all about, but mostly we just have a laugh. I think we're friends.

One day, over lunch, he asks me to join him for a drink after work. I hesitate for a moment and then agree. We settle into the Palace at seven. It's my first time in the place and the portraits of writers, poets and musicians chime with my ongoing exploration of literature within the walls of Trinity, just around the corner. Joe seems to know half the people in here, as well as the barmen.

'The Friday evening pint is one of the rituals of the working life of probably every city under the sun,' Joe reckons.

'Is it now?' I ask. 'For men or women?'

'Ah, I can see you're a bit of a feminist. I liked the way you took on that fat solicitor. There's no flies on you,' he says.

'I don't like anyone touching me up,' I say. 'You don't have to be a feminist to feel like that.'

Some of his friends are here, having clearly skipped the last hour at work to get on the high stool early. They've been downing pints for a while, by the look of things. Joe couldn't be more of a gentleman, refusing to let me buy a round until I insist. Then I say I've had enough, up early, study to do, stuff like that. I know he's keen on me, the way he looks, touches and talks to me, eventually relaxing into conversation. I'm not sure I'm ready for that kind of relationship.

'You don't need to walk me to the door. I know my way home,' I say as I polish off my last sup of stout. 'I'm off this weekend, so I'll see you Monday.' I walk away and feel him watching as I leave. I don't look back.

***

As the deadlines for end-of-term assignments and exams approach, I'm flat out. As soon as I've done some study, as long as I don't have to do a shift in The Bistro, I head home to help Mam. In this way, and without us being quite aware of it, we've become closer than ever. She's recovering slowly but surely, but there are still things that she can't do. She misses her knitting and sewing. Her poor eyesight means she finds it impossible to thread the needle. But she is gradually getting back to her other love: baking. Soon she is producing brown bread and apple tarts, which I bring to The Bistro with me to have on my break. When Pierre rather huffily asks me why I prefer to bring my own food rather than eat his, I give him a taste. He is so impressed, he says he wants to serve the bread with his soups.

When time allows, I like to chat with Pierre. He can be excitable under pressure and it's difficult to ignore the tension that sometimes pervades the kitchen, often compounded by what he considers the unnecessary interference of the boss and his even more irritating wife. But when things are quieter, he takes an interest in what passes for my taste in fashion and in men. Particularly one man. He likes Joe and thinks we'd be a good match.

I've gathered from the start that Pierre is gay, and over the weeks and months, he gives me and Joe an insight into his upbringing in a rural town, his repressed sexuality and the homophobia that pervades our Church-dominated society. I soon discover that he's a sensitive and funny soul, and we find ourselves chatting during our breaks about anything and everything. He came out when he was in Paris and quickly discovered how liberating that city is in more ways than one. Compared to Dublin, where being gay can be a dangerous and dark experience.

The upcoming summer season means a busier lunchtime trade, including the construction of an outdoor eatery for warmer days and a gradual expansion of my responsibilities. 'You might even become a successful entrepreneur yourself one day,' the boss says to me after he consumes a slice of my mam's now famous apple tart, following a tipple or two of his own best wine, 'as long as that Joe fellow doesn't fill your head with mad notions.'

He likes that I'm a Trinity student. Says it brings some class to the joint. Paula went there too and she seems to like me, for whatever reason. As she is not around as much these days, I find myself playing bistro hostess, even though there are older and more experienced waitresses on the job.

The reason for Paula's absence is revealed to me by accident one day, when I discover her in tears in the ladies' loo, having just emptied her stomach. She has recently discovered, to her absolute shock, that she is carrying her first, and unplanned, child.

As I help her clean herself up, her inner torments flow. 'I mean I've been diligent with the pill,' she reveals in absolute confidence to me. 'I get them from an old friend in London. She can buy any amount of them over the counter, not like in this godforsaken place. I don't know what I'm going to do. I'm not ready to be a mother. I'm scared. And I don't know what to say to Aidan. He'll die of shock. I'm hoping you can take over some of my jobs. I'm not feeling the best these mornings.'

A couple of weeks later, on one of the rare days that she turns up for work, Paula reveals something else about the baby that has her in a constant state of worry. She is unsure of the paternity of 'this thing' growing inside her and thinks it may have something to do with a regrettable incident after some government event she attended at Easter.

'We all went to a club after the dinner but Aidan went home because he wasn't feeling well. By the end of the evening I was quite drunk and I don't remember much but there was a guy there that I've met a few times and …' She senses what I'm thinking. 'No one you would know.'

We are not close, but it seems like she has no one else to confide in. She certainly can't talk about it with her husband by the sound of things.

'I'm sorry, Paula. If there's anything I can do. Or you just want to talk or whatever,' I say, gently touching her arm.

'No, it's okay, but thanks for listening,' she replies, rubbing her eyes with a tissue. 'I'm nearly twelve weeks gone and I don't know what to do. Aidan is wondering what's up with me, but he's so clueless. I'll have to tell him soon,' she says and bursts into tears again.

***

Playing hostess one afternoon, I greet Fenton, the advisor, who on this occasion is accompanied by a man some of the customers appear to know on sight. He also looks familiar to me, but I don't know from where.

Fenton asks me to secure a table indoors 'near the back with a little privacy'.

As they order, he thanks me and asks, if I'm not too busy with my hostess chores, that I apply my waitressing skills 'to the needs of our appetites and thirst'. Pompous git.

'I couldn't help but notice that you were the height of efficiency and discretion on my last visit. A bottle of your best Beaujolais to start,' he continues.

'That's no problem, Sir,' I reply.

The pair set about eating, drinking and talking, mostly in low tones, only breaking off to order coffee and dessert.

'I haven't had this here before. It's delicious,' says Fenton, taking a bite of apple tart.

'My mother bakes it,' I reply, regretting it immediately.

'A woman of talent. Like her daughter, I'm sure,' says his portly friend.

I smile, but I don't fall for the bait. As I top up their glasses, the advisor thanks me and decides, for some reason, probably related to the one and a half bottles of wine they've consumed, to introduce his friend.

'This is Robert Clarke,' he says. 'You probably know him from his appearances on the occasional chat show, if you like that sort of thing, politics you know, the high end of the game.'

His friend seems to revel in the moment of flattery directed at him, even if it is for the benefit of a girl less than half his age and with not the slightest interest in the shenanigans that pass for serious politics in the chambers of Leinster House just down the road. 'You must call me Bob,' he says.

Later, as 'Bob' rises from the table to take his coat from me, I feel his hand on my back. Fuck, I think, this guy is coming on to me. The touch and the thought make my stomach lurch. Lucky for him, his hand does not wander further down, so he doesn't warrant the sort of treatment the sleazy solicitor received.

'At least no one stormed off this time,' I say to Joe as I wipe the plates into the bin and tell him of my second encounter with Fenton and some big-shot politician who's been on the telly. I don't mention the back stroke.

'Bob Clarke, that fucker. He's the man whose name was on that napkin. Greedy bastard,' is all Joe says before resuming his battle with a dish of cooked crabs who don't want their shells removed. I'd forgotten all about the napkin, the notes and the name. Joe hadn't.

SPRING 1976

9

LEINSTER HOUSE

As the government stumbles from crisis to crisis, Bob Clarke finally gets the opportunity to shine when he sets out his party's position on the conflict in Northern Ireland. Addressing a commemoration for the heroes of the War of Independence, including his late father, in his native Clare on a cold Sunday in late February, he calls on the British government to declare a commitment to withdraw from the six counties of the North and advance the unity of Ireland. The speech goes down well with the party faithful, who have been confused and embarrassed by the failure of their leadership to confront the government over its increasing censorship and repression of nationalist opinion.

Clarke knows that he needs to bring these people with him if he is to build on his growing support base. But he also has to be careful not to antagonise the other party factions, who are divided on what approach to take to the security measures employed North and South against the various republican gangs. His leader is trying to sit firmly on the fence.

As well as this, Clarke has to take into account the revelations made by the British embassy official, Martin Crawley, to Fenton during his advisor's chat with the slimy bastard in The Bistro almost a year ago. So far there have been no repercussions, but the fact of the matter is that what they know could be used against him at any time. He is desperately trying to juggle the need to placate his restless troops while staying in favour with those whom, in time, he may find himself in delicate negotiations with – whether it is to resolve the bloody conflict, or advance his interests, or both.

The day after the trip out West, he feels invigorated by the positive reaction from the troops. 'If the Brits think that they can bully me with their old divide and rule tactics, they've another think coming,' he says to Fenton.

'Your speech has certainly buoyed your popularity among our crowd, well most of them, but I fear the boys in Ballsbridge won't be too happy,' says Fenton cautiously.

'Well it's your job to keep the embassy crowd sweet, so why don't you bloody well do it? They must know that we have to keep up the hard-man talk or people will drift into the arms of the gunmen, especially down the country. It doesn't take much to lose them. Besides, we have to distance ourselves from the law and order brigade in the Blueshirts and their new garda commissioner. He'll have us all locked up if he has his way.'

'I'd be more concerned about the offshore business that Crawley was on about. He seems to know more than his prayers. Is there anything else I should be worried about, Bob?' asks Fenton.

'Whatever he has up his sleeve I can tell you it won't go anywhere. That's all done and dusted and above board. All handled by respectable accountants and lawyers. Good party men. Besides, the paperwork is tucked away in my safe at home. Not even the taxman will find it. I'm already up to my eyes dealing with those bastards over my holiday home and yacht in Cork. They screw you every way. No wonder half the businessmen in Dublin have monies hidden abroad in case of a rainy day.'

'What about the oil company in Canada? He was very specific on that,' Fenton persists. It suddenly dawns on him that he hasn't seen the napkin with the notes on it that Martin Crawley passed to him in The Bistro since that day. He doesn't mention this to Clarke. A cold sweat breaks out on his brow.

'We've met with loads of people who want to invest in a business-friendly environment. Oil, gas, nuclear energy, you name it – they want to come here. We need every cent and job we can get out of the Americans. I won't take any fucking strong-arm tactics from Crawley and his friends. I won't back down because of his threats, veiled or otherwise. Stay in with them, though. Enemies closer and all that. Keep an eye on the Brits and also on that bastard Cooney. I hear he's ramping up new laws to lock up anyone who doesn't agree with him. No one will be safe until we get his crowd out of office.'

'Cooney's due to make a keynote speech in the next few weeks. I'll go along to lend an ear. It won't be anything like your one to our boys yesterday, I'm sure. Somewhere in Dublin, I'm told. It'll be thick with Blueshirts. I doubt you'll get an invite,' says Fenton, smiling.

Clarke laughs and they move on to more pressing matters.

10

JOE

A brainwave by the boss sees me preparing what passes for canapés at the upper end of the city's luncheon market. Aidan Murphy has identified, with the help of a food supplement in one of the English Sunday papers, another revenue-generating prospect – supplying food for public functions in and around the business and political 'quarter', as he likes to refer to it in the marketing leaflets promoting the new service. I'm to serve the food, including cocktail sausages, pâté on toast and smoked salmon on fresh brown bread, for the first away game for The Bistro. I ask Angie to give me a hand, after getting the okay from the boss. She's happy to earn an extra few bob on her day off. Murphy, who was approached to provide the catering by the event organiser, is excited by this new departure, though he's less than enthusiastic about the occasion. For political reasons, he is not inclined to attend, being a diehard Fianna Fáiler. For financial reasons, he's up for it.

The occasion is an important speech by the Home Affairs Minister, Patrick Cooney, in St Ann's church on Dawson Street. Sections of the script, the provocatively entitled 'Violence, Revolution and War', have been kindly 'advanced' by the minister's handlers to the newspapers.

Setting up in the back of the room, with its cushioned pews so unlike the hard benches I was used to in my frugal Catholic Mass-going days, and overlooked by homages to a mix of dead clerics and First World War heroes, I calculate that I have just about enough to feed the assembled crowd. They're busy gulping the free wine as if prohibition is coming in tomorrow. The plan is to distribute the food after the minister is finished, allowing the guests to simultaneously digest both the delicacies of The Bistro and the political intricacies of his latest foray into the intensifying public debate over government policy on the deepening conflict north of the border.

Controversial is the word most associated with his speeches. This one will be no different, according to the journalist from *The Irish Times* who was provided with a taster of the speech for the morning edition. The collection of mainly Fine Gael politicians, party funders, uniformed guards and army officers, a purple-soutaned senior cleric or two, diplomats, hacks and the politically curious are not disappointed. Cooney delivers a tour de force of reactionary bile, which leaves me a little shell-shocked while I'm adding the finishing touches to the serving trays. It's April Fool's Day but that does not appear to be a contributory factor to the objectionable claptrap the hard-line right winger dishes up to his enthusiastic audience. They cheer like a bunch of half-pissed soccer thugs at a Millwall game every time the speaker draws another analogy between the terrorists stalking his country and communist plotters from Peking to Moscow.

'There are two sources of subversion in Ireland, the Provisional IRA and Official Sinn Féin,' Cooney thunders, 'springing from a Sino-Hibernian version of the Communist Manifesto. Revolution and its techniques are international.'

Banging the rostrum, and raising his voice several octaves, he declares his intention to crack down on these subversives. He warns 'there might have to be a derogation from some laws on individual rights but this should be temporary, debated in public and reviewed'.

Angie thinks he's scary. She's never been in a room full of grown men hooting and screeching during a forty-minute torrent of abuse hurled at enemies of the State. Neither have I, but I've heard the red-faced minister ranting before.

'But the last defence against the terrorist and revolutionary war is a vigilant public, constantly on the alert to the burrowing and infiltration of revolutionaries. Student and youth organisations are particularly vulnerable to infiltration by people trained to do it,' Cooney rails.

Nodding towards the few hacks furiously scribbling their peculiar shorthand into their small notebooks, he goes on: 'The media must realise that the continued strength of democracy is the best guarantee of its own freedom. Communicators cannot just be neutral in reporting terrorism but have a duty to align themselves with the democratic government.' To another round of applause the minister leaves the stage and the voracious crowd falls on the plates of food. The wine is flowing again.

A while later I see Angie with tears in her eyes.

'Jesus, Angie, are you okay?' I say, touching the arm that isn't holding a tray of dirty glasses, plastic plates, knives and cocktail sticks.

She shakes her head. 'I just served our friend from The Bistro. Over there,' she points.

I look around and spot Fenton. Angie tells me the other guy is the Englishman he had the row with. The man who scribbled on the napkin.

'They didn't notice me at first. The English guy was talking about the minister being so courageous, direct, no nonsense; that he's going to root out the evil subversives and restore good relations between our two countries. "Not like your man Clarke with all his nationalist nonsense," he said. Then he says, "Those three big bangs in May two years ago really concentrated the minds of your people. And I imagine it won't be the last time, if you don't destroy those murdering IRA bastards soon." Three bangs, he said. Then Fenton copped me and the conversation quickly changed to rugby. He even said he hoped he'd see me in The Bistro soon. I would have hit him on the head with a bottle of his favourite plonk, if I'd had one.'

She's angry, upset and starts to break down again. I catch the tray she's holding before it crashes to the floor.

'Angie, come over here.' I put my arm around her and draw her towards the back of the room.

'I didn't really know what they were on about until I heard them talk about the three bangs, and I knew it could only be about the bombs,' she says as the tears start to flow again. 'Did you know my mam lost the sight in one eye that day and nearly lost it in the other?' she says, wiping her face with the bundle of napkins I give her.

'Jesus, Angie, I'm sorry. I didn't. Look, you go on home and I'll finish off here.'

'No, I'm okay. Sure, we're nearly done. I'm sorry. I just can't ...'

'Don't worry. Come on, let's clear this up and get away from these fucking creeps.'

As we finish tidying up, composure restored, she wonders aloud why the minister has not given his admiring audience any insight into who bombed Dublin that day. He spoke of a host of brutal killings that have recently numbed people across the country, and in England, but no mention was made of the single biggest loss of life in this city, or anywhere else on the island, since the Troubles erupted.

'He was playing to the crowd,' I say, 'drumming up fear. Is it any wonder the Brits love him? No mention of the loyalists killing and bombing this town to bits. Blame everything on republicans. But from what you overheard, it seems to me like the Englishman was saying what a lot of people think. The dogs on the street believe his crowd had something to do with the Dublin bombs in '74. They have plenty of motives. For years, the Brits have been pushing the government to crack down harder on the IRA and their supporters in the South. One way to do it is to frighten the life out of people here, especially the politicians. You heard how they love all the new security measures introduced by Cooney and his promise of even more. At the same time they've been working hard to deflect rumours that their agents, working with deranged loyalists, were the ones that actually conspired to wreck this town.'

'And my mam's eyesight,' Angie reminds me.

***

It's well after the end of the morning shift when we return the residue of our labours at the single most important political event of the day to The Bistro, which has also added a significant wedge to the week's financial returns, much to the delight of the boss.

'A few more of these and I might switch my allegiance to Fine Gael at the next election,' he jokes. He has no interest in the bullshit we have just witnessed and no idea what Angie has just gone through. We aren't about to tell him.

As we walk along the college wall in the dry early evening, I tell Angie about the explosion here almost two years ago. I point to the pockmarked and darkened spot where the car bomb detonated, leaving poor Carol lying in agony on the footpath. I tell her how I tried to help the young woman, her leg mostly torn away, her eyes pleading. How stunning she was, the yellow coat, the red handbag. How I've thought about her since and wondered whether her leg was somehow saved. At the spot, there is nothing left to see from that horrendous day but a few scars on the wall, and even some of these may have come from earlier wars and insurrections. There is no memorial to mark what happened that evening – no plaque, no flowers, nothing. I tell her about my interrupted visit to Holles Street to see my sister, the blood on my clothes, the crashing glass. I don't say where I was coming from. I'm fucked if I'm going to ruin it now.

Angie talks about searching the morgue, the kid she calls Lazarus, who woke from the dead wrapped in a bloody sheet, the awful scenes in the casualty unit, finding her mam in the Mater, the young doctor, her dad, and her mother's slow and courageous recovery.

'I'm sorry about getting so upset earlier, at work. You must think I'm some sort of whinger, crying over spilled milk.'

We are looking over the wall, into the college grounds. I turn and look into her eyes. I take her hand.

'I think you are anything but. You're smart, strong and, if you don't mind me saying, beautiful beyond words.'

She squeezes my hand and holds on as we walk towards town. My heart is pumping.

We part at the front entrance to the college, me heading for the Palace and my Friday evening pint-swilling friends, she to the library to finish an assignment on Yeats. Before I let her go, she suggests meeting up in the Music Place the following night.

'Bring some of your mates. My friend Terry will be with me,' she shouts as she disappears through the big wooden door.

All the talk in the Palace is about Cooney's speech and the government's plan to bring in even more special laws to defeat subversion. He's now called 'Concrete Cooney' after he ordered a republican hunger striker's grave to be covered with cement to prevent an IRA burial with full military honours. The general conclusion is that the law and order brigade must be preparing for an election in the not too distant future and is making the promise to eliminate the republican threat its main platform.

'Did you know that the bastard minister in Posts and Tele-graphs is taking the names of any letter writers to the *Press* who question government policy on the North?' says Donal. He's getting some freelance work from Dev's newspaper.

'Between the Cruiser and Cooney things will only get worse for everybody. More censorship, more repressive laws, more Heavy Gangs,' I venture.

Then I tell them of the scene in St Ann's that upset Angie. I recount, to the few still listening, the words she overheard. '"Three big bangs in May," he said. The Brit was thrilled with Cooney and clearly not so happy with Fianna Fáil.'

After a few more pints my blood is up. 'Some of those fucking journalists, when they're not swigging bad wine at government receptions, should take the time to dig up the truth of what goes on in this shithole republic. Or if they won't, someone should.'

11

ANGIE

The place is hopping when I arrive with Terry just after 9 p.m. and before the lads from the Palace. She is already attracting looks and a few dog whistles from some of the five or six men standing at the downstairs bar. They've never seen someone with pink streaks in their hair before. It's an experiment on which Terry is working with her hairdresser sister and it's becoming all the rage in Coolock, where the family moved a few months ago. Bay City Rollers gear, rolled-up jeans, bovver boots and pink or red dye are in, and the kids are queuing outside the door of their salon to join the latest trend.

We've been back here a few times since our first visit, but she didn't look like Debbie Harry then. When Joe and his two friends, Tim and Donal, arrive, Terry is puffing a joint passed down to her by some of the locals, perhaps in compensation for the slagging they gave her over the hair. Joe pretends to be shocked. The locals here are funny and irreverent, not unlike the crowd in Humphrey's. But they're not used to being answered back by women and, with a few drinks on board, me and Terry are well able for them. We ask how they manage to stay in the pub all day, who looks after their kids, when do they bring their women out? We wreck their heads about contraception, divorce and the lack of it. Joe says I'm a different woman when I'm not playing the polite hostess in The Bistro.

'I didn't think I'd see you passing joints in a pub. You know that's illegal,' he laughs.

'When in Rome,' I say. 'Besides, I don't smoke.'

I think he'd like to know more. I'm okay with that.

The gig upstairs is about to start and the five of us make our way through the throbbing crowd and sounds, to a side table against a wall hung with pictures of music legends: Thin Lizzy, the Clancy Brothers, Rory Gallagher, Joni Mitchell, Sandy Denny and Leonard Cohen.

Christy Moore and Jimmy Faulkner kick off with a powerful set of trad and folk tunes.

The young doctor from the Mater, Brian, who is still running the upstairs bar, is on first-name terms with the musicians and some of the rougher-looking characters hanging out at the back smoking long, fat joints. There's a dark side to this place and the doc wants me to know it.

'You can get any sort of contraband in here, including every kind of hash, uppers, downers, you name it. Most of the lads here are on the dole, but they manage to make enough of a living from other pursuits to let them drink pints all day, most every day. A lot of hard work is done on the phone downstairs. But they're a good bunch unless you cross them.'

My sociology lesson is interrupted by Joe, who introduces me to an old friend from his neck of the woods. 'This is Steelie. He went to school with me in Crumlin. He's a regular here.'

'Nice to meet you, Angie,' says Steelie, with a wink. 'Joe was always the bright one in our class. The only one to go to college. And well got with the chicks.'

When the music comes to a noisy end, we move downstairs for last orders. Standing at the crowded bar, I notice the public phone comes with a health warning. Inscribed on the unwashed wall beside it is the message: 'Be careful. You're not the only one listening.'

The doc joins us for our last pint.

'I see you're enjoying the dark side of the moon,' he says.

We laugh together, but there's a certain edge between Joe and Brian.

'Not my problem, but aren't men so precious?' I say to Terry in our taxi home.

'Better to have them chasing you than ignoring you. Two fine things they are, but imagine you and Doctor Zhivago. I bet he knows his way around,' she says. We're in hysterics.

AUTUMN 1976

12
LEINSTER HOUSE

Bob Clarke is relieved. The press and, more importantly, his party leader have accepted that his problem with the taxman is the result of an unfortunate oversight. With a lot more on his plate and plenty of fish to fry, being dragged into a controversy over his private wealth, which is in the ha'penny place compared to others he could mention in the party, would have been an unwelcome distraction. Now he has to prepare for fresh challenges with the hot summer almost over and a fresh political season looming.

This morning he has his scheduled Monday chat with Fenton. Then he has the front-bench meeting where he has to face questions about his recent statements on the North, which have both sides of the divided parliamentary party on his back. Not to mention the short but decidedly angry missive from the British embassy seeking an early meeting to discuss the view of the leading opposition party on cross-border security and the investigation into the brutal assassination of their ambassador and his secretary in Dublin.

Meanwhile Eileen has been asking about the late nights and early mornings when he's not at home. The bird from the Indo *is no less demanding of his time, his attention and any stories that will keep her name on the front page.*

To make matters worse he has a hangover, while his advisor is his usual irritating, unflappable self.

Fenton clears his throat and starts. 'Okay, it looks like we've a busy new term ahead and that's just dealing with the things we know about.'

'What do you mean, know about?' replies the suspicious Clarke.

'Well, there's your policies on the North, your recent financial troubles, the fallout from the British over the murder of their top man in Dublin, the Heavy Gang stuff and whatever you're having yourself. Who knows what tomorrow will bring?' says Fenton.

'What I know is that our troops are restless. They don't like the IRA but they hate us kowtowing to the Brits. It's a thin line, Myles, and it doesn't help when their soldiers treat our border counties like their backyard. Cooney is still flavour of the month with the Brits and the boss is worried that the Blueshirts will call an election on the law and order ticket.'

'The Brits may love Concrete Cooney since his rant in St Ann's and his crackdown on republicans, but they're realists. They know the coalition can only last so long. Then it's back to business with Fianna Fáil and people like you,' says Fenton. 'But we need to convince them that you are the man of the future. After your speeches to the party faithful since February, they think you're beating the republican drum just to make yourself popular. You need to change the rhetoric, especially with their ambassador getting blown to bits just a few miles up the road. Crawley wants you to meet a guy who's coming over from Whitehall in a few weeks. Nothing formal.'

'So no afternoon tea with the Queen?'

'Not quite,' laughs Fenton. 'It will just be a get to know you sort of meeting, given it seems likely you'll be sitting at the cabinet table sooner rather than later,' says Fenton.

'If he's anything like Crawley I'm not sure I want to meet this man from the Foreign Office, or whatever he is. At the same time we have to mend our fences and build relationships. I'll do it as long as we control the arrangements. No smoke and mirrors. We meet in open view. After all, we have nothing to hide,' Clarke replies.

'Fine, what about The Bistro? I noticed you like the service provided by that pretty young waitress,' Fenton smiles.

'We're not as friendly as you and the owner's wife, from what I hear. Let's have lunch there some Friday and we can prepare for the encounter with our friends from London.'

13

JOE

It's late September and a new, slightly nervous, young waitress has asked me to fetch a bottle of wine from the pantry and bring it to a pair of impatient, noisy and unpleasant gentlemen who have already polished off two bottles of the boss's best Beaujolais. The kitchen is fairly quiet, as it's well past the lunch-hour rush, so, like the gentleman I am, I help her out. When I get to the table who do I find but Clarke and Fenton.

I display and open the bottle like a waiter from the Gresham and half fill the long-stemmed glasses. I've developed quite a fascination with the politician and his circle since the napkin incident and the scene in St Ann's that upset Angie so much. I decide to take my chance.

'Mr Clarke, isn't it? I recognise you from the news. The boys are back in town,' I quip. If there is one thing an ambitious politician appreciates it's instant recognition and Bob Clarke is no exception to this rule.

'Indeed and I am, and I must say this new Beaujolais is going down a treat.'

'Was everything okay? How was your meal?'

'Excellent, our compliments to the chef, top class as ever.'

I introduce myself.

'I'm Joe Heney, the commis chef here. I've followed your career with interest, Mr Clarke – I've always been fascinated by politics.'

'Well, son, it's good to see that some young people can see beyond the nose on their face, isn't that right, Myles? This is

Myles Fenton, by the way, fixer and spin doctor *extraordinaire*. If you want to know the inside story of the House, this is your man. He knows every nook and cranny in the place, or should that be every crook and his granny,' laughs Clarke, taken with his own joke.

I've been reading a lot about Clarke recently, particularly about his settlement with the tax authorities. It seems he had failed to declare ownership of a holiday home and sailing boat in west Cork when listing his assets for the Revenue. It wasn't the size of the mansion or the luxury yacht that captured my imagination when I saw the photos on the front page of the *Press*, but the lame excuse proffered by the Fianna Fáiler for his previously hidden wealth. He claimed that he had simply forgotten to declare them at the appropriate time because it was the anniversary of his father's death.

The story had broken in early summer and I had read the details aloud to Angie and Pierre over croissants one morning. 'Mr Clarke intended to declare the recently acquired assets, but the date for returns coincided with the twentieth anniversary of the sudden death of his late father, Seán,' the newspaper said, adding that 'Seán Clarke, who had fought so courageously in the War of Independence and the Civil War, was a founder member of the party and a popular and effective minister in Dev's administrations from the mid-1930s up to his unfortunate, and sudden, demise twenty years later. Celebrated in story and song, the elder Clarke was one of the golden generation of revolutionaries who had fought for, founded and served this great State over the decades,' the author gushed. Because of his family connections, Dev's paper seemed happy to let the matter of the dodgy tax scam rest. But whatever about his father, the younger Clarke is no republican revolutionary, that's for sure.

It seems unlikely that I'll glean any insight into the men's conversation over the previous two hours, but before I leave them to their wine and coffee, I ask whether they think the government can last its full five-year term.

'Good question, young man. We've just been discussing that ourselves, right, Fenton? I'd give them no more than six months and if they keep bending their arses to the Brits it could be a lot sooner. I'm telling you my father would be turning in his grave if he knew what they were at. The fucking SAS running riot in our own country and not a cross word from this shower of Blueshirt bastards. Not to mind the mess they've made of the economy …'

The rest of his tirade is drowned out when the sound of Abba blares across the restaurant. I can see that Clarke's loose remarks have provoked a pained look on his advisor's face. I'm tempted to ask Fenton how he squares the remarks he shared with the Englishman in St Ann's a few months back with the nationalist rhetoric of his boss. I don't.

Clarke finally winds down and takes another swig of wine from his glass. 'Before you go, young man, we have some sophisticated British friends to entertain early next month and we'd like to book a table here, isn't that right, Myles?' Fenton's face is stony as he nods in agreement.

I call over the hostess to sort this out for them, but remain close by so I can hear the details. 'That's no problem, Mr Clarke, I will put you in the book for that Friday, say 1 till 3?' she confirms.

'So they'll be back soon,' I say to myself. In less than two weeks.

As I return to a bag of spuds that need peeling, I'm thinking about Clarke's reference to the SAS. The story of how eight SAS men were arrested on the wrong side of the border was big news earlier in the year. The new British Secretary for Northern Ireland, Roy Mason, went ballistic and threatened all sorts of reprisals over the arrest of his men. Unfortunately for him and them, the gardaí who picked up the Brits, who happened to be carrying bags of guns around the back roads of Louth, were not thinking in terms of healthy Anglo-Irish relations. Charges inevitably followed. Of course, so did their early release on bail and the speedy return of the 'Daredevils' across the Irish Sea. There's not been much of a political fuss over it. Unlike when the British ambassador was killed by the IRA in Dublin and the political temperature, like the weather, soared.

I've no doubt that today the politician was playing to the gallery with his remarks to me. But he chose the wrong audience. Clarke is a significant player in Fianna Fáil, who likes to wrap himself in his own green flag and show off his republican family baggage. At the same time, his closest advisor is tight with an English guy who was showering praise on Cooney in St Ann's. The Englishman was almost boasting about 'three bangs' as if he knows who did the bombings, and yet Fenton didn't bat an eyelid until he noticed Angie. There's something strange about the relationship between the advisor, the politician and the Brit. I'm certain the cryptic notes on the napkin Angie found could explain a lot, if only I understood them more clearly.

As the peeler mechanically slices skin from the spuds, my mind is working overtime, wondering how I can find out more.

***

Over a quiet pint in the Palace the next evening I tell Angie about the comments made by the half-pissed Clarke when I served his wine. We've become closer since that day at St Ann's, watered by occasional nights in the Palace and the Music Place, and I can't stop thinking about her. She's definitely less reserved around me now, and every now and again she throws me a look that gives me hope of more intimate times ahead.

Last night, when I got home, I took another gander at the napkin, which I've kept. I've had a feeling from the start that it might be important. It reinforced my original assumption that the Englishman knows something about Clarke which involves a lot of offshore money. And I'm wondering if he plans to use that information to get what he wants. The Brits are not stupid. They must know that Fianna Fáil is likely to take back power in the next election, and they need a way to make sure that a new government will continue the hard-line policies towards republicans. And Clarke is likely to be a senior player in the next cabinet.

I outline my theory to Angie. 'They need to turn Clarke away from his nationalist bullshit. Fenton is probably the go-between, trying to find a way to keep his boss and the Brits happy at the same time.'

'A conspiracy of agreed lies,' says Angie. 'That's what my da calls it when he hears the latest political scandal to hit the establishment and smells a cover-up.'

'My dad is the same,' I say, 'but he just cries into his pint and says, "Sure what can you do?" But we need to do something, we need to find out more, expose the crap that's going on. Those bastards in the Dáil have been screwing this country up with their underhand dealings. If we could expose even one of them, it might just make something change.'

I proceed to tell her about the crazy plan I've come up with to find out more about Clarke and Fenton and especially what they are up to with the Brits.

'Look, we know Clarke is coming in for lunch on Friday week with "some sophisticated British friends" and there's a good chance if we can hear what they're saying we will learn more. And the only way to do that is to bug their conversation. They won't have a clue that we're listening in.'

'Joe, that sounds a bit nuts. How exactly are we going to bug their table?'

'I have a mate who can plant the recorder. The problem is you'll have to be the one to turn it on.'

She doesn't respond to this, so I break the silence. 'I know it's a bit of a gamble and nothing might come of it, but we have to give it a try. What if we find something out about the bombings? Don't you want to find out the truth?'

'Of course I do, how can you even ask that?' She pauses for a moment and then, 'I suppose, if it's the only way to find out what's going on … it's not as if we're planning a murder,' she says.

'Hardly the crime of the century,' I agree.

'Not compared to blowing innocent people to bits. And you're right. You've helped to open my eyes about how our politicians play with the lives of innocent people, people like my mam. And I don't like it. I'm in.' She reaches out and takes my hand. An electric shock runs up my arm.

We discuss the ins and outs, the profit and loss on this risky deal. It may not be a crime to be curious, but I'm really not sure of the legalities of bugging a private conversation. At best we could both lose our jobs, or in a worst-case scenario be charged with something or other. I wonder how I'd feel to be back in the 'Joy. Not good.

'So how is this going to work?' she asks.

'I think I've found a way to get the recording equipment put in place. I talked to Murphy this morning, told him that the acoustics around The Bistro are all wrong and that customers have been complaining. I told him that I know a skilled musical engineer who can install a modern Bose system so the music can be centrally controlled and monitored, with an added facility that allows for different sound levels across the house. And that because he's my mate, he'll do it for cost. Murphy fell for it hook, line and sinker. He's even agreed to allow me to try something new in the music department, as long as I don't frighten the horses with some "Bob Marley shit or the Rolling Stones".'

I explain that my mate, Jimmy 'the Red' Macken, who I know from the Music Place, will hide a small microphone underneath the window ledge immediately adjacent to the table that's been booked by the politician for his meeting. He'll put it behind the curtain so it can't be seen. The microphone will be linked by an extended lead to a small cassette tape recorder placed on the floor of the cloakroom in the back of the restaurant near the table. Jimmy, known as 'the Red' because of his hair colour not his politics, can install the mic and Waltham cassette recorder in no time and he'll be happy to oblige. The score for fitting the Bose system is a bonus. I can make sure that the music is turned down at the back of The Bistro when our targets are having their lunch so it doesn't interfere with the sound.

All Angie will have to do is switch on, and off, the recorder at the right times.

14
ANGIE

On an early October afternoon of sunny spells and scattered showers, I welcome Clarke and his advisor, Fenton, when they arrive at the appointed time. I give them my most endearing smile.

'You're looking well, Angela,' Clarke says. 'How is your mother getting on with the tart business?'

'I presume you mean the apple tart business?' I smile.

'I do indeed,' he laughs. 'I might have a gin and tonic while we're waiting for our guests, if that's okay, my dear?'

'The same for me,' says Fenton.

He thinks he's a charmer, our Bob. I can feel his roving eye on me as I walk away to fetch their drinks.

I'm ready and waiting when two well-dressed gentlemen, folded umbrellas in hand, arrive at The Bistro some five minutes later. One of them is the Englishman from before, the other a taller version of John Steed from *The Avengers*. I direct them to the table at the back and ask whether I can take their coats and brollies.

The lunch is likely to be quite a serious affair, if their demeanour is anything to go by. The tall one seems agitated. As he hands me his expensive, fur-lined coat, he remarks to his colleague, 'We may as well have met in the window of the damned Shelbourne.' I pretend not to hear. He takes the seat opposite Clarke at the window and closest to the curtain.

After hanging up the coats, I reach down to the Jacob's cream cracker box under the table in the small cloakroom and press the red record button on the machine, making sure the tape, already inserted, is whirring before I replace the box cover. In just under forty-five minutes, I have to remember to come back and switch the ninety-minute cassette to its B side. This is possibly illegal and certainly unprofessional behaviour. I'm in at the deep end, drowning in nerves.

I've agreed to go along with Joe's plan for the simple reason that I believe these men can possibly reveal who was responsible for the bombing that killed, crippled and maimed hundreds of people in my town, including my mam, and scarred the minds of so many more.

As I return from the cloakroom to hand out menus and take drinks orders, introductions are being made. 'Bob, you know Martin Crawley from the embassy?' asks Fenton.

'Of course, good to see you again,' says Clarke. 'We met at the memorial service for the ambassador. The poor wife. Sad affair.'

'Yes,' says Crawley. 'We miss the ambassador deeply. Let me introduce Alan Richards, from the Foreign Office. Alan is only here for the day so I'm afraid we're on a tight schedule this afternoon.'

'Welcome to Dublin, Alan. Is it your first time?' asks Clarke.

'Not quite and I'm sure it won't be my last,' says Richards.

'Sorry to hear about the sudden departure of your president,' says Crawley. He's referring to the sudden resignation of President Ó Dálaigh after the Minister for Defence, Paddy Donegan, while drunk, called him a 'thundering disgrace'. The shock and scandal had the country on the verge of a nervous breakdown for weeks. Donegan retired to behind the bar of his pub in Louth.

'Messy business,' Crawley says.

'An honourable man,' says Clarke. 'But don't worry, we'll have another one of our own up in the Park before long. The Irish people don't like the government messing with the president. Separation of powers and all that. We're not a monarchy, you know.'

'How's life at the embassy, Martin?' Fenton quickly changes the subject.

'Better, thanks. The new ambassador is due any time now,' says the diplomat. 'There's been a delay in his arrival because the car we ordered collapsed under the weight of the armour plating it now requires. But we've time enough to talk about that. How's the family?'

'All fine, thanks,' says Fenton as Clarke quickly polishes off his G&T.

Once the pleasantries are exchanged, talk turns to the choices on offer, with me providing some useful information about the starters and specials not written in the menu, which include fresh Atlantic mussels and, for the main course, beef bourguignon. From the wine list, Clarke recommends they try the Burgundy, which will go down nicely with the beef.

'Unless you lads prefer white,' he says graciously.

'Water is fine for me,' says Richards.

'Of course. What about you, Martin? Surely the diplomat in you will rise to the occasion?' Clarke laughs.

'Just one perhaps. Red is fine,' Martin says politely. I'm thinking he didn't spare the wine the last time we met, in St Ann's. Must be on his best behaviour.

I'd love to hear what the man from the Foreign Office has to say. I'm not hanging around longer than I have to, though. I'll find out soon enough.

As the meal progresses, I try not to concentrate on any of the conversation, as advised by Joe. I carry on my business diligently and just about remember to turn the tape, without being observed, and without a perceptible clicking sound, as it reaches the 45-minute mark. From a distance, their conversation seems heated. By the time they reach, and refuse, dessert, there is a cold, almost icy atmosphere, which Fenton tries to dispel with some light-hearted remarks when I approach to clear away their dishes. They don't seem to be getting along so well. I reckon lunch will be over well before the full ninety minutes of tape are up.

Before I know it, the two Englishmen are signalling to me. Crawley asks me to fetch their coats and brollies, and makes their excuses about urgent business back in Ballsbridge. Richards offers to pick up the tab for the meal.

'Of course not,' Clarke booms, 'this is on us. We don't expect you to come all this way for just one meeting, Alan, and not enjoy a meal at our expense. Sure is that not what the Irish welcome is all about, the *céad míle fáilte* and all that?'

Richards nods, thanks him for his generosity and adds that he will return the favour in the event of a suitable occasion arising in London in the future, perhaps in the Savoy. With that, he turns to leave.

'Sorry about the rush, lads, but you know what it's like when you try to crush so much into one day. I'll call you later, Myles,' Crawley says to Fenton, before rushing to catch up with his swiftly departing colleague.

A clearly relieved Clarke insists that Fenton stays for another drink. 'That Richards is some ignoramus,' he complains as I clear the table. 'I don't mind him refusing a drink, but who does he think he is flying in here like some fucking member of the royal family expecting us to bow and scrape. He wants us to apologise for stuff we didn't do. Like blowing up Ewart-Biggs. I didn't hear him apologise for Bloody Sunday, the fecker. Does he not know we are a proud sovereign people in our own right? Isn't that what my father and his comrades fought for, God rest them?'

The politician vents his frustration and anger without paying any heed to the few remaining customers scattered at tables around the restaurant, or to me, as I fill his glass with more of the expensive Burgundy. I make it quick, as I'm conscious of the warning from my favourite commis chef about giving any hint that I might have even a passing interest in the everyday life and conversations of a prominent politician, his advisor and the Englishmen.

Two glasses later, Clarke pays the bill with a ten per cent tip.

'Thanks, Angela,' he says as he and Fenton put on their coats and head out into the rain, in much poorer form than when they entered two hours earlier.

I quietly lift the tape from the recorder, place it into its casing and slip it into my apron pocket. I disconnect the machine from the extension lead and close the biscuit box. I can collect it later when the afternoon business is complete and the restaurant is quiet.

15

JOE

It is some hours later when we repair to the Palace and a much-needed few pints to decide where we are going to listen to the results of our intelligence gathering. We're excited that we've pulled off our secret mission, and more than a little giddy when we leave the bar three or four drinks later. I manage to bum a bit of draw off Eddie, a part-time dabbler who always has some stashed away for a rainy day, or a drought like this one. We head for my place, having decided it is a suitable base for operations, where we can also enjoy the few large bottles of stout I have in the press.

The tape starts with some general shuffling and background noise as they settle into their seats. It's not until the food is served that the really interesting discussion begins.

Richards: 'Let's get down to business. Your so-called "honourable" president refused to sign the new version of the Offences against the State Act, which, with its new powers of arrest and detention, would have been a great help in defeating the subversives who killed our ambassador. If that is the way your people are going to behave against the greatest threat to our way of life since the Second World War, then we are going to have problems. We know a lot about dealing with communists and subversives in our own country. The blasted Labour government is riddled with them, for God's sake. We are using every weapon in our arsenal just as you will need to use yours if you are going to defeat these bloody murderers.'

Clarke: 'And we intend to, but all within the constitutional parameters. President Ó Dálaigh was merely doing his duty. You can be assured that the Irish people are appalled at what happened to your ambassador. They will not tolerate …'

Richards: 'Cut the platitudes, Clarke. We've heard them all before. Let me get down to brass tacks, no beating around the bush and all that. You let a mob of hooligans burn down our embassy two years ago and now we've just lost one of our best to these IRA killers. And all we hear is you bleating about a few SAS men accidentally wandering across the border in the middle of the night. We don't, of course, get involved in the internal affairs of another country, but we have interests to defend, as you know, considerable interests that require careful nurturing and protection. I believe you expect an election soon and I'm here to establish which horse we should be gambling on when the race starts.'

Clarke: 'Of course, Alan. Can I call you Alan? Certainly, we are all in agreement that the curse of subversion must be resisted for the sake of our democracy and the values we hold, ones we share with your people and your government. At the same time, we can't forget that there are historical complexities at play here, and we can't be seen to be subservient, in any way, to the wishes of another state or government. Of course, we have a shared interest in sorting out the relationship between the two parts of this island once and for all, but it doesn't help if excessive force is used by either side. That only plays into the hands of the gunmen. We condemn utterly the assassination of Mr Ewart-Biggs, a fine gentleman whom I met at your embassy when he arrived just a week or two before he was callously murdered. Wonderful host, and his wife of course, a very generous lady.'

Richards: 'Mr Clarke, I won't mince words here. First, we want you to support every effort being made to track down the cowardly bastards who blew up Ewart-Biggs and his secretary, including a guarantee that the new emergency powers which your man up in the Park refused to sign will be pushed through. When I said Ewart-Biggs was one of ours, I meant that he was more than just the ambassador – he was the liaison between the Foreign Office and MI6. A key man, brave too, lost an eye in the Alamein. The boys in Whitehall are none too pleased that this could happen in the country of a supposedly friendly neighbour. And speaking of the good Jane Ewart-Biggs, she is indeed a wonderful person and her husband did not go around the night spots of Dublin shagging anything in a short skirt like some people we know. That lady from the *Independent* you meet in Grooms and the Gresham, Robert, might get you into trouble yet ...'

There are sounds of coughing and spluttering and then the clanking of dishes as Angie collects the empty starter plates. Once she moves away the talk continues.

Clarke: 'Now that is unfair, all completely innocent, two grown people, consenting adults who meet on a professional basis. Surely ...'

Richards: 'Cut the bullshit. We have assets in this town at every level – in the papers, the police, among politicians – and we will deploy them to take down you or any other snivelling politician who wants to run with the hare and hunt with the hounds to get elected in this miserable backwater. Either you are strong on terrorism or you are not our friend. So forget about the perfidious Albion and your precious fourth green field. And don't forget that little matter Martin raised with your associate here some time ago in this very establishment, I believe. Surely you didn't think deposits in our protectorate in the Caribbean would not come to our notice? Are you completely naïve? Who do you think sent the very bright young chap with a first-class honours in banking and finance from Cambridge to set up this elaborate offshore system? Yes, we know all about him. Another one of ours, you might say. We can splash your little stash across the front pages any time we want, including the source of that nice little wedge that arrived in from Canada not so long ago. Two for me, one for the party, is that how the game works? Now that would make for an interesting read on a Sunday morning and would certainly not help your re-election prospects, Robert.'

Clarke: 'I strongly resent the implication here. Are you suggesting that I am somehow involved in some elaborate international financial network? I mean, that's preposterous …'

Richards: 'I'm not suggesting anything, I'm stating a fact and you know it.'

For a moment silence descends and then there is some small talk between Fenton and Crawley as Angie serves the main course.

Richards: 'So let's talk about where we are now so that I can brief my people, including our new man in Dublin, and advise on our progress. By the way, the new ambassador is one of those who believe that you people are trying to have your cake and eat it. Letting us deal with the terrorists while you wave your green flag and utter platitudes. But be sure of this, when those IRA bastards blow up our ambassador and bomb our cities they have declared war on the Empire, and you are either for us or against us. Make no mistake, the dogs are unleashed and we need to know who our friends are. We need you to prove that you are our friends and that includes putting an end to your mutterings about further inquiries "into this, that and the other" and your torture case against us in Europe. And we expect you to play dumb when our SAS men are let off with a slap on the wrist when their case comes to trial. If you are going to win the next election as you have been bragging about and want to continue your rise to the top, you need to take on what I'm saying. We won't tolerate nationalist coat-trailers in government in Dublin. Is that clear enough, Robert? And besides, if you don't help us, who's to say what could happen? Who says there won't be another attack on your beautiful city that we might have been able to prevent if we got the co-operation we needed?'

At this point I press stop. Angie and I look at each other in complete shock.

'Did he just say what I think he did?' I ask.

Angie nods, the horror written all over her face. I rewind and we hear it again.

'Let's listen to the rest,' I say.

Clarke's response to the Englishman's onslaught is to

reassure him that his message is understood, while pleading for some reciprocation and an end to the cross-border provocations and the incessant demands from London for more and tougher security measures against the IRA and any other perceived enemies. Richards is having none of it. Clarke is expected to deliver by persuading his Fianna Fáil comrades around to the British way of thinking in whatever way necessary, or the shady deals and illicit affair will find their way onto the front pages. He is explicit about the consequences of failure.

Richards: 'I can tell you, Robert, that this is only the start if your crowd do not heed our warnings to crack down on the republican murder gangs. If you think I'm bad you should meet some of my friends in the service, the secret service, I mean. They're prepared to take out the Labour government in Britain. Do you think they'd hesitate for a second if they wanted to take out yours, or you for that matter? Do you honestly think the loyalists could have done the '74 job on their own? Three bombs, high explosives, plastics, timed to go off within minutes of each other, on the route to the main train stations during a bus strike. One just a hundred yards or so from your excuse for a parliament. That's called military precision, Bob.'

Clarke is genuinely shocked.

Clarke: 'Are you telling me that you people did that? Who in the name of God do you think you are, coming in here and threatening me, our people? I've a good mind to –'

Richards: 'What I'm saying is that we have people who are capable
of doing those things, and they can only be reined in if we
work together in our common interest to defeat subversion.'

Then Fenton speaks up. He realises things are getting out of
hand and moves to calm tempers.

Fenton: 'It would be wrong if there were a misunderstanding
about the financial matter you raised. I mean Bob is not the
only wealthy individual who has availed of this facility, which,
after all, is perfectly legal and above board, and simply facili-
tates high-worth individuals accessing their funds without all
the bureaucracy involved in declaring taxable income. It is a
system, as you know, that functions for respectable individuals
across many jurisdictions, including your own, and of course
brings certain benefits to your economy through the hefty
commissions that pour into your banks from offshore activities. The depositors in tax-light jurisdictions are people of the
highest integrity and, indeed, influence in the business life of
this city, of different political persuasions and none, and some
have strong links to our vital trade with Britain across many
sectors.'

Richards: 'Rubbish, Myles. We all know that in Bob's case it
is a racket to receive money and hide it from prying eyes.
There's a tidy sum of £100,000 sent through the bank of
Nova Scotia and now lying in a Bermuda account which has
your name on it, Robert. We know the source of the money
is Canada's leading oil and gas exploration company, which
has an interest in Ireland's Atlantic riches. They are hoping to

get valuable exploration licences from your crowd, isn't that it? It doesn't take a genius to work out why they would be paying large sums to leading and influential politicians like yourself. I'll say it again; what do you think it would do for your chances if this juicy little tale hit the headlines, especially around election time? You might think that the only details are hidden in your safe at home. But of course we have a copy of everything. You know what we Brits are like for keeping records.'

The message appears to hit home. With assurances that the 'robust' exchange has indeed brought clarity to their relationship, Clarke promises to share Alan's very justified concerns with his party colleagues, or at least with those he believes are sympathetic to their way of thinking, who understand the value and necessity of close co-operation with London on security and other matters of common interest.

The rest of the meal is largely consumed in silence with Fenton and Crawley exchanging small talk about the educational progress of their offspring in different, but elite, private institutions. Up until then the man from the embassy had hardly spoken a word. While Crawley seems to be a senior official at the embassy, dealing in security matters, Richards is clearly a notch or two higher up the ranks.

In just over sixty-five minutes, the tape has given Angie and me a shocking insight into how the other half lives, how the power brokers converse in private and how our city and country are at the mercy of forces neither of us will ever understand. Some of the references to people and transactions are beyond us, but there is enough in the recording to keep us up talking half the night. Richards all but admits to the British role in the bombings, while the Brits clearly have their foot on Clarke's neck over his offshore bank dealings and an affair he is having. The £100,000 deposit from Canada must have been paid in return for a promise that Fianna Fáil will grant a licence for oil and gas exploration to one of the world's largest mining companies when they regain power.

Angie yawns. I'm knackered too, but I could go on all night. I look at her tired, beautiful face. I can hardly resist the temptation to kiss her. But I do.

16

ANGIE

After the tape reveals its secrets and we've exhausted our interpretations, my tired mind shies away from the terrible implications of it all and, instead, absorbs the living space of my friend and co-conspirator. The walls are plastered with posters of Led Zeppelin, the Who, Che and John Lennon, as well as covers from *Rolling Stone*. An impressive selection of albums from Muddy Waters, Van Morrison, Cohen and Janis Joplin through to the latest from the new wave of punk bands, The Sex Pistols, The Clash and Patti Smith, are scattered on the floor. There is a touch of the brother about him, similar age, same taste in music, laid-back; but at the same time he's different, more real and committed. Novels from Russia, South America, Connolly, Pearse, various communists, Angela Davis, Malcolm X and Mandela, poems and pamphlets litter his shelves. Sartre, de Beauvoir. Joe is more serious, more passionate about politics, civil rights and all that stuff, than Tony will ever be.

As he clears the empty bottles and the debris from the joints made of his home-rolled tobacco laced with the screed of hash he managed to extract from his small-time dealer friend, he invites me to stay. He keeps his place fairly neat, I'm thinking, for a man. Even the tiny bathroom is not unclean. There's a faint smell of garlic and herbs in the air. He must do a bit of home cooking, maybe with ingredients liberated from The Bistro.

I feel comfortable with Joe. I like his sense of humour and the non-threatening air he has of someone who really likes me, but seems willing to wait until I'm ready for something more. I think that day will come. When Terry joked that she could take him off my hands, even for a quick shag, I just laughed, but I wasn't one bit amused. She can't understand why I'm not sleeping with this fine thing. I'm not sure, either.

There's just something that nags at me about Joe. He clams up whenever I ask about his past. Like girlfriends, college days, family. The closest I've got to finding out anything about his past life is from his childhood friend Steelie and he's no angel. Is there a mother and child out there he's not telling me about? Or something else? He's a closed book and he won't let me in. I'm wary of what I might find if and when he does. But the more time I spend with him the more I want to know everything, no matter what.

'It's too late for you to go now,' he says. My eyes are beginning to droop. It's after three in the morning, cold and pitch black outside.

'I could do with some sleep right now,' I say. 'It's been a long night. We can pick this up later.' I yawn again as he directs me to his small bedroom. I told Mam I would be staying with Terry, so there's no rush to get home.

'I'll sleep on the couch,' he says, the unspoken desire hanging in the air between us. I take his hand as he moves away. I pull him towards me, wrapping both arms around his neck. I press my lips to his. Soft and moist. One long, warm kiss. I lead him to the small bed. He strips to his shorts and lies down. When I come back from the bathroom, naked, I crawl into the bed beside his long and slender body. Within seconds, I'm fast asleep, or so he tells me the next morning.

I wake to a midday sun streaming in the window, in a strange but comfortable place, rested and hungry. I don't recall any dreams or disturbance. Joe's arm is stretched across me. He is gently snoring. There is a look of contentment on his face. I slip from the bed quietly so as not to disturb him and tidy up the kitchen in silence, then sit at the table with a cup of tea and watch him through the open door. A short time later he wakes up with a start and looks for me beside him. He smiles. I don't go back to the bed and he doesn't seem to mind. We can wait.

I have time for a coffee before I head home. We go to one of the few places that match The Bistro for quality, and resume the conversation from the night before: the contents and meaning of the recording and, more importantly, what to do with this newfound knowledge. We hold hands across the table. Clearly Richards is no ordinary diplomat. He has to be of the intelligence variety, an Ian Fleming character without the flash car and the poison pen. Joe read somewhere that Ewart-Biggs, the British ambassador killed by the IRA, had served with MI6 in a number of locations around the world where his country's strategic interests were exposed. It makes sense that his colleagues would be determined to avenge his death at the hands of the IRA.

As Joe talks, I suddenly sense the danger we might unleash on ourselves by poking around in this particular hornet's nest. 'You should try to keep your voice down a little. You're always telling me the walls have ears,' I say. He nods and looks at the few other customers in the café.

'Anyway, it's one thing to have a recording of all this but what do we do with it?' I say. 'We now have concrete evidence of what you and most of the world have suspected all along, that the British are influencing politics on both sides of the border and are prepared, if necessary, to blow our city, and my mother, to smithereens if they don't get their way. And that at least one of our politicians knows about it.'

'We could just go to the papers with the tape. But the chances are they'd run a mile and wouldn't print the stuff. Besides, these are dangerous people and if we release this tape they will figure out exactly who was in a position to record it,' he says. 'Who knows how they would react? I'm not willing to put you, my family or yours in danger for this.'

The possible cost of this adventure is very clear in the cold light of day. We are tempted to destroy everything, the tape and the napkin. After some discussion we agree to hold onto them both for a while, but not to let anyone else know what we have. We'll return the bugging equipment to Jimmy the Red and tell him that the plan we had, to record two self-important and much disliked showbiz celebrities for a bit of craic, failed when they didn't show up.

For now, we need to check out a few things, take our time to come up with a proper plan. As Joe says, if the contents of the illicit tape are circulated in raw, unedited form, it will not take long in this small town before the dogs in the street are barking and it is traced back to The Bistro.

'Then we'll be toast, literally,' he says.

'Thanks for the bed.'

I kiss his cheek, then his lips and run for the bus to town coming down the street. I'm flushed. So this is what it feels like. He waves as I look back.

SUMMER 1977

17

JOE

During my morning break, I read about the new British ambassador 'presenting his credentials' to the new Fianna Fáil president, elected unopposed. The political correspondent gushes at the symbolism of it all and speculates on whether the change in personnel will lead to a 'rapprochement of sorts between our most important neighbour and the State's largest political and authentically republican party'. The front-page report goes on to suggest that the strains and tensions evident in recent years between the main opposition party and the government over policy and action on the North, which have involved explicit criticism by Fianna Fáil of the British armed forces and their night-time meanderings along the border, may also be on the wane.

In the image of the new president and the ambassador that accompanies the piece, the Englishman called Crawley is standing almost, but not quite, out of shot behind them. Martin Crawley, British *chargé d'affaires*, the caption reads. There's no sign of Richards.

When I read a shorter piece on page five of *The Guardian*, where only the president and ambassador are shown, I notice a similarity in the political message. A quote from Fenton, in his role as press officer for Fianna Fáil, sees him welcome the evolving harmony in relations between his party and 'our friends across the Irish Sea'. The article also mentions that Fenton is a likely candidate for government spokesperson after the seemingly inevitable accession to power of the party following the next general election.

On an inside page of both papers, it is noted that the SAS men were fined £100 each for possession of arms and ammunition without the appropriate licences during their border crossing, one of fifty-four such incursions last year. They got off on the more serious 'possession with intent' charges. Another piece says that the government requires yet 'more time to consider' a report on the torture of internees in the North prepared by the European Commission on Human Rights, and by all accounts extremely critical of the British authorities. Amnesty International is claiming that republican and criminal suspects in the South are being beaten brutally in police stations. The main opposition party has no comment on any of these matters, at least none is reported.

'Why am I not surprised?' I say to myself.

Usually, Fianna Fáil people would be up on their hind legs complaining about the lax treatment of armed Brits running across the border and using torture against nationalists in the North. Now they are silent, complicit even, maybe afraid of the consequences if they raise their voices too loud. There's a good reason on tape why Clarke should hold his tongue and work hard to persuade his colleagues to do likewise. This is heavy shit.

I worry again about what I might have dragged Angie into. We've left the question of the tape and our struggle for justice on the back burner, but ever since the night she spent in my flat I can't get her out of my head. Things haven't moved as quickly as I'd hoped – she's been so busy with college work that we've only managed to snatch a few evenings together in the Palace.

I'm hoping once the academic year ends we'll get to explore each other more. The last thing I want to do is get in the way of her studies. I'm willing to wait as long as it takes.

It doesn't help that Murphy is particularly irritable as he tries to come up with new ideas to attract more punters. The Bistro, he says one day, is under threat from the other eating establishments that are popping up around the city centre, with ever more varied menus, special offers and drinking options.

'It's simply not enough to do a few selections of French red and German Liebfraumilch any more. People are sick of Blue Nun. We have to sell wines from the New World, Australia, South Africa, even the Argentine, and cold beer, bottled and on tap, that sort of thing. We have to meet the expanding tastes, and waistlines, of our sophisticated and modern consumers,' he says to anyone who'll listen.

Today we have no choice, as he's addressing the gathered staff at the end of the lunchtime shift. He says he worries constantly over the prospect of a bad review or worse still about complaints from customers over the service and standards at the restaurant.

'People will always be jealous of success,' his wife never tires of saying. 'Fuck the begrudgers,' she continues if a couple of glasses of white are involved. Like this afternoon.

A few weeks later, the spring is back in Murphy's step when he reveals that he's been approached by some of the Fianna Fáil politicians that frequent the place to organise a fundraising event in The Bistro. 'As long as the cost does not reach into my pocket or antagonise any customers who might kick with the other foot, as it were. That's what I told Myles Fenton, the man who approached me, and a regular here, as you know,' he adds.

Murphy doesn't want to make a wrong move in the mine-field of politics, no matter how good it makes him feel about himself or, more importantly, how grateful the future ministers and hangers-on may be for his efforts and the rewards this could bring. He makes it clear that we will all reap the dividends if his ambitions succeed.

'I told Fenton that people like me, entrepreneurs, should have an input into party policy, on tax, crime, that sort of thing, if we are to help with fundraising,' he tells Paula within earshot of the kitchen staff. '"Splendid idea," he says. "Why not join one of our policy groups? They're always looking for new ideas. You don't have to bother with boring old *cumann* meetings. Sure you can come and go as you please, throw in your tuppence worth and when we get back in sure you could be on the board of the Food Promotion Authority or something."' I'm a little surprised when his wife does not look impressed. I thought that sort of political smoozing would be right up her street.

Of course it is me, Pierre and the other staff, who'll bear the brunt of Murphy's latest plans. It's us who'll be doing all the hard graft for little reward beyond the goodwill of the boss, assuming all goes well, or for the criticism that will come with any perceived failures or shortcomings, no matter who's to blame. As it is we're taking home less than £50 a week and already working all the hours God gives us. The boss thinks overtime is a privilege he bestows on his workers, and pays little or nothing above the normal hourly rate.

Days later the government, as widely predicted, is forced to call an election in June, just a few weeks away, after some internal and soon forgotten row sees the leader of the junior coalition party walk out of office and into history.

18

ANGIE

By mid-May I've finished most of my third-year assignments and have only two papers to go. I take on more shifts in The Bistro and am immediately charged with the task of organising the front-of-house responsibilities for the forthcoming political fundraiser. The great and the good of Fianna Fáil will be attending, despite it coinciding with their grinding duties of canvassing in the middle of an election campaign. Myles Fenton, of all people, is the chief organiser, which means I'm helping him with seating and other arrangements, placing guests at the appropriate tables, and ensuring that the most generous donors are afforded the best view of the hastily erected platform and proximity to the anticipated incoming Taoiseach.

I have a list of those who have accepted invitations. Some 150 are expected, which will stretch both the physical capacity of the restaurant and the patience and endurance of the kitchen and waiting staff. I have to find space to guarantee the comfort and enjoyment of the paying guests. The party is charging £1000 per table of ten, which by any standard is sure to raise a tidy sum, even after expenses due to the boss are deducted. It seems an enormous amount to me and gets me thinking about what other use might be made of such money; maybe to build a monument to those killed in the bombings three years ago this week.

After what I've learned about Clarke and Fenton, I don't see how this crowd will be any better than the one leaving office. They're all the same, parties for those who have it good already.

After months of hardly seeing each other, I'm back in Joe's company and eager to catch up on lost time. I know he's found it frustrating, but he understands that I have to concentrate on college. I'm glad we can spend more time together now. He's happy too.

During a tea break at work, I mention Fenton's fawning over the list of rich and powerful who are about to descend on The Bistro to splash a small fortune on his party. Joe says he has an idea he wants to discuss with me later, and suggests going for a pint in the Music Place after work. 'Bring the guest list too,' he says.

The list is a veritable 'Who's Who' of Dublin's business and political high-flyers, including a lot of their addresses and phone numbers. So sneaking it out to a pub full of gangsters and dopeheads doesn't seem that wise.

'We'll have to be careful with it,' I say.

'No problem,' he smiles.

I've been warned by Fenton and the boss, more than once, to keep everything confidential. The exclusive event is strictly private, Murphy insists, and no prying reporters or photographers are to be allowed near the place. Fenton is supposed to ensure that the privacy of the guests is maintained, especially concerning details of the party benefactors and their interactions on the night. But in his eagerness to impress us with his access to and influence over the high and mighty, he gave a copy of the guest list to both me and the boss, with instructions written on it as to where each guest should be placed.

With Paula's help, I am to make sure that anything needed is provided in terms of eating and seating requirements, table decorations and entertainment. Some of the country's best performers and dancers are lined up for the night.

As we go through the invitation list that evening, Joe says that the cream of the establishment – business owners, hoteliers, industrialists, beef barons, representatives of the most powerful countries in the world, as well as the chosen few from print, stage and screen – have moved in behind the clearly unstoppable return of Fianna Fáil to power. The owners and editors of the main papers are included, of course, but can be expected not to reveal the identities of the other guests, as are diplomats, bishops, senior gardaí and army officers and, more importantly, rich and influential political donors along with their wives.

'This is how the game works,' Joe says. 'The party slogan to "get the country working again" is really about working your friends and supporters into the right positions. This fundraiser is not just about making donations but about making connections and making money in the future, lots of it, for those who already have it.'

'That's all very interesting, but what do you plan to do with this?' I ask.

'The whole establishment is lining up behind Fianna Fáil, and by extension Bob Clarke and his lackey Fenton,' Joe says. 'We can show how the election is being bought to put them back into power. Meanwhile the Brits are threatening to expose Clarke if he doesn't follow their orders on the North and cover up their role in the bombings. They have him over a barrel because of his corrupt offshore riches. Clarke, the British ambassador and Crawley will all be there along with the other high and mighties. It's all part of a bigger jigsaw. We can get photos of the main characters in this little plot together. We can show how the people who run the country behave when they let their hair down. They pretend to have these great principles until they think no one is watching. We need to expose Clarke and the greasy bastards who blew this city apart. If my idea works we might just get other people in politics and the media interested, and we may get to the truth. I know it's a long shot, Angie, but all we can do is try.'

'That's good enough for me,' I say, gripping his hand tight. I still haven't much of a clue about what his plan really entails.

A lot of people who I don't recognise come up to chat with Joe. He must have been spending a lot of time in the Music Place over the months when I was preoccupied with my studies. He's even become known to some as the 'meat man' due to his generosity. He says they are not accustomed to the fine cuts he sometimes brings to the pub after rescuing them before they are binned at The Bistro because they are deemed not fresh enough for the punters.

'I don't see why perfectly good sirloin steak, fillets of beef and cuts of lamb and pork should be dumped because Pierre says he can only cook produce freshly purchased, one or, at most, two days from the farm gate,' he explains. 'Besides, there are a few men here with big families. I'd say their wives are lucky to get fatty mince a couple of times a week after the publican takes his whack of the family income.'

Joe tells me more about some of Dublin's most gifted criminal talents whom he has come to know and whose only mistake is to have fallen victim, sometimes more than once, to diligent detectives and their most essential police tool, the informer. Some of his newfound friends make me nervous, not least the ones who look and sound like they'd rob their own grannies.

I watch as he passes a package of well-wrapped steak to Heno, a rough-looking character whose successes in life include an infamous theft of a large pile of cash, gold and silver from one of the city's most exclusive jewellers. Heno, Joe explains, served five years in the 'Joy, not because his safe-cracking technique was immediately apparent to investigators, which it was, but because he stupidly, with drink on him, gave a silver bracelet he had intended to hide for a long time to a hooker friend who sometimes provided services to a Branch man in Store Street. The garda was not long in finding out the source of her new and expensive adornment, and Heno was arrested, charged and convicted after his fingerprints were matched to those conveniently found on the handle of the safe. He proclaimed that this was impossible to all who cared, and to his weary lawyer, who advised the outraged thief against telling the judge he was wearing gloves the entire time and therefore could not have left prints. Heno took his brief's advice, kept silent and did the time.

Joe says that many of those who frequent the Music Place are graduates of one reform school or another, for crimes like robbing apples or skipping school. Some claim they are victims of terrible abuse by the clerics who brutally raised them, and a fair few met while spending time in one or other child, juvenile or adult detention centre. They feel no compunction about armed bank robberies, or jump overs as they call them, car theft, cheque fraud or selling copious amounts of stolen liquor, tobacco, fur coats or leather jackets. Their only concern is being caught.

After a few more pints, supplemented by the odd joint

passed over from Heno and his mates at the bar, Joe explains the elaborate plan he has hatched. I'm not used to the Guinness after a few months of exam-induced sobriety and feel it going to my head pretty quickly. I listen to his idea, which sounds ever more credible and ingenious in direct proportion to the amount of drink I consume. I don't think too much of the possible consequences. By the time we leave, we confidently expect that with a few more days of preparation we will make the political fundraiser in The Bistro a night for everyone to remember.

As we cross Dorset Street, Joe nods towards a dark-blue Ford Cortina with two men inside. 'Branch men. They're on the look-out for the scoundrels, subversives, suspected but uncaught bank robbers, rapists and other scum of the earth who frequent this place. And the odd man on the run. Some job,' he says.

I feel a slight chill down my spine. I say goodnight. We kiss gently at first, but soon harder. The need we both feel takes over. I pull back. My head is spinning and I'm too pissed to take up the offer in his eyes. 'Soon,' I say, 'I promise.' As my bus pulls up he whispers, 'I'll hold you to that.'

Among my roles in Joe's complex scheme is convincing Murphy and his wife to hire a few extra staff for the evening, given the expected large attendance. While the boss counts the cost in his head, Paula instantly agrees with me.

'I could do with a few more staff on the floor. It will leave me free to look after our guests properly,' she says.

I say I know someone, a college friend with waiting experience who happens to be at a loose end.

'That's a start, thanks, Angie,' she says, as Murphy nods a reluctant head. He's stopped arguing with her, at least in public, for reasons that she confides that same afternoon. Why she tells me the innermost secrets of her relationship is beyond me. We have nothing much in common, with me just going on twenty-one, a poor student from East Wall, and her an ambitious professional from Foxrock in her early thirties. Maybe she hasn't many close friends, but whatever the reason, she clearly feels that she can trust me. As we work on the details of the party she relays the outcome of her unwanted pregnancy. She tells me she went to London to 'deal with the problem' without ever telling Murphy about it. She told him she was going to visit a college friend for the weekend. But the abortion left her more troubled than she expected and after weeks of sharp exchanges punctuated by long silences, he confronted her and she confessed.

'He went ballistic, but I said that it was my business whether I wanted to have a baby. "I'm not ready," I said. Neither is he, but I didn't say that. For weeks afterwards, we barely spoke and I was getting ready to walk out. Then I realised that for all his palaver about abortion and the law and the Church, it suited him down to the ground. A baby wasn't on his radar. He hardly has time for me, not to mind parental responsibilities. And, better still, I had made a messy choice for him so he didn't have to fight with his conscience. Best of both worlds. Little did he know it wasn't his. I'm not even sure he would have cared,' she says bitterly.

I pat her hand awkwardly, not sure what to say. She thanks me for listening and for being a shoulder to cry on, then quickly reverts to her normal self, preparing for the crowd due to assemble in less than a week's time. Later, she reminds Murphy that we still need two or three extra staff. Murphy agrees to go along with the idea on condition that they are vetted by him to ensure they are suitable.

'We can't have any old chancers and troublemakers in The Bistro on Friday. Only persons of impeccable credentials and background. Blueshirts and commies need not apply,' he jokes.

This gives me a chance to bring in Joe's mate, Donal Dunning. We tell him that he'll get exclusive photos at this party of the political and financial elite. He's mad into the idea of working undercover. Late one afternoon, I introduce a well-presented young man with waiting experience called David Gunning to Murphy. The boss assesses his educational background, his culinary knowledge and table-serving skills, and they briefly discuss his family history. It includes the not insignificant detail that he has an uncle in the gardaí. That, along with the fact that he is a friend of me and Joe, gets him the gig for the night's work at a more than reasonable £2.50 an hour plus tips. Another two staff are acquired on a 'once-off temporary basis' from a respected establishment nearby whose proprietor plays the occasional round of golf with Murphy.

As the day approaches, other arrangements are put in place to ensure that all goes smoothly on the night. These are ones that have nothing to do with the boss and his ambitions, but are intended to further the pursuit of justice which commenced in The Bistro all those months ago.

19

THE BISTRO

As he drives down Booterstown Avenue and past the spot where Kevin 'that Blueshirt bastard' O'Higgins was killed on his way to Mass, Bob Clarke can't help but admire the quality of his election posters and the smiling, yet determined, image that adorns every second lamp post. The campaign is going well and if the opinion polls are anywhere close to the mark, the party is set for a comfortable victory.

'It looks like we are going to make it but we shouldn't take anything for granted,' he says to Eileen. She agrees and makes the astute observation that he looks the epitome of leadership and gravitas compared to his rivals on the hustings. Their posters are already coming apart at the seams due to some recent inclement weather and the weak cardboard they used. His, in contrast, are made from a light plastic material that just came on the market and has a greater resistance to the wind and rain blowing in from the Irish Sea. Just to be sure, though, the lads weakened the ties holding the dull posters of the opposition candidates, so that many of them are flailing in the wind and about to blow away.

'Just like they will when the votes are counted next week,' he chuckles to himself. He's on course to top the poll in the southside constituency and, with a bit of luck and a lot of energetic positioning around the party leader, will have his arse on the back seat of a ministerial Merc within a few weeks.

'All the hard work and sacrifices you've made over the years will finally be rewarded,' says Eileen, with her irritating knack of discerning his thoughts. On this occasion, at least, she's in harmony with his own disposition.

*'Yes, my dear, and I couldn't have managed it without you. It's
time for both of us to reap the rewards. I just have to convince that
Cork bastard to give me Finance, or Industry and Commerce at least.
Or maybe you'd prefer Foreign Affairs? We could see a bit of the
world.'*

*'Shopping on Fifth Avenue, now there's an idea. The best shows on
Broadway and all funded by the hard-pressed taxpayer,' she laughs.*

*It is not often that they have time to share a joke. He works day
and night in his relentless drive to get to the top of the political heap
while she, with the help of a housekeeper and cook, keeps the home fires
burning.*

*She has long given up the notion of a marriage fuelled by deep
love and mutual understanding, and has settled for the comforts of the
detached mansion on Cross Avenue, the luxury of her own sports car
and two holidays a year, one foreign. The three children, now in their
later teens, have the best of everything.*

*'It's a long way from west Clare,' she muses. When they started out
it was in a house with an outside jacks near Inagh. Love and poverty.*

'Now, we have neither,' she thinks to herself.

*On the Merrion Road he puts the boot down and the new Audi
practically purrs on its way to the fundraiser which should mark
another step on his steady journey to political power. At the back of
his mind he grapples with the threat hanging over his head from
the English spymaster and wonders again whether he should tell his
boss, and the world, what he has learned about the attacks in Dublin
and Monaghan. For now, his conscience is on the losing side of that
argument.*

*When they arrive, not too early, not too late, there are a respectable
number of guests already nibbling at platters of food and chatting*

while soft traditional music plays in the background. Murphy and his wife are arguing over flower arrangements.

'*They can't eat fucking pansies, darling. How are you going to get the plates and goodies on the table? It's like the fucking Chelsea flower show,*' *he hisses too loudly.*

'*They are carnations and lilies if you must know and they are staying where they are,*' *she retorts.*

The row is suspended when they see Clarke and his wife hand their coats to Angie. Clarke, wisely, does not greet the attractive young hostess by name.

'*Bob, Eileen, how wonderful to see you,*' *Murphy gushes. Paula stands back a little, then comes forward and takes the politician's wife by the arm.*

'*Come, I'll show you to your table. For the special guests,*' *she says, leaving Clarke free to work the room. Already the local Catholic and Protestant bishops, accompanied by a handful of dressed-down clerics, are here, all of whom, no doubt, are looking forward to the quality wine and food at one of the city's most prestigious eating establishments. They are soon joined by healthy numbers of senior gardaí, army officers, industry magnates, bankers, legal eagles, newspaper owners and editors, and celebrities – more than were expected due to a last-minute surge of requests. Extra tables have been squeezed in to accommodate the bulging crowd.*

'*Full house, Bob. We've covered ourselves in glory this time,*' *says Fenton, beaming.*

'*We're out the door with twenty grand at least,*' *Clarke says, rubbing his hands. Not including anonymous donations. He's chuffed.*

At exactly 8.30 p.m., as planned, the party leader and his large entourage arrive, fresh from the hustings. Clarke joins him as he steps on a small platform discreetly placed near the entrance so the large crowd can see him. The sounds of the Beach Boys blare from the speakers, giving a modern, sort of JFK effect, to the occasion. A crowd approaching 200 are milling around when the music is lowered and the Taoiseach-in-waiting welcomes the guests, speaks confidently about 'our prospects for a historic success' at the polls and reminds all present that extra financial assistance is badly needed if Fianna Fáil is to be restored to its rightful place in government.

'As the bishop says, we don't want too much noise in the church so a silent collection will do,' he says to loud guffaws from the crowd. 'In the meantime, enjoy yourselves tonight, but not too much. There's work to be done tomorrow.' More laughs, loud applause and cheers.

The waiters are filling glasses with red and white wine. Clarke joins Eileen as those assembled are invited to take their seats for the food and entertainment. They are placed with the new British ambassador and his henchman, Crawley, as well as the American envoy, a young, clean-cut, handsome bachelor. Eileen is beside herself. Fenton is busy rushing from table to table, glad-handing and making complimentary remarks to the wives. He whispers something to Paula Murphy, who blushes, composes herself, pushes his arm away and stomps off. The leader has the bishops and the garda commissioner to himself. Clarke is pleased with that. Not so pleased is Eileen, who's watching the flattering and flabby food critic from the Indo stroking her husband's arm.

'Could be a long night. Must watch the sauce,' Clarke says, taking a gulp of wine and the hard look from his wife. Fenton joins their table, stuffing a brown envelope into his inside pocket. 'Make sure you put the donations somewhere safe,' Clarke whispers.

David Gunning is discretely taking careful note of the assembled guests, who's conversing with whom and, where possible, what they are saying. Every now and then he checks the camera he has installed on a shelf overlooking the main dining area, a strategic location with a full view of the elite gathered for the occasion. All but the lens is hidden by a conveniently placed, lavish flower display.

As instructed by Joe, he takes a particular interest in Clarke and the circle that forms around him, including the man from the embassy whose photo he had seen in the newspaper with the recently appointed ambassadorial replacement. The new envoy appears to be enjoying the night and in particular the charms of Eileen Clarke, who is following her husband's advice to mix with the people whose influence and position could make all the difference to them someday. Besides, she likes his cultured accent and very English manners, and he's not bad-looking for an ambassador, although not as nice as the American one, who is the target of half the single women in the room, and quite a few of the married ones. She is also taking some pleasure in the knowledge that most of the other women, for all their finery, are not about to become the wife of a government minister and a potential future party leader, assuming that all goes well.

Chicken wings, steaks and wild salmon are rolled out in copious amounts from the kitchen and the wine flows freely into thirsty mouths. From every perspective the night is a great success – for Clarke, Fenton and their leader, for the guests, for the Murphys and for the party, which by all accounts is fighting the most expensive election campaign in the history of the State.

As the night progresses and alcohol-induced relaxation sets in, the camera manages to get copious shots of supposedly celibate or happily married men indulging in more than intimate contact with some of the young women brought in by Fenton to add some colour to the *occasion. The Catholic bishop is no slouch when it comes to pressing the female flesh, while several politicians, including a number about to put themselves before the people as icons of moral integrity, are out of their skulls before the end of the main course and groping any woman in sight. Their wives, also taking the chance to imbibe, don't notice or don't care.*

Clarke is among those whose inhibitions and self-control have been diluted by the steady flow of Beaujolais. He sees Angie with a tray of full glasses. As she nears him, he reaches to take one, whispers in her ear and puts his hand on her backside, pulling her close. He leers down the front of her blouse, red-faced and puffed-up with too much booze. Angie looks both shocked and distressed as Donal surreptitiously clicks the borrowed 35mm Canon AE-1. Discreet. Continuous shots. No flash. Worth its weight in gold.

20

BOOTERSTOWN

Heno watches as the Audi emerges from the driveway just after 8 p.m. An hour later, the son leaves in a red Mini and doesn't spare the horses as he lashes down Cross Avenue and towards the city. Not long after, a taxi arrives to take the two girls, dressed to the nines for a Friday night out, in the direction of Blackrock. That just leaves the dog, he reckons, and enough time to have the job done well before 10 p.m. He has cased the joint on a number of occasions over the past two weeks and has worked out the weekend routines of the family, which was not that hard as they are fairly predictable. He has already discovered that he can make an easy entry by a back door which leads into a pantry off the kitchen. Breaking the side window will allow him to pull the bolt inside. The red setter barked and howled for at least half an hour after his nocturnal visit last Friday, but he has a solution to that problem. It won't be the first or last dog to enjoy top-quality sirloin from The Bistro, which the 'meat man' gives him assuming it's feeding his five kids in west Finglas.

'I'm well able to feed my own family but never look a gift horse in the mouth,' thinks Heno as he waits for the optimum moment of entry. 'It comes in very handy for a hungry mutt.'

The dog barks at nine bells as Heno approaches the back door and louder again when he breaks the small window with his towel-covered hand and pulls the inside bolt. The mutt is in the pantry howling at the door when the lump of meat lands at its paws. Heno hears the sound of chewing, then groaning. Two minutes later the Red Setter lies down as the heavy dose of rat poison takes effect.

'His last supper and he didn't feel a thing,' says Heno to himself.

With the aid of a torch strapped to his forehead, Heno does a reccie of the downstairs rooms but has no doubts, from years of burgling experience, that what he wants will be in the master bedroom. At the top of the landing to the left is the large en suite room, curtains drawn, with a king-sized bed and a huge walk-in wardrobe. At the far end of the room is another door which opens into a smaller room with three walls of shelving holding books of all shapes and sizes. Family photos hang on the remaining white wall and a large landscape of the Burren is suspended above a teak desk containing a myriad of small drawers and cubby holes. Some documents and files lie scattered on top but nothing that signifies anything of importance and certainly not what he is seeking.

Carefully removing the painting, he finds the safe. It is a model he has come across before, in the homes of similarly well-endowed people of importance, all of whom are convinced that their security is impregnable until they discover otherwise. In this case, it takes Heno all of four minutes to disable the electric cable connected to the keypad on the front of the safe. It's a simple procedure employed by the manufacturer as a back-up to allow entry in the event that the owner forgets the code.

'Pretty stupid,' he thinks, 'but to be fair it's meant to be a trade secret.'

Inside, he finds an envelope containing a large wad of fresh twenty-pound notes, a tidy selection of jewellery and a bundle of documents marked confidential. He also finds what his latest accomplice is looking for. The words 'Royal Bank of Bermuda' and underneath 'Client account: Mr Robert Clarke esquire' give the game away. Joe the 'meat man' was right. The job is worth Heno's time and *effort. The bundle of money and sparklers are his — all his new friend wants are the papers, which are of no value to Heno. So he's happy to purloin them in return for the tip-off that the owners, some big shot and his wife, will be out for the night. The name Clarke rings a bell, but not loud enough to trigger any doubt about his mission.*

A walk in the park and a dog with a weakness for a bit of steak. In less than fifteen minutes the main job is done. A brief expedition through the other rooms, opening drawers and strewing stuff around the place to make it look like a random attack on a rich house in the suburbs by some local tea leaves, and he's done. He doesn't take any of the whiskey or rum from the cabinet, doesn't shit on the floor like some scumbags and doesn't leave any prints. Heno is a professional, or at least he likes to think so. Gloves, balaclava and silence — the key assets of a successful thief. At 9.40 p.m. he's on the Merrion Road heading into town for a few scoops after a successful night's work. First, though, he has to stash the goods in the lock-up he rents in a lane off Dominick Street. He's the only one with the location and the keys. Professional job. Good stroke.

His unsuspecting victims are among the last guests to leave The Bistro. When the doors close for the last time, Murphy and his wife sit down to bask in their undoubted triumph, a truly wonderful occasion, a very successful fundraiser for the party and a healthy dose of revenue for their own bank account. Even the party leader went out of his way to praise and thank them. He gave a not-so-subtle prediction that either or both could find a role at some significant level in the ranks where their organisational skills would be very useful in the challenging times ahead, post-victory. Murphy almost had to bite his tongue in case the words Bord Fáilte fell out. Paula was equally chuffed, as compliments about the food, wine, flowers, music, her outfit, hairdo and her all-round excellence rebounded off the walls.

Even the staff, especially Angie, Joe and the new waiter, David, seem to be pleased with how the night went.

'And why wouldn't you be?' Paula says. 'You were wonderful and I think a bottle of champagne is in order.'

21

JOE

When we escape the clutches of our inebriated employers we make tracks through Dublin's late night revellers towards Sloopy's night club, near the Palace.

'You could buy a house with the sparklers on some of those women in The Bistro,' Angie says.

'And that's just the women,' I reply.

She gently slips her arm through mine as we cross Dame Street. I like it. At the nightclub, I go straight to the top of a long and winding queue, greet Andy the doorman and drop him a fiver. Half price.

Amid the noise and flashing lights, the mini-skirts and flares, we assess the results of our night's work. Donal keeps his camera close to his chest in his small carrier bag. He is full of talk, spouting on about the assembly of the privileged and what the news editors wouldn't do to get a few shots of the glittering occasion. He's getting excited and loud. With a gesture to my lips I ask him to tone it down. Donal takes the point.

'Dead right,' he shouts through the Stones and 'Satisfaction'.

But it's hard to resist the temptation to gloat, and after two vodka and cokes, we are laughing and joking about the various guests we encountered and the state they were in.

Donal tells Angie of the shot he thinks he got of Clarke grabbing her arse and staring down her blouse.

'I was only topping up his wine, not giving him the come-on,' she says. 'What a grubby sleazebag.'

I'm thinking about Heno. We have agreed not to get in touch, not to visit the Music Place, not to do anything until whatever heat is generated by his side of the operation subsides. I'm uneasy at keeping Angie out of that particular loop, but have decided that what she doesn't know won't hurt her. Besides, Heno's job might not have come off, or he might not have found anything useful, for us at least.

Angie wants to dance. I tell Donal not to move. The nerves and excitement of it all have me wrecked. Fleetwood Mac. Our first slow set. She leans close. Our bodies move well together. We leave after another round. I arrange to collect a set of the photos and the negatives from Donal once they are developed. He can bring a selection around the newsrooms. She gives him a hug.

'Fucking gorgeous,' he says to me as he jumps on his bike.

'I know. See you later.'

'You know what?' says Angie, smiling and taking my arm.

'That you're fucking gorgeous.'

'You're not too bad yourself,' she says, her head now tucked into my shoulder.

We walk back to my flat.

Once inside, I ask, 'Do you want a cup of tea, a bottle of –?'

'Just you,' she says, walking me to the bedroom.

She pulls me to her, her warm soft lips on mine, and we share a long, deep, tongue-filled kiss as she opens the buttons on my shirt. We strip in seconds until there is just us, our naked bodies together again. I explore her breasts, her stomach, her most tender places. She guides me into her soft and damp spot, deep inside, deeper. As one we find the pleasure we seek. We've waited so long. She calls my name as she comes. She pulls me closer, tighter until every drop is shed. When it ends, we lie together in silence.

'I'm sorry,' she says finally.

'For what?'

'For taking so long to do this, to make love to you.'

'You were worth the wait.'

We kiss and fall asleep.

I dream of canapés and wine, long gowns and black ties, shop windows blown out with shoes on the street, a car burning, a girl with bloody hair, fat bishops, politicians and a dark-blue car. I am dancing a slow set with Angie to 'A Whiter Shade of Pale', then she's disappearing through the crowd, gone. I see Clarke crouching over her. She's strapped to a bed made of glass bottles. It's shaking and shattering with the wine spilling over her naked frame. Blood red. I jerk awake, sweating. Now I remember why I never drink vodka.

'What's wrong?' she asks, still half asleep.

'Just a nightmare. I'm okay,' I say, pulling her closer.

Soon we are making love again.

22
BOOTERSTOWN

Bob Clarke is a happy man, more than slightly pissed, when he pulls into his driveway after the fundraiser. The wife is rattling on about someone she met from the newspapers who is interested in her idea for a new fashion magazine. He's thinking it's only six days to go before his destiny is secured, when the people of this borough will place their trust in him as their parliamentary representative in such massive numbers as to make him a certainty for high cabinet office. He struggles to pull the key from the ignition and climb out of the car. Eileen is already through the front door and in the house before he manages to lock the Audi. As he reaches the top of the steps, he hears an unmerciful scream.

'What is it? I'm coming,' he shouts, tripping over the doorstep and crashing into the hall, head first.

'Jesus, I think my fucking arm is broken,' he curses as he stumbles to her side. There on the kitchen floor lies the cause of his wife's anguish. Their red setter is stretched out with its tongue lolling out on the tiles beside what looks like a half-eaten raw steak. There is a foamy substance around the animal's mouth and head and he guesses that the poor creature suffered some form of seizure. It's clearly dead.

'He must have had a heart attack or something. I'll bring him out to the shed for now,' he says as he tries to console his better half. She's down on her knees, sobbing and stroking the animal's head over and over.

'Who gave him the sirloin? We didn't have one in the house. He must have choked to death,' she says, crying. Clarke eases her up and

guides her into the living room, sitting her down on the couch. He goes back to the kitchen and just about manages to drag the dog out to the shed without falling again. Then he pours two stiff Jemmys. Eileen gulps hers down, then resumes her keening.

He sits with his arm around her for a while until she falls into an exhausted, drunken and noisy slumber. Laying her gently down, he gets up and refills his glass. He turns on a light on the desk. Only then does what she said strike him. Even if she's wrong about having sirloin in the house, the mutt wasn't in the habit of making himself a steak dinner. Sobered by the thought, he notices the drawers of the cabinet in the living room are open. A pen he is certain he placed in its holder on the desk that evening is lying on the floor. It hits him like a smack on the head.

'Oh my good Jesus,' he says aloud. The safe, check the safe! Gripping the banisters to keep himself steady, he clambers up the stairs to the master bedroom and into his study. The safe door is ajar and it doesn't take long to establish that the cash and most of the wife's jewellery are gone. Although the house deeds and other papers have been left behind, the envelope containing his Bermuda bank details is missing. That's when he sobers up completely.

His mind racing, he calls the sergeant in Blackrock, a friend of his and the party. Tom Taaffe is a heavy sleeper but is roused by his wife to take an urgent call from Bob Clarke, on whose request, or rather instruction, he acts immediately. Taaffe says he will have a squad car dispatched from the station to Booterstown to secure the scene and preserve any evidence. In the meantime, he will personally take charge of the investigation into the burglary and will have detectives over to Cross Avenue as soon as possible. He takes Clarke's advice not to bother the commissioner, who left the party rather tipsy not long before Clarke, at this ungodly hour with something that might be a minor incident. He agrees that the Special Branch should be informed given the political profile of the victim and, of course, the unique circumstances prevailing in the country with the Troubles and an election campaign in full swing. He calls the station, gives a string of instructions and promptly falls back to sleep.

After his discussion with the sergeant, Clarke sets about preparing his best response to this invasion of privacy, the attack on the integrity of his family home and the theft of some items of jewellery precious to his wife, including her mother's wedding and engagement rings, and her own favourite necklace. The death of their beautiful and loyal dog, Rusty, has greatly upset the whole family, especially the children, he will say. It appears to have been a callous and brutal murder carried out by the thieves, who will be tracked down and convicted of this heinous crime with the assistance of our friends in the gardaí.

These are the thoughts he will convey to the party's press officer and his own advisors when it comes to dealing with any public fallout from the incident. Look on the bright side. It can be used to leverage votes he might not otherwise get from a sympathetic public in a wealthy constituency. Fear of their homes being robbed is a serious concern among the otherwise comfortable middle class.

On the other hand, he does not want to feed the current narrative put about by the Blueshirts that they are the only ones hard on the lawbreakers and delinquents. They have promised, if returned to government, that they will increase spending tenfold on the fight against criminals and subversives. He can win both ways, he thinks, if he pours cold water on this promise. He can present himself as a living and courageous example of how government policies on crime have failed. He will gain sympathy for the manner in which he emerges, with his family of course, before the cameras at the earliest possible opportunity to state that he will not let the attack on his home deter him from his political responsibilities, including his party's promise to deal with the breakdown of law and order in society.

His rambling mind is disturbed by the doorbell. The men in blue from Blackrock responding to his call to Sergeant Taaffe. A squad car in the drive, blue light flashing. He's not ready to deal with their questions yet.

'Sorry, lads, for dragging you out at this hour,' Clarke says. 'The house was robbed when we were out last evening. But we're all right. Except the dog. My wife is asleep and I don't want to upset her any more.'

'Sorry to hear that, Mr Clarke. Yours isn't the first house burgled on this road,' says the taller one. 'There's a few right scumbags prowling around. We can come back tomorrow. We'll get the crime squad and forensics on the job. If you need anything just call us.'

With his head still pounding and his thoughts racing, Clarke ponders what he's going to tell his leader and party advisors and the media, when they find out, about the possible motives for the burglary of his home. For this has him flummoxed. Why the fuck would some lowlife looking for valuables take bank documents? Even if it has the Bank of Bermuda and his name all over it, it's no good to anyone but him. Unless that's what they came for and not the cash and jewels. 'Jesus, fuck, I need another drink,' he moans. As he downs another Jemmy, Clarke decides that he'll make no mention of the missing papers to the police, or to anyone else, just talk about the stolen cash and jewels.

His next move, before anyone else arrives, is to alert Fenton to the potential nightmare that could be unfolding before their very eyes just days before the election and his expected elevation in the ranks of Irish political life. As he dials the number, his head begins to throb even more as the night of heavy drinking takes its toll. His mood turns to one of anger and revenge. There's no answer from his advisor. He hangs up.

'The robbing fuckers will pay for this. Fifteen years at least and a good beating won't be good enough for them,' he raves. He has a sneaking suspicion that the burglary could have something to do with the political state of affairs and its disparate players, including the Blueshirts, his own jealous party colleagues and opponents in the battle for high office, the left wing and republican subversives seeking to damage anyone held in respect, or the fucking Brits.

Less than two hours ago he had been in the company of their ambassador and that snivelling little rat, Martin Crawley, who was quick to remind Clarke, quietly, of what they expect of him in the new regime given what they know of his various illicit activities, including his fling with the reporter and, worse, his en-tanglement with the elaborate offshore fund which is under their ultimate financial management. And how the fuck did that bastard, Richards, know the documents were stashed in his safe at home? Must ask Fenton about that, he reminds himself. He's the only one I told about them. Then again the Brits don't need the papers – they already know everything. He decides that none of his rambling suspicions make any sense.

He falls back in the armchair and drifts away to the sound of his snoring wife on the couch across the room. They are awoken by the sound of the doorbell and she is soon making tea for two imposing members of the elite unit of garda national security and intelligence. They say they've been instructed by the commissioner to urgently investigate the break-in at the home of a man tipped to be a cabinet member and possibly the next Minister for Home Affairs. When asked how the commissioner knew about the break-in, when Clarke had agreed with the sergeant in Blackrock that it was not necessary to disturb him, one of the men explains that Dublin Castle received a tip-off from an ambitious detective in Blackrock about the burglary. It did not take long for the ghost shift at the Castle to realise that this could have potential ramifications at such a crucial stage of an election campaign and that it would be wise for anyone concerned about his job and future prospects to alert the commissioner.

Commissioner Edward 'Ned' Gavin was not impressed when he was rudely awoken by his wife telling him to answer the phone on the hall table.

'It's not for me at this hour,' she said. He rose unsteadily and took the call.

'Get down to Clarke's house before the local detectives,' he advised. 'Don't mess the scene up. Gather as much information as possible but don't disturb anything. The lads in Blackrock will want to handle it. Don't take anything for granted, either. Find out what's missing and report directly back to me,' he barked. I need this like a hole in the head, he'd thought, as he sank under the blanket and fell back asleep.

The two Branch men survey the crime scene, upstairs and down, closely observing the victim as he is asked what is missing from the safe. It is immediately apparent that this is the work of an experienced burglar. Clearly the thief, or thieves, had watched the family leave the house, probably from across the wide tree-lined avenue. Then, once they were gone, gaining access to the kitchen through the pantry window was simple and the dog was handled with a ruthless efficiency, by a steak probably laced with some sort of easily available poison. From there it was simply a question of finding the valuables. It would have been guesswork that there was a safe of some kind and where else to start looking but the study? But getting it open was not that easy and had to be the work of someone with the required skill set. The cut wires showed that the burglar didn't know the code, so this was probably not an inside job, but that couldn't be entirely ruled out. 'Don't take anything for granted,' the commissioner had said.

'Can you give us an account of your movements, and those of the rest of the family tonight?' the detective inspector asks politely as he sits on the armchair across from Clarke while his junior partner, the detective sergeant, re-examines the scene upstairs. The wife, who is still the worse for wear, is back in the kitchen making more tea. This allows the sergeant to investigate without the suspicious eyes of her ladyship watching his every move. It doesn't stop her expressing her concern to Clarke about 'that man snooping around our bedroom'.

'An account of our movements,' huffs Clarke, shaking from the effects of booze and strained nerves. 'I thought that's what you ask of suspects, not the fucking victims.'

'Perhaps I should rephrase that. Where were you all when the burglary took place?'

Clarke explains that the kids are off gallivanting with their friends, while he and the missus were at a function in the city. They arrived home sometime after 1 a.m. to discover to their shock and horror that the dog was dead and their home in a state. He says that the kids are staying with friends for the night. The eldest is eighteen, just finishing the Leaving. He went into town. The girls are twins of sixteen. They are allowed to go to Stradbrook, the local rugby club disco.

'No drink of course,' he assures the detective.

'Would you mind if the lads from Blackrock have a chat with them at some stage, just in case they witnessed anyone suspicious in the neighbourhood over the past few days?' the inspector asks.

'Not at all. As long as myself or my wife is with them during the interview,' says Clarke. He's as wary of the police as he is of the average member of his own parliamentary party and equally protective of his kids, his unruly but lovable son in particular. Jonathan does not have the wit to organise a robbery of his own house, not to mind my safe, he thinks, dismissing the theory he is sure is going through the devious mind of the detective sitting in his favourite armchair.

Detective Inspector O'Malley is discussing the event in The Bistro when they are rejoined by Detective Sergeant Mullen, followed closely by Eileen with the tea and ham sandwiches.

'The elite of Dublin society was present, all the key party donors, the leader and his team, front-bench spokespeople like myself and various dignitaries. Commissioner Gavin was there too, as you may be aware,' says Clarke, in a less-than-veiled warning to the pair of hungry savages not to lose the run of themselves.

'Indeed. As we've explained, it was the chief who insisted that we came out here at the first opportunity. He is personally going to oversee the investigation, wherever it leads,' says O'Malley. The veteran is quick to grasp the potential political minefield he has just stumbled into and the need to avoid a turf war with the local crime squad. He informs Clarke that the Blackrock detectives will be back to take prints and statements, including from the kids. The dog will have to be examined. He adds that they might even have a lead on some local robbers and the unfortunate business could be wrapped up before too long.

'You've had a rough night. Try to get some rest. We'll be in touch. Good luck with the campaign,' he says as he and Mullen make their *exit through the hall where a pile of election posters with Clarke's toothy smile and carefully coiffed hair beams up from the floor, in stark contrast to the hungover wreck they have just interviewed.*

They don't have anything in the way of a lead but there are several lines of inquiry to be followed. The thief must have known that the family would be out of the house on Friday night and that they had a dog. The question is whether he was looking for something specific or if this was a simple robbery for high-value goods. As they travel back to the Castle they also weigh up the possibility of insurance fraud, which is all the rage among the more squeezed end of the middle classes. They rule it out on the grounds that a man with the prospect of becoming a government minister within days is unlikely to engage in such a scam. And he would hardly kill the family pet in the process.

The prospect of Clarke becoming Minister for Home Affairs has also clearly crossed the mind of the commissioner, who is not taking any chances with this investigation as it could have an impact on his career, as well as all those involved down the ranks, including O'Malley and Mullen. For this reason alone, they determine to get to the bottom of it, no matter how complicated or embarrassing it might become for all concerned. They decide to check the list of guests at The Bistro to establish whether there were other break-ins at any of their homes. The list is provided within hours by the politician's advisor, Myles Fenton.

Within forty-eight hours, with the help of a pliant security correspondent at the Independent, *and in return for some selective information on the crime, they manage to get more than they expect. The name and address of a freelance photographer who is touting photos of the fundraiser, taken without the permission of the owners or the organisers, it seems.*

'Although a link to the burglary at Clarke's home is tenuous, to say the least,' O'Malley says when he is updating his superiors, including Ned Gavin. 'What makes it significant is the presence at the fundraiser of the British ambassador, some of the wealthiest people in the country and half of the future cabinet if, as we all expect, the party is returned to power within the coming days, and of course yourself, Commissioner. This is a pretty serious breach of security and there are potential political consequences to whatever the hell is going on, whether or not this turns out to be linked to the break-in.'

Gavin agrees, and ensures that O'Malley is given extra man-power and resources and the green light to use whatever methods are required, however unpalatable, to uncover the truth about the events of that evening.

23

JOE

After a few days, Donal complains that none of the photo editors in the *Press*, *Times* or *Indo* have come back to him with an offer for his exclusive shots. Well, some of them, as we held back the more salacious, including the photo of Clarke with his filthy paws on Angie. He is considering other outlets, or just sticking them on the walls of every pub jacks in the city. I advise against the notion and say their contents will be lost on the average punter without proper context and explanation.

At first I'm surprised there is so little interest in the photographic record of an event that is certain to shape the outcome of the election in just a few days. Every bigwig in the city from bishops to bankers had been letting their hair down, and most members of the incoming government. Then it dawns on me that the owners of these papers were present at the event by private invitation of the party that is almost certainly about to enter government with an unassailable majority, if their own polls and predictions are anything to go by.

'We should have thought of this,' I say to Donal. 'Why would they shit on their own doorstep? They were there, they know what went on and they clearly hope to benefit by being on the inside track with the new crowd in power, getting all the best stories fed to them by our friend, Fenton. They're also cleaning up on election ads. The last thing they want is a row with the party.'

The Sunday papers, with their gossip columns and celebrity bullshit, are a possible avenue of approach but they could trivialise a good story. It will be lost among all the inches of crap about new heels and hairdos and the fashion sense of the city's finest, or lack of it. At my suggestion, he leaves the full collection of photos and negs with me. Later, I give them to Angie to keep in her college locker.

On the morning of the election the *Indo* runs a front-page story, off lead, about a burglary at the home of a prominent politician on the southside, no name or address. It reports that local gardaí are investigating and are satisfied they will apprehend those responsible within a reasonably short period. Detectives at Blackrock are in charge, with the assistance of the Special Branch and C3 at Dublin Castle, given the identity of the victim and his political significance.

I finish my coffee and croissant and fold the paper, leaving the sports pages on top. I have yet to meet Heno. Reading about the hunt for the burglar makes it all the more real and dangerous. It hadn't occurred to me that the Branch or C3 would get involved. I need to talk to Heno and fast. Who knows where this could end up? I decide to head for the Music Place after work. I wonder if I've bitten off more than I can chew, placing my friends in danger. I fear the worst.

As I slip in the side door to the pub there is no sign of the Branch outside and Heno is in his usual spot at the bar. Then again, I suspect he does not take the *Indo* of a morning and is blissfully unaware that his little break-in is front-page news. He's a little chuffed when he finds out.

'Don't worry, there's no chance they'll get me on this one,' he tells me after explaining that he cleaned out most of the safe, including 'the papers you wanted'.

'Details of a bank account in Bermuda. Cash and sparklers,' he says. 'Clean as a whistle. In and out in less than an hour. The dog took a hit but he died happy, eating your steak.'

'My steak. What do you mean?' I ask.

'Your best sirloin with a heavy coat of rat poison,' he says.

'Jesus, you killed the family dog?'

'At least it wasn't one of his crazy kids,' he says, laughing. I try to stay calm.

Heno has got us proper physical evidence of a sensational political secret that could destroy the career of a potential minister. Not least because it has put the politician under the thumb of a man who looks and talks like an English secret agent. Alan Richards, who knows more than he should about the Dublin bombs and who's not afraid to blackmail the pathetic Robert Clarke. I'm frozen with a mixture of amazement, fear and paranoia. I order a pint to settle my nerves.

Heno sees only the funny side to the whole affair, providing a description of Clarke leaving the house with his wife looking like she was dressed for the horse show, the girls heading for a night out with skirts so short they were barely there and the son booting it in his new Mini so fast that you could hardly see him for smoke. And to think they thought a dog and a common-or-garden safe would be enough to stop any self-respecting thief when there was such a stash of money, jewels and secret papers to be found.

I quickly down my pint, make my excuses and tell Heno I need to collect the papers by the end of the week.

'No sweat,' the crook says, probably wondering why I look so freaked out. It was a walkover, he says again, and he now has enough to cover the family holiday for the summer, Courtown or Butlins, whatever the missus likes. He suggests we meet in a different pub next time, given the state I'm in. Joxer's, down the street.

'What about Friday lunchtime?' he says.

'That'll do, I'll see you then,' I reply.

As I walk through the city centre I reflect on the outcome of our risky operation and the next steps. The bank details, the words on tape explaining what they mean, the reference to the three big bangs and the graphic photos of the main characters in this sordid little drama. The question is how do we tell the story and at what cost?

24
THE BRIDEWELL

At 6 a.m., Donal awakes to a heavy knock on the front door, then another, and several more before he opens it with his T-shirt on backwards and inside out and his jeans just about hanging on him. Four burly men force their way past him, with one firmly propelling him into the living room of his top-floor Gardiner Street flat. The place is littered with books, magazines and photographs, hundreds of them stacked in boxes on half a dozen shelves and more in the bedroom.

'Right, where are they, you little bollox?' says the main burly man, whose name Donal hasn't caught because it hasn't been thrown.

'What are you on about?' asks Donal, still half asleep.

'The fucking photos of the party in The Bistro? We're told you're trying to sell them, you fucking pedlar. Grotty little business, isn't it? Taking photos of people behind their backs and selling them for a living. Sleazy journalism, is that it? Now hand them over.'

'I don't have them,' says Donal, who quickly realises he's in serious shit. 'I got rid of them,' he lies.

'And why would you do that?' the main burly man asks.

'No one wants them,' he says, truthfully this time.

One goon finds his photos from Talbot Street on the day of the bombs.

'Very grisly. Do you like this sort of thing? Pictures of human misery caused by scumbags like you,' says the garda, throwing the pictures of body parts and scattered effects on the floor.

'I'm a freelance photographer. It's my job,' Donal protests as a pair of cuffs is snapped round his wrists.

He soon finds himself in the back of a Renault van on the way to the Bridewell, while other cops are left to go through every single photo, letter and document in his untidy flat. He knows that it could be a long day and night. He's not in any position to warn Joe and Angie that they could be due an early morning visit. But he can't understand what the big deal is. It's just a few photos. The subjects might not like it, but he's fairly confident there's nothing actually illegal about snapping them, however secretly taken.

These thoughts are not long fermented when he gets a painful dig in the kidneys from the heavy cop sitting beside him in the back.

'You know, Donal, your life would be a lot easier if you just gave us the full set of photos instead of fucking us around. We know you have them. The Press guy told us you were hawking them. You'll not get a job in this town after this caper,' he sneers before planting a jab into his prisoner's private parts. Donal's loud moan falls on deaf ears.

In the interrogation room in the Bridewell, the approach is more civilised. A polite, or less ignorant, man begins to write his details on a long, lined sheet of white paper. Name, address, date of birth, family history, job, hobbies, friends?

'Do you know any subversives, Donal?' he asks, almost kindly, like a nurse inquiring about any sexually transmitted diseases he might be carrying.

'Like someone with a mask carrying a machine gun? How would I recognise one?' Donal says calmly.

'You know what I fucking mean, smartarse,' says the detective, letting the mask slip. 'I can keep you here all day and tomorrow and the next day if I want. I'm in no hurry. We know that you worked in the restaurant for the night. We'd like to know who asked you to take photos or was that your own crazy idea. And why? In particular, we'd like the current whereabouts of Angela Whelan. The one who got you the job in The Bistro, and her friend, the chef. Did you know Heney's a fucking jailbird?'

'I'm not saying anything more without a solicitor,' Donal says, to a hostile reaction.

25

ANGIE

I'm walking out of the Exam Hall, feeling pleased with myself. My English paper went well. Only the Irish one left. I'm about to make my way from the college to The Bistro when I see Joe leaning against the wall pulling on a smoke. I'm not expecting him. Not long afterwards, we are whispering anxiously over bad coffee in Trinity's student bar, the Buttery. I'm learning of his crazed invasion of the privacy of one of Ireland's most powerful politicians.

'Are you stark raving mad?' I say when the full details of the break-in at the minister's house emerge. No unnecessary information such as the names of the actual perpetrators are revealed in his convoluted account of the nocturnal activities in leafy Booterstown. To add to the drama, he heard just an hour ago that Donal was taken away this morning and is most likely in the Bridewell. That information came after an angry encounter with Murphy, who wanted to know what the fuck the police were doing in his establishment the previous evening, asking about someone he had hired for a couple of hours on my recommendation. Joe explains that his first reaction was to deny any knowledge of Donal's complicity with wrongdoing and instead ask the agitated Murphy, as calmly as he could, what all the fuss was about.

'He says, "This guy Donal has been touting exclusive photos of our private party to the papers all over town. How many times did Fenton say the event was private? He kept going on about keeping those nosey fucks out of the place and here you and your girlfriend bring this sneaky little bastard dressed up as a waiter to a party fundraiser with the leader and half the next fucking cabinet, not to mind the commissioner and the bishop skulling wine by the bottle. He told me a bare-faced lie, that his father or uncle or whoever was in the guards. Well if there's one thing the cops don't like, it's someone taking their name in vain. I hope they knock the complete bollox out of him. As for you and your pretty friend, I'll have more to say when I get back from the accountant. This could fucking ruin me. I've a good mind to fire the pair of you." Then he rushed off.'

He takes off the boss's angry reaction, accent and expressions perfectly, but this time it's not remotely funny.

'He was hardly out the door when that geeky darkroom friend of Donal's pulls up on a bicycle and calls me outside,' Joe continues. 'He tells me the cops were in Donal's gaff this morning. Your man was about to drop in to collect some negs for developing. He saw them carting Donal off and said more cops were still in the flat. Probably tearing the place apart looking for something. He said he knew Donal and me were tight and that he thought he'd better tell me in case Donal needs a solicitor or something. Also said he hopes he gets out soon because he owes him a score for printing work. That's when I told the chef I had a stomach problem and came down here to catch you before you walked into the shitstorm.'

'Well, thanks for that. As if we don't have enough to worry about,' I say.

'Anyway,' says Joe, 'the cops are chasing the guy who robbed Clarke's house. It was in the *Indo*. It seems they haven't a clue who they're looking for. Or what was taken in the robbery. Our man got the Bermuda bank details. We'll have them soon. This could put a stop to Clarke's gallop and expose his dealings with the Brits and their role in the bombings.' He sounds excited and nervous.

When I grasp the significance of the documents taken from the safe, a snake of fear runs down my spine. I had no problem keeping the photos and negs until we came up with an alternative plan to get them published, but Joe's little side venture is now front-page news and there's a full-scale search going on. These bastards could descend on us at any minute. They might go to the house and frighten the life out of Mam.

And there's the little matter of the tape with the Englishman boasting about the bombings. If the police get their hands on it, all hell could break loose. What has Joe done? Breaking into a rich politician's house wasn't part of the plan he sold to me.

'They have to suspect there's a connection between the party, the photos and the robbery at Clarke's house,' I say.

Shamefaced, Joe replies, 'I should have told you what was going on. Shit, I'm sorry. I thought it was safer for you not to know. I've fucked up, placed you and Donal in danger. '

'That's an understatement. What a mess. Maybe we should get rid of the photos and negs, the tape, everything?'

I feel a twinge of guilt for criticising his behaviour given that it was at least partly my mam's trauma that motivated his quest for truth and justice. But this thing is getting out of hand altogether. I can almost feel my life imploding around me. And I'm in no hurry to see what's in store for me when I get back to East Wall. The cops could be outside the door already.

Joe says we need to calm down and decide what to do next.

He says the safest place for us at this point is his place. Even the boss has no idea where he lives.

'In fact,' he says, 'the only one that has ever visited my gaff is you.'

I call in sick to The Bistro from the public phone at the college gate. As I sit at his kitchen table a while later, I silently contemplate how we got into this fix. Over the first cup of tea, and his tenth apology, Joe tries to make sense of it all.

'So Donal is under arrest, which means they'll be looking to talk to you since you got him the job,' he says. 'But you haven't committed any crime. You knew nothing about the burglary until now. They'll learn quick enough that Donal is a mate of mine. So they'll want to talk to me as well, but there's nothing to link me to it, unless Heno is caught and spills the beans.'

'Heno, the ex-con?' I say.

'He did the job and got some cash and jewels as well as the bank stuff,' Joe replies. He seems calm again. I'm shaking. 'The cops probably suspect a connection between the theft at Clarke's house and the party in The Bistro. And they'll be looking for any photos that could embarrass all those politicians, bishops, diplomats and their own commissioner. That must be why they picked up Donal after he showed some around the newsrooms. But taking pictures isn't a crime.

'We could destroy everything but then all our work is for nothing. And look at what we have. The English spy on tape talking about the bombings and Clarke's hidden stash, the details of the bank account and where the money came from, and photos of all those fuckers wining and dining. They're a nest of vipers but we have the goods on them.'

'And they're about to knock on our front door at any moment,' I say.

'At the same time,' Joe says, 'we've enough to prove that people in high places know more than they'd care to admit about who blew up Dublin and your mam. The tapes, photos and bank statements show who they are and the corruption and lies they're covering up.'

Now I'm thinking of the devastating consequences of that day in May: Mam unable to sleep because of the headaches, the gaping hole on Talbot Street outside the shop with the new shoes in the window, the boy Lazarus with the penetrating eye, Da crying at the bed in the Mater. With what we have we might even get an investigation into the events which transformed my family life. It seems wrong to give all that up. But I'm terrified of being arrested and how that will affect my family, my future.

My rambling mind is disturbed when Joe hands me another cup of tea.

'Thanks,' I say. 'This isn't all your fault. We got into this together and we'll get out the other side. It could be worse.'

Moving the photos from my college locker to a safer hiding place, given that they are now the subject of an investigation, would seem to be the most urgent matter. If the guards are after me, they will check every possible spot I might use to store them. Then there's the issue of what to do with the incriminating tape. If Joe is found with that we'll be in serious trouble.

We discuss all the possibilities, our possible arrest and even conviction of a crime. The guards will be at our homes sooner rather than later and we need a good solicitor. Whatever about Donal, there is no question that Murphy handed over every bit of information he has about us to the police and probably added in a few suspicions of his own just to make matters worse. Such as how Joe was always going on about politics and revolution and trade unions, reading out all that stuff in the newspapers about the bombings and the Brits, and spouting all sorts of conspiracy theories.

'The stuff we have may be our only protection. I still have the napkin as well. We have to keep everything safe, hide everything quickly. We might also be able to use some of the photos from the fundraiser as a bargaining chip,' Joe says.

I know he's thinking of me in the crude clutches of the drunken Clarke. I think of the shot of his red lecherous face, his face almost on my breasts and his hand clutching my backside, and I agree. Clarke would not want that out in public.

'If it comes to it I'll take the rap,' he says. 'I'll tell them you had nothing to do with it.'

'Why should they believe you?' I say.

'It's the truth. Anyway, the real guilty ones are the people we have in the photos, the ones whose secrets are exposed on tape, and Clarke, with his offshore bank account. Sure we had to use some devious methods to get our evidence, but at most the only crime here is possession of stolen property and I'll take responsibility for that. It's no big deal,' he tries to convince himself.

I'm not so sure. I say the jails are full of people who've done a lot less. He drops his eyes to the floor.

By noon, we have a plan of sorts, which involves me getting the photos and negs to a safe location while he looks after the tape, napkin and the stolen bank papers, for now. We need to get them offside before we're hauled in. And I need to get home soon, police or no police.

I'm terrified at the prospect. But the only way to avoid it, it seems, is to do a runner and that's not on with my mam still needing help. We agree we should both go back to work as soon as possible. He says to ask for Gerard Neilan if I'm pulled in by the gardaí. They have to get the solicitor you ask for, he says, although it might take a while. Neilan is the only solicitor in town he knows of who has a reputation for successfully defending those accused of subversion, innocent or not. Joe is due back in work tomorrow afternoon, by which time he will have got the documents from Heno and hidden them with the tape. Hopefully, he can also make contact with Donal, if he gets out of the Bridewell.

'We're in this together,' I say and kiss him quickly before I go.

My first stop is my locker, to collect the photos. On the bus home to East Wall I pass the morgue with its memories of blackened bodies, torn limbs, the smell of antiseptic and Lazarus. Further on is Humphrey's and the church which dominates the skyline of our streets. It's a hive of social and religious activity for the community, especially the older women like my mam. I sang in the choir when I was younger.

That's when I get an idea that might just go some way to resolving our current dilemma. As I walk up Church Road I place the envelope of photos on a ledge behind the bin at the back of the Black Widow's shop. We used it as a hiding place when we were kids. It'll be safe there for a while.

When I open the front door to an expected confrontation with Mam, I smell baking bread.

'I thought I'd have some ready for your next shift,' Mam shouts from the kitchen. 'Would you like some with a cup of tea, love?' I can't refuse. She carefully fills the cups and slices the bread. Her new glasses have helped her no end.

As we sit together over the cup of tea she reveals the disturbing, not unexpected news. 'There were two guards here this morning looking for you, dear. Nice enough lads, they were. Well one of them was polite anyway. They didn't say why they wanted to talk to you, but they want you to call them. They wrote down a number. It's here somewhere,' she says, searching the kitchen shelves. 'I told them you're up to your eyes with exams.'

I fake surprise, trying not to show how scared I am.

'I wonder what that's all about,' I say, taking the number from her hand without directly looking her in the eyes, the good or the bad one.

'Detectives they were, in one of those unmarked cars. I have to admit I got a bit of a fright. I thought something had happened to you, or Tony, bless him. Anyway they said it was nothing to worry about. Something about work. But I know you, Angie, I know you wouldn't be involved in anything bad.'

'Thanks, Mam,' I say as I silently plan my next move.

Mam continues to make soft but futile attempts to get some useful information as to what it is the gardaí could want. But I can't tell her, not yet anyway. I get up to go.

'There's nothing simple in this world anymore. Heaven knows where it will all lead to,' she says as if suspecting that there's something in the ether. She suggests I call the police back quickly, if only to let her mind rest.

'I'll say nothing to your father. You know what he's like with the worry.'

'I've got to get new pens and a notebook for college. I'll call the guards while I'm out. Do you need anything in the shop?'

'We could do with a half a pound of butter for your lordship's tea.'

I run down Church Road, retrieve the envelope and pray silently that I can offload the material burning a hole in the inside pocket of my coat before all hell breaks loose.

Father Bennett answers the presbytery door and sees my flushed face. He is concerned that something has happened to Mam.

'Is something the matter, Angie? Is it your mother?' he asks as he leads me down the hallway.

'No, no, she's fine, but thanks for asking, Father Bennett.'

'Rory, you can call me Rory.'

'Yes, Father, Rory.'

He mentions that I'm not a frequent visitor to the house of God, or the one next door. Says he hasn't seen much of me these past few months. I'm usually on my way out as he visits for prayers with Mam and a few neighbours on selected feast days. He rambles on about how Mam is well able to make her way to the church now and is recovering so well from the terrible events of a few years ago, and how I'm a great help to her in that regard. Hadn't it been a great thing to go to Trinity and me turned into a diligent student with good marks all the way, making Da and Mam so proud.

'I'm here to ask you a favour,' I say, breaking his flow.

'Tell me,' he says as we sit in his large, sparsely furnished living room.

I explain how I'm trying to help out a young photographer who's been arrested and whose pictures I have promised to keep. 'They were taken at an election fundraiser but for some reason no paper wants to publish them even though they're clearly newsworthy. There's nothing illegal about them, Father, but the guards were at the house this morning and I think they're looking for these pictures. I could just hand them over, but that could cause more trouble for Donal, who's been in the Bridewell since this morning. I don't know what to do and I thought you could advise me, or better still hang on to them until we clear things up. They are pretty harmless, just photos of some rich and famous people and politicians that you would see any day on the news. You can look for yourself,' I say as I pass over the sealed envelope.

'I will take your word for it that there is nothing illegal in this,' he says gently. 'I don't need to pry into matters I know nothing about. You're a good person, Angie, so of course I'll put them away for you and keep them for as long as you need me to.'

The visit by the Special Branch to our house prompts me to go further. If anything happens to me, someone has to look after Mam and the priest seems the most likely ally. It's better someone she can trust can explain things to her, if needed. I take a leap of faith.

I explain that the whole thing is connected with the bombs three years ago. How myself and a friend have found out that they were planted in order to get the government to go harder on the IRA, that it was not just loyalists from the North involved.

'The British had some role, we don't know what for sure. No one has been caught for killing more than thirty people that day. We're trying to find out why. I can't really say much more.'

'You don't need to, Angela. I will look after your envelope safely until you need it back,' he says.

I was hoping that would be his reaction. Anyone else would have asked more questions and sought more answers. But he isn't like that.

'I've not broken any law, Father, I can promise you that,' I say as my mind reverts to the dark confession box of my past. He holds his hands up to stop me saying any more.

'That doesn't bother me,' he says. 'My only concern is for the soul, not for the government or any other worldly authority, with the possible exception of the Pope. I've seen too many young people like you, in places much worse than this city, caught between the forces of good and evil. You are searching for the truth about your mother's tormentors. That is a worthy cause. For her and for you. Sometimes you forget that you are a victim too. During those black days in May, I saw the dead and maimed as I went around the hospitals seeking out the relatives of my parishioners too weak or afraid to search themselves. I found a boy who woke up in the morgue. A young man scarred and injured for life, trying to rebuild his body and his life. He was a fine little footballer, you know, just bought a new pair of boots to bring with him to England. His father, Harry, was bringing him across for trials with Spurs and Forest on the mail boat that night. The poor boy had his whole life before him until … Well, the Lord works in mysterious ways.'

His words struck like a bolt of lightning.

'Father, I was there when he woke up,' I say. Tears are welling up. From somewhere very deep. He can see my pain at the memory.

'Perhaps you should meet this brave young man some day. See how well he's doing now, all things considered. Danny Ryan is his name. His dad passed away a year later. Harry was in poor health, but the bombs and what they did to the young fella finished him altogether. Poor boy spent three months in a coma, then nine in rehab, a body full of car metal. Ten operations later, young Danny came home to see his father carried out in a coffin. On the day the Miami Showband was massacred.'

He takes the envelope, rises from the chair and brings it to a large desk. He puts it carefully away in a locked drawer.

'There you are, Angie. Now I've got to prepare for confessions.'

I regain control of my wavering emotions. 'Thanks, Father, and I was going to say that I might be able to help out with the choir sometimes.'

'Well, Lord be praised, I was just about to ask you. I'm told you have a beautiful voice and I could do with some help with the youngsters. You might give us an evening at practice every now and then.'

'That's a deal. I'll need to brush up on the "Ave Maria". Thanks again, Father Bennett … Rory,' I say, waving as I close the gate behind me. I feel as though someone just lifted the Rock of Cashel off my shoulders. I'm not sure why.

26

LEINSTER HOUSE

The fever of the election has pushed the incident of the stolen files and the poisoned dog to the back of Robert Clarke's already crowded mind, but not too far. For sure, the kids are devastated over the death of poor Rusty, but he can always replace the animal. He topped the poll, as expected, in south Dublin and brought in a running mate. He is on course for nomination to cabinet as the party reels in an even greater than expected majority. The pundits put it down to the outrageous promises made to cut house rates and car tax, along with other sweeteners for the hard-pressed middle classes. He suspects there has also been a backlash against the increasing hysteria of the previous crowd about the threat of subversion, with reds under every bed, as well as a media fomenting anti-government sentiment at every opportunity.

His own campaign leaned heavily on the republican credentials of his late, lamented father.

'We are not going to lie down to the demands of any foreign power, not least the British, when it comes to maintaining our country's hard-won independence and sovereignty. We will deal with subversives as we always have and we don't need instructions from anyone. We remain committed to the unity of our country by peaceful means,' he repeatedly told voters on the hustings and during the one television debate in which he participated.

Considering the complex state of affairs with Richards and Crawley, he knows this is all pretty meaningless, but it contrasted neatly with the incessant and unnecessarily harsh threats of the incumbents, who were forever going on about the need 'to curtail the precious freedoms to which we have become accustomed in the face of the subversive threat'. At least that's what Fenton said.

'People don't want to hear how bad things are. They want good news and someone who paints a bright future,' he said.

It seems to have worked.

The only dark cloud on the horizon for Clarke as they survey the mounting evidence of a landslide, bigger than anything Dev achieved in twelve out of thirteen elections, according to the all-knowing Fenton, is the possible fallout from the break-in.

'It's not fucking Watergate,' Clarke moans, and not for the first time, but the failure of the gardaí to apprehend a suspect, or anyone, after a full week of investigation is annoying to say the least. The sooner they can close the whole thing down the better. There's a country to run and he is about to join the high command. Besides, he desperately needs to recover the bank documents taken from his safe. He will be hard put to explain them if they fall into the wrong hands.

'Not yet,' says Fenton drily, with his typically pessimistic assessment of the situation. They know that in the course of the investigation the guards have tracked down a photographer who sneaked into the fundraiser that night disguised as a waiter. But it seems he has no subversive or political connections and was simply trying to make a name for himself. So, although the incident was embarrassing, not least after Fenton had taken it on himself to ensure there would be no unwanted media intrusion, it seems it's not linked to any wider plot. It's a godsend he had the foresight to invite the newspaper owners. That almost certainly guaranteed their co-operation in declining to publish, and indeed alerting the police to the ambitious opportunist.

That is as far as the investigation has gone, according to the latest briefing from the commissioner. His men spoke to Murphy and his wife, and have a couple of staff at The Bistro to question, but there's no indication that there's anything more to it. The only slight worry is that Gavin had also observed that if some thief wanted to use their attendance at a party fundraiser to rob their home, then Clarke would not have been the obvious choice from the list. He may live in Booterstown, but there were at least a dozen millionaires from the horsey set, the big builders and the ranchers in the room that night and they weren't burgled. So we have to examine other angles, the commissioner said in his imperious manner. Not what Clarke wanted to hear.

'Can you think of any possible reason why you would be singled out?' he asks as Clarke almost physically squirms on the other end of the phone. Which got him and Fenton looking at the British and their dirty tricks department. The Brits are the only ones who know anything about the Bermuda angle.

'But why would they bother when they know the story and have their own copies of the bank statements? Sure they've rubbed my nose in it already,' says Clarke with a pained expression. 'I have to meet the next Taoiseach tomorrow and he's bound to ask me about what's happening with the investigation. What will I tell him?'

'Stick to what the guards have told you until you know something better,' Fenton advises. 'Say nothing about the missing documents until you are forced to. I will make some discreet inquiries of our friends at the embassy.'

'With friends like that, who the fuck needs enemies?' Clarke snorts. 'And by the way, how did that snob Richards know I had the bank stuff in my safe at home? You wouldn't by any chance have shared that piece of information with your friend Crawley?'

'Surely you don't think I'd discuss such delicate personal matters with a foreign diplomat?' Fenton protests. Too much, perhaps.

'I'm beginning to wonder what you actually discuss, Myles, and with whom. I trust I've no problems in that regard,' Clarke says, giving the startled advisor his most piercing, threatening gaze.

The commissioner has taken a personal interest in Clarke's plight, not out of any sympathy for the politician, but because he's determined that the incident will not blight his seamless career as he looks to the sunset of retirement. He has informed the secretary of the Home Affairs department of what he regards as a routine burglary at the politician's home, but one that he believes should be handled with the utmost professionalism and sensitivity given the identity of the victim and his expected appointment to high office. He has placed his best security detail at the disposal of the local detectives and is confident of an early breakthrough.

What is bothering him a little is this matter of the fundraiser and the photographer. The snapper did not co-operate with the investigating officers, on the advice of his solicitor.

'If he has nothing to hide why doesn't he come clean?' he asked himself and the department secretary simultaneously.

He just can't shake the feeling that there is more to this burglary than meets the eye. He has instructed Detective Sergeant Mullen to bring in the known associates of Donal Dunning 'or David Gunning or whatever his name is', who is due to be released within hours unless they can link him to some subversive conspiracy and charge him. According to Mullen, one of his friends has a history with criminal republican elements. Some drugs business in Holland. Did a spell in Mountjoy. There might be something there, although he is not sure what. The Russians maybe. That Official IRA crowd and

*the communists are beating a path to their embassy in Orwell Road,
arranging their so-called study trips to Moscow.*

*And of course there is the security embarrassment of the man
secretly photographing senior politicians and members of the gardaí,
including himself, along with the British ambassador and his crowd.
What if the photos find their way to the English tabloids? Senior
diplomats, including a good chunk of the top personnel from the British
embassy, politicians, bishops and police on a wild night out on the
town, raising money for the incoming Taoiseach and his boys. Those
bastards would have no hesitation in publishing them with a view to
embarrassing the security forces in both countries and damaging their
recently restored relations as they seek to defeat a common enemy. If
there is one thing he hates almost as much as the fucking IRA it is the
gutter press.*

*Gavin is firmly of the belief that his most important responsibility
is to protect the State from any threat and that the co-operation and
assistance of the country's powerful neighbour is far more beneficial
in this regard than mutual hostility. In this, he knows he differs from
some of the political gobshites who are about to take power, but it is
an outlook and disposition that has helped him on his way to the top of
the greasy pole that is the Irish police service. He isn't going to change
now. It's also brought him into contact and friendship with people
in London who appreciate his insight and talents, and who will, no
doubt, continue to do so in the years to come.*

*The more he thinks about it, the more Gavin is convinced that the
robbery of Clarke's house and the photo session at the fundraiser that
night, which he himself departed in a less than sober state, are in some
way connected. He just doesn't know how or why.*

'It's a fucking hand grenade ready to explode and it's under

my arse,' he thinks before barking his latest orders to his assembled underlings. 'And this time don't spare the horses. I want them talking from the get go,' says the commissioner as the dogs are unleashed on the commis chef and the student waitress from The Bistro.

27

JOE

It's just before the holy hour when I approach Heno at the bar of Joxer Daly's. The safe-cracker is reading the form for the horse racing at Leopardstown. Results from English tracks are droning from a radio on the counter. Every other customer is doing the same thing, some kind of ritual for gamblers on their lunch break. There's a fair bit of movement between the pub and the bookie shop next door as the runners for the next race, and the odds, are broadcast from the crackly wireless. I hope Heno's having a lucky day.

'Order a drink, then follow me into the jacks when I finish this pint, but not too quick,' Heno says without looking up from the paper.

I ask the barman for a glass of cider, nothing too strong, but something that doesn't make me out to be a complete eejit in a room full of pint suppers. I'm due in work later and don't want to be half cut when I meet Murphy. As Heno folds his paper and polishes off his drink, I notice the brown envelope in the features section.

'I'd go for Shining Example in the next race or maybe Rough Diamond,' he mutters as he slides off the stool and heads for the men's room. I follow a minute later.

When I open the door to the smelly pit that passes for a toilet, Heno is pissing in the cubicle.

'Wait till I'm gone and take it from in here, from behind the cistern,' he says.

When he leaves I retrieve the envelope and stuff it down the front of my trousers. Back at the bar I polish off the Bulmers and look at the horses for the next race. Heno is spending his ill-gotten gains on Second to None, the second favourite in the two-thirty, the second race at Leopardstown. It came second last time out. Superstitious or what? I don't hang around for the result. I'm afraid I'm being watched as I leave the pub but I don't look around to find out.

With the papers tucked in and sweat on my brow, I turn off Dorset Street and head for the city centre. The crowds give me a chance of getting lost if anyone is behind me. Down Moore Street and into Henry Street where the shoppers are thick on the ground, then across Liffey Street and over the Ha'penny Bridge, nearly there. I don't know Heno well enough to be sure that he's not already talking to the cops to save his own skin and I've no idea whether I'm being followed. I'm scared. I've no notion what the guards are up to and Donal has not resurfaced from his detention to provide any information in that regard. I desperately needed to get the bank documents before they fell into the wrong hands, or made their way back to their rightful owner. Now I have to find a secure place to stash them.

The only person Angie and I feel we can trust to help is off work this afternoon and at home, in Fownes Street. It's on the way to The Bistro, where I have to start my shift at 4 p.m. sharp. We discussed the options and both agreed that if we didn't turn up for work it would be a sign that we are guilty of something or other. Angie is not due in today so there's no mystery over her absence. I left the job suddenly yesterday when I got the news from Donal's friend, but made a play of feeling unwell, stomach pains and the like, which is pretty much what I felt when I heard of the arrest. Pierre said I was as white as a sheet and should go home to bed. He's no fool and gathered from the hysterical reaction of the boss that me and Angie are in some sort of trouble. He seemed to enjoy the spectacle of Murphy threatening to fire us both on the spot or at least as soon as he gets the chance, but then he pointed out to the boss that it was too late to find a replacement for me in time for the busy days and evenings ahead.

Besides, he went on, there are laws and regulations that prevent an employer from sacking people on a whim and the last thing Murphy needs is a picket outside the door of Dublin's most popular eatery, unionised or not.

Turning the screw on the almost apoplectic Murphy, Pierre observed that someone as keen on politics and current affairs as me had no doubt joined a trade union. The militants in Liberty Hall would be only too willing to make an example of The Bistro, if they got even half a chance. That's how he saved my skin and my job, for the time being at least.

Pierre opens the front door of the dilapidated four-storey house he shares with friends and ushers me in. I ask him can he mind something for me and Angie for a few days.

'Of course,' he says. No questions asked. 'Anything for my favourite couple.'

I know he has a soft spot for both of us, especially Angie. Looking at my flushed and nervous face he adds, 'I don't know what you're up to and I don't care. Just promise you'll look after Angie. She's a good kid.'

'It won't be for long, I promise,' I say as I take out the envelope with the bank statements in his hallway. I hastily put the case with the ninety-minute cassette tape, along with the red napkin, into it and seal it again.

'Don't worry, I'm well used to hiding things I don't want other people to see. I've more than one secret spot in this place,' he says as he takes it from me.

'It's not drugs or anything, though the cops are looking for it,' I try to reassure him.

'I commit a crime every night I sleep with my partner,' he laughs. 'Do I care?'

It isn't ideal, given that we work together, but it's the only safe place we could come up with that the cops might not think to look. Angie insists we can trust Pierre. I agree.

According to Pierre, Murphy has accepted that he cannot sack us for no reason, and with no hard proof of any wrongdoing. He took the chef's point about finding quality staff at short notice. He also knows that the whole affair, although under wraps for now, has the potential to do enormous damage to the reputation of his restaurant, not to mind himself, if it is made public that two of his staff members were involved. And nothing would scream our guilt more than being suddenly fired.

The boss says little or nothing to me when I walk in the back door, other than to suggest that the next time I fall sick I should try to give the chef some notice, rather than suddenly leaving him in the lurch, personnel-wise. The reason he doesn't immediately confront me with a barrage of questions about my friend Donal and the illicit photo shoot is occupying two seats at the front window of The Bistro, sipping tea. Two goons, just waiting to pounce. I feel the blood drain from my face and my stomach pain is suddenly back.

'There are a couple of gentlemen here to see you,' Murphy tells me before I have time to don my apron. The stocky one approaches, tells me his name is Mullen and says something about arresting me under the provisions of the Offences against the State Act. The other guy says nothing. Next thing, I'm sitting between two large gardaí in the back seat of an unmarked Ford Cortina on my way to the cop shop, leaving Murphy to complain to the fresh air about being a team member down with less than two hours to kick-off.

Now I'm nursing a severe pain in the ribs, inflicted in the back of the police car by one of the heavies bringing me to the Bridewell. My second visit. When we land my pockets are emptied by a sergeant in uniform. He says I won't be leaving until I confess to everything. I'm roughly pushed into a cell. At this stage I've not been told what I'm being asked to admit to, but the message from the cops is that I'm fair game. The professional foul in the kidney leaves no marks. It's a warning shot to soften me up in advance of interrogation.

'We'll crack you like the gang we got for the Sallins job.'

I've heard stories of brutality emanating from this place over the years, including the savage beatings given to republicans who were suspected of a massive train robbery at Sallins last year.

'I'm not in that league,' I assure myself. I sit on the hard mattress pondering my fate, scouring the dozens, maybe hundreds, of names and messages scrawled on the filthy walls, and wonder what's next. I'm shaking and it's not from the cold. I decide that I'll ask for a solicitor and stay silent. Pick a spot on the wall. They can only do so much.

They're looking for a few photos and maybe a link to Clarke's house, but they haven't anything to go on. Jesus, I hope Angie is okay.

The sergeant comes in to ask whether I'm ready for an interview to deal with potential criminal offences. I politely explain that I won't be answering any questions and want to see a solicitor.

Five minutes later the door flies open and two different men in plain clothes come at me. One picks me up and throws me clean out the door, the other puts me on my feet and steers me down a corridor past closed cells. He pushes me down a set of wooden stairs. I land head first in a darkened, empty passageway. I hear doors close heavily behind me just as I get to my feet. I take a hard blow above my left ear, another to the right. My head is ringing. As I fall to the ground again, the two brutes kick the living daylights out of me, ribs, back and sides, legs and arms unspared. All I can do is crouch in the foetal position and hope they'll stop before I'm dead. I cry out, then scream and scream again. I hear the echo of my own pleading voice and nothing else but the grunts of two grown men kicking the shit out of me as I lie helpless on the ground. Now I know what that means. I can feel it in my jocks.

'Think about this, you fucker,' says one as he lays another boot in the direction of my lower back, just where the sore kidney is hiding.

'Fucking jailbird,' says the other. 'We know all about you, fucking drug-dealer scum. You should have been left to rot. You won't get an easy ride in the 'Joy this time.'

For some reason, I think about a Cork accent before I fade into the unconscious world. When I wake up, I have more than a sore kidney to think about. I'm aching all over. I've no idea where I am and I don't care. All I want is the severe throbbing from top to bottom to stop.

No one comes near me for a long time. I lie across the mattress, in darkness, sobbing and moaning, wishing the pain would go away. I've been in and out of consciousness for hours, or days for all I know, when the light comes on and a plastic plate of greasy mince and mash with a tin mug of water are thrown across the floor by someone in a uniform. I stumble across to the hole in the floor and puke up whatever is in my bruised and battered stomach. I try to sup the water but drop the mug. I watch as it spills across the floor towards the hole that smells of excrement and piss. I cry again, louder, and pass out on the bed.

When I come to, I'm asked by the uniform whether I'm going to eat my food or leave it lying there on the floor.

'If not, some other poor fucker can have it,' the man laughs. 'You'd better get used to it, sonny. You'll be here a while yet.'

'I want … I want to see my solicitor,' come the words from somewhere behind my broken teeth.

'Now which one would that be?' replies the garda. 'Sure there's no one awake at this hour of the night. Besides you'll be busy for a while. There's a couple of lads here who want to see you.'

This time I'm not dragged down to a dark passage but into a brightly lit room a few doors the other way. I'm placed on a chair in front of a wooden table. On the other side are the two men who met me in The Bistro, both dressed to the nines like they're going for a job with the bank.

'We heard you were acting up a bit last night, Joe,' says the one who calls himself Detective Sergeant Mullen. 'It doesn't do to mess around with the boys in here. I thought you'd know that with all your experience and knowledge. I hear you read the papers every day.'

'Where are you staying now, Joe? Your current address, like, and I don't mean this place,' says the other smiling man whose name I didn't catch.

'Those animals beat me up. I want to see my solicitor.'

'That will come in time but sure we'd not be able to reach him at this hour. Which one have you got in mind?' Mullen asks.

'Neilan.'

'Oh, Gerard. Sound man, if a bit of a lefty. I'll see what I can do.'

As the pain travels up my legs, into my kidneys and lower back, across my arms and chest to my ears, I try to consider my options. If I keep my mouth shut I could end up in the dingy basement with the two heavy lads again, no question. If I don't I might get myself into deeper shit, for a long time.

'We know you had something to do with bringing that cheeky bastard Dunning or Gunning, or whatever, into The Bistro. Your girlfriend recommended him to your boss, but he's your mate. So what was the plan? Sell the photos and make a lot of money for yourselves? What about your famous cellmate in the 'Joy? Is he involved in all this carry on? It won't be long before we have you back inside again. You've breached the Offences against the State Act which outlaws sedition, Joseph, and which can send you to jail for a long stretch. You took photos of people who are high-risk security targets, including diplomats like the British ambassador. Did you not notice there's a war going on?

Remember what happened to the last one, the ambassador, I mean. If those photos get into the wrong hands we could be talking of murder or, in your case, accessory to murder. So let's get real. Detective Inspector O'Malley has a few questions for you and you'd better answer them good and sharp.'

The one called O'Malley finally speaks. 'I have a file here that puts you in cahoots with known republican terrorists a few years back. That dirty business in Amsterdam. You were lucky to get just two years. Could have been a life sentence if there was proof you were involved in the death of that poor fucker found in the canal. Your friend who helped our inquiries said you were only the front man for the job, the innocent student. From where I'm sitting you're up to your neck in it. Subversion, drugs, crime and now we think you might know something about a break-in at the new minister's house. Have you ever been in the Russian embassy?'

'The what?' I say aloud this time. This is getting out of hand.

'The Russian embassy. Orwell Road, Rathgar.' O'Malley repeats the words slowly.

'Never,' I say.

'Have you ever spoken with anyone from the embassy or anyone who has been there?'

'How would I know? I want to see my solicitor.' They think I'm a fucking Russian spy.

'Do you know the politician whose house was robbed?'

'No, who is he?'

'Bob Clarke, Booterstown. But sure you knew that already, didn't you, Joe? Have you been in his house?'

'No.'

'And where do you live, currently? You're obliged to give us your address, solicitor or not,' says Mullen.

'I live with my ma.'

'Where?'

'59 Plunkett Gardens, Crumlin.'

'That's better,' says O'Malley. 'Now we're getting somewhere. Tell us. Where are the photos?'

'Don't know. Never saw them.'

'Come on, Joe. Sure Dunning says he gave them to you for safekeeping,' the cop says.

He's lying, I'm sure. Donal's no snitch.

'Not true. Anyway what's the big deal about a few photos of people at a party? Everyone already knows who was there and it's long over, so where's this security risk you're talking about? And since when do you beat people up who've done nothing wrong? I want to see my solicitor, and a doctor.'

'Listen, Joe. So you fell down the stairs. Tough shit. Your pretty girlfriend is currently under our temporary care, or will be shortly, and you wouldn't like anything to happen to her, would you?' says Mullen. My heart beats faster and my eye starts to twitch.

'We will arrange for Mr Neilan to come in first thing in the morning. But it wouldn't be necessary if you would just answer a few of our questions honestly and no more fucking us around,' says O'Malley.

'I want my solicitor, now,' I say, deciding it's time to clam up. I pick a spot on the wall, over their big heads.

'If that's the way you want to play it,' says O'Malley who rises from the table and walks out leaving his sergeant behind.

'Inspector O'Malley is a reasonable man, Joe, but I'm not and neither are some of my squad. They hate commies and IRA men, Gardiner Place or Kevin Street. All the same bunch of fucking subversives to them. Did you think they'd go easy on you with your record? They haven't even started yet. An ex-con, drug-dealing piece of shit with blood on your hands. You tell us what we want to know or you'll have another accidental trip, if you know what I mean. I'll let you stew on that for a while.'

The police strategy is simple. Bring in both of us separately and use us against each other. Divide and conquer. I pray silently for Angie.

28

ANGIE

I'm at home. Mam is with her sisters at Humphrey's. I saw the dark-blue car with two heavies parked at the end of the street when I went out for tea and milk this morning. Just like the one Joe pointed out to me near the Music Place. But I still never clocked they might be there for me. Mam left just after Da went back on his rounds after lunch. There's a knock on the door just after 4 p.m.

The visit is not unexpected. But I didn't imagine being disturbed by two heavies in mid-afternoon when I'm alone at home for what seems like the first time in years. They come into the house uninvited, after one of them flashes a piece of paper. He mentions the word 'search warrant' and something about the burglary at a minister's home. He sits me down on the couch while the other rambles from one small room to the next lifting books, cushions, photos, opening and closing presses and drawers along the way. It doesn't seem like much of a search to me, but the invasion of my privacy and my family home, and my fear of these two big men go to the pit of my stomach. I thank God Mam isn't here, but I'd give anything for Da to come home. He'd have no time for these bastards taking over his house. But it's the day he goes to the credit union after work, so I'm on my own.

The pair don't say much.

'How is your mam getting over the bomb?' says the one looking down at me. 'Must have been an awful shock.'

'You know what we're looking for, Angela. You can make this easy for yourself if you just hand over the photos,' says the other as he comes in from the kitchen.

'I don't know what you're talking about,' I say.

Once they're finished, and having found nothing, they bundle me into the back seat of the Ford Granada. I'm hoping someone on this street of squinting windows sees me being dragged off, even though Mam will be mortified. I've heard of young women being disappeared and tortured by police in other countries. Electric shocks and cattle prods. These are the thoughts, irrational or otherwise, that race through my overactive mind as we drive at speed up the Ossory Road, onto the North Strand and down to Store Street garda station, passing Humphrey's. Mam is probably in there supping a glass of stout, blissfully unaware of her daughter's sorry plight.

I soon find out why they chose this station. The bean garda doing an intimate search of my body mentions that we're just beside the morgue where the body parts of people killed by 'fucking terrorists like you' had been scattered. For good measure, she sticks her gloved fingers up my rectum for a second time.

'Just checking for any drugs or stolen gear,' she laughs.

In the interrogation room, the two Branch men from earlier advise me to co-operate and I can be home by teatime. I don't believe them given all I know and have discussed with Joe in anticipation of this very set of circumstances. I wish he was sitting beside me.

I ask to see the solicitor. Neilan. I sit tight. The longer it goes on the tighter I sit. Strength comes from somewhere and I glide from cell to interview room and back like a nun on retreat. Not another word comes out. I sit in my cell reciting Irish poems in my head until I conk out in the dark.

29

LOCK-UP

Gerard Neilan has a busy morning ahead of him. First to Store Street and then the Bridewell and it's only 8 a.m. There is no end to it these days. People dragged in for no good reason. Complete waste of garda resources and his precious time. War against crime, against drugs, against subversion. The wars go on and on. Still, it brings in a few quid to pay the bills, he says to himself as he bounds up the steps opposite Busáras, briefcase in hand. Lucky for these kids the State will pick up the bill. Free legal aid is a great invention.

The young woman he meets in Store Street is not your normal thug or terrorist. A Trinity student no less, and a bit of a looker.

'What brings you to this dump?' asks Neilan after he introduces himself in the interrogation room.

'Those bullies outside,' she says.

'And for what reason?'

'They claim I'm involved in a conspiracy to sell photos of some politicians and diplomats. They also mentioned an investigation into a burglary at a minister's house.'

'And?'

'And what?'

'Are you in some conspiracy to sell these photos?'

'No.'

'Or involved in a burglary?'

'No way.'

'Is that all they want?'

'They've been at my house annoying my mam. She was injured in

the bombings. I don't want them upsetting her or my dad.'

'Tell me, Angela, why do they think a good student like you would have anything to do with some political conspiracy and theft? Have you been arrested before?'

'Never, and I haven't stolen anything.'

'What have you told them?'

'Nothing.'

'Well, keep it that way. You have the right to remain silent. Tell them I advised you to keep your mouth shut and if they want to charge you with something so be it. I can contact your family, if you wish, to say you are okay. Have you been abused in any way? Did they feed you this morning?'

'I'm okay, but I couldn't eat the muck they offered me. Please don't contact my mam. Not yet. But I would like to get word to a friend of mine. He works with me in The Bistro where the stupid photos were taken. Just tell him I'm okay.'

'What's his name?'

'Joe Heney.'

'I'm just on my way for an appointment with the same gentleman.'

'Where?'

'The Bridewell. I'll tell him you're okay. Take my advice and you'll be out of here before long. I'll check in with you later.'

As he leaves the station, Neilan has a quick word with Detective Inspector Tom O'Malley, who is leading the investigation into the elusive photos. It seems this is not some routine criminal investigation. O'Malley is a top guy in the national security squad. The officer mentions the possible link to a robbery in Booterstown, which they are investigating along with the local detectives, of course. Neilan asks if this is about the burglary at the home of the politician Clarke. It's the talk of the Law Library, the original source of most political rumours in the city, true and false. Gossip central.

'It is,' confirms O'Malley.

'Then why was Miss Whelan not arrested by the local detectives who have jurisdiction in this matter?' asks Neilan.

'There was too much urgency. Not enough time. Besides she lives near the city centre. A bit of a journey for the 'Rock lads. We are working closely with them. There is also the matter of her helping a photographer to infiltrate a private function involving some of the country's highest security risks.'

'She told me you searched her home. Can I see the warrant and a good reason why it was issued to you and not the local gardaí handling the case? This all appears a bit unorthodox,' says Neilan. He mentally scrambles for any other embarrassing questions he can come up with.

'Everything is above board and your client has been treated very well, as you have seen. I can show you the paperwork later.'

'When can she expect to be released?'

'Hopefully in the morning if she can satisfactorily answer a couple of queries we have. It's a sensitive political and security matter, you understand, Mr Neilan.'

'I have advised her of her right to remain silent and I expect she will stick to that, so I wouldn't waste too much more of your time, or hers. I take it you won't be disturbing her mother again. She has been through enough, as you should know. The basis for the warrant looks very thin to me. I'm not sure this will go down well before another judge, if it ever gets that far. What crime do you think my client actually committed?'

'We've yet to establish all the facts, Mr Neilan, and her role in any of these matters.'

O'Malley opens the door to let the solicitor out. 'Smart fucker,' he says to himself.

When the solicitor sees the state of his next client, he realises this case is more serious than he had reckoned. The young man in the interview room is clearly traumatised. Joe Heney is in severe pain when he lifts his T-shirt to show the damage inflicted on him by unidentified gardaí. He can barely stand. The red marks on his face, the blue bruises on his arms and body are evidence that the Heavy Gang has been let loose in the Bridewell again.

'They'll tell you I fell down the stairs, but they beat me black and blue in some fucking dungeon underneath this place,' Heney says, barely holding back the tears.

'The stairs in here have an unfortunate reputation for causing injuries,' Neilan replies. 'Can you tell me why they would mistreat you in this way? Have you been arrested before, any previous convictions?'

'I did time for possession. Dope. Fifteen months in the 'Joy. They are looking for photos of the fundraiser in the restaurant where I work. But I don't have them.'

'The same place where Angela Whelan works?'

'Angie. Yes, how did …?'

'I just left her in Store Street. You'll be glad to hear she hasn't suffered the same kind of rigorous attention as you. Did they offer to get you a doctor?'

'You must be joking.'

'I will give you the same advice I gave your friend. Maintain your right to remain silent. If they want to charge you so be it. They can only hold you without charge for another thirty hours unless they look for an extension from the court. We will oppose that, obviously, and may seek an order of habeas corpus.'

'Habeas what?'

'It literally means present the body, but what it means for you is that the guards can be ordered to charge or release you immediately. I suspect they won't want you appearing in this state before a judge after what happened to the Sallins crowd last year. But they can be nasty if they want. I suggest you try to rest. I'll talk to them before I leave. O'Malley and Mullen are in charge. Top men in security so there is something serious going down. Have they asked you about anything else other than the photos?'

'Yeah. They mentioned something about some politician called Clarke who was at the fundraiser. He comes into The Bistro now and again. Someone robbed him, they said.'

'Bob Clarke. His house was burgled. There's almost a news black-out on the story. They asked your friend Angie about that too. I will lodge a formal complaint over your injuries and demand that they send in a doctor to examine you, but there is no guarantee that he won't officially accept their version of events. Either way we will have to get you out of here.

'There is one stumbling block, however. They went to your house and your sister told them you don't live there any more. Why did you give a false address? This won't play well if it goes to court,' Neilan says.

'Because I only moved to a new flat in the last while and I don't want them tormenting the landlord. It's hard enough to get a place these days.'

'If I was you I'd tell them where you live. They'll find out anyway. All they have to do is check with the ESB or the gas company or whatever. You must have some bills to pay.'

'Suppose so,' says his new client. The kid doesn't come across as the *experienced criminal and terrorist the guards are making him out to be. But you never know these days.*

'Look, I'll be back later to see if they got you that doctor. In the meantime, hang tight and keep your head.'

'If you see Angie, don't tell her about the beating. I know she'll find out later, but I don't want her worrying.'

'Did you think about that before you decided to launch your one-man campaign against the system? O'Malley mentioned your friend was taking pictures at a private function. He wouldn't be on the case if he didn't think there's a major security issue here and who knows what else? I'll need a full statement from you on all these matters. As soon as you get out and your injuries are dealt with. Is that clear?'

'Sure.'

The solicitor nods as he pushes back his chair.

'A Trinity student and a commis chef threatening to overthrow the State. That's a new one on me and there's no excuse for beating the shit out of the kid, whatever he is,' Neilan thinks as he takes up his briefcase and leaves. 'The guards are on thin ice here and I'm going to help break it.'

As it turns out, he already has. Despite his calm in front of Neilan, the inspector has run into a dead end and decides to release the Whelan woman early due to the potential embarrassment he might face in court if the issue of the search warrant is fully and publicly explored.

'Neilan was on the ball when he noted that our team did not have the authority, which rests with the Blackrock squad, to obtain the warrant,' he tells Mullen over their morning brew of coffee. 'Worse still, the lads told the girl they were investigating a burglary in Booterstown when they should have just mentioned the photos we're looking for. The problem is having a copy of photos taken by some-one else is not in itself a crime and does not justify a search warrant. Besides, there is no case against her and the solicitor could have applied for her release on those grounds alone. It was better for all concerned to let her go.'

'It might even look like an act of kindness,' Mullen agrees, 'espe-cially after all her mother's gone through. But we'll keep an eye on her, just in case.'

On the other hand, Mullen wants to hold on to the lad. Heney is an ex-con and dope dealer and who knows what else. Fair game. He gave a false address, which is a sure sign of guilt. Besides, if they hold him for the maximum forty-eight hours it will give the unfortunate bruises he sustained in the Bridewell time to fade a bit, at least the ones on his face. These days he'll have no problem finding willing allies in the media to highlight his treatment and Neilan is well capable of rattling the human rights cage.

O'Malley is more inclined to let him go. He's sure Heney is up to something but can't find any links to known subversives. Mullen's team searched Heney's flat, once he admitted the address, and found nothing incriminating. Nothing to back up the commissioner's obses-sion with the Russians except for a poster of Che Guevara and a copy of the Marxist manifesto on his bookshelf. And there's no evidence that there was any sinister plan for the photos beyond making a few quick bucks. Plus, Neilan's threat to apply for an order of habeas cor-pus for Heney is not an idle one and could cause more trouble than it's worth.

As for the theft at Clarke's house, it appears to be a random inci-dent. Nothing more than a few stolen jewels and cash.

'Why the commissioner is so worked up about this robbery is beyond *me,' he says to Mullen as he signs the release form for Joe Heney at 3.30 p.m., half an hour before the forty-eight are up. 'Besides, we've bigger fish to fry.'*

30

LEINSTER HOUSE

There's no sign of the boss behind his ornate wooden desk in the leader's office when Clarke is ushered in. Bad sign. Instead the party chairman, Liam Lynagh, stands with his hand outstretched and his best fake politician's smile plastered on his face. Clarke knows that Finance has gone to the Taoiseach's main rival. The gobshite with two languages and the posh Gonzaga accent is to get External Affairs. The next most senior post is Home Affairs and though it is a poisoned chalice of sorts, at least it would keep him within spitting distance of the main title and his long-held ambition, indeed destiny, to lead the party and the country. He's sure that's what's coming to him. Besides, he's had the brief in opposition for over two years now.

'Robert, the Taoiseach asked me to have a chat with you. He's gone up to the Áras to see the president,' Lynagh says as he directs Clarke to a comfortable armchair close to the window overlooking the lawn and fountain.

'You deserve some congratulations, Bob, topping the poll and bringing in that extra seat on the southside. We had the wind at our back for sure, but that is no mean feat in solid Blueshirt country,' the party chairman says. 'As you can see from the long line outside, I'm under a bit of pressure so I'll get straight down to it. How is Eileen, by the way? She must be pleased.'

'Very much so. She's looking forward to the challenges ahead.'

'How are your personal finances, Bob?' Lynagh says.

'My what?' comes the shocked reply. 'My personal finances? Of course, yes, well, in rude health I must say, never better.' Clarke

swallows hard as he waits for the next bombshell and wonders, almost aloud, 'What the fuck does he know?'

'I'm sorry I have to touch on these delicate matters, Bob, but we can't have cabinet members going bankrupt during their term of office or indeed open to any sort of temptation or compromise.'

'Of course not, Liam,' comes the reply from Clarke's mouth. 'Rich, arrogant fucker from Cork with a farm of a thousand acres,' is the thought in his head.

'Now, I want to touch on something that has crossed our minds, the Taoiseach's and mine, since he came up with the notion of you as our next Minister for Home Affairs. There are a lot of pressing and sensitive issues facing us in this area, not least the British insistence on a harder clampdown on subversives. I know you parade your republican credentials and, like myself, are proud of them and your late father of course, one of our great heroes. Would you be comfortable having to defend some of the measures we may have to introduce if we are to defeat the IRA and their like? The last crowd made a virtue of it and look where it got them. The worst defeat for Fine Gael in history. But now it's our watch. I had the British ambassador in yesterday demanding that we do something along the border. There's an SAS man missing and they want us to turn the place upside down for him. It seems like this sort of thing is going to be a regular occurrence for the foreseeable future.'

'Yes, I heard about that. Dreadful business. I think my father would be quite proud and happy to see me in a Fianna Fáil cabinet in whatever position you wish to offer. Home Affairs is an area I am passionate about and of course I will follow Dev's example. I understand the realities of the situation. We won't tolerate so-called republicans trying to destroy the State we have built.'

'Excellent. It's a challenging post and you've been doing a decent job with it on the front bench. On another note, I must ask you, Bob, is everything all right at home, domestically speaking? It may seem crude, but, if I'm to believe what I hear on the grapevine, we can't have a member of cabinet playing away from home.'

'Excuse me?'

'The journalist you've been seen with, out and about. And not so discreetly, in the Gresham and Grooms and such.'

'Oh, there's nothing to that. Just a casual friendship, which of course I will terminate if you feel it necessary.'

'Well, it's really not my business, but a Minister for Home Affairs must be above all else a man of the highest moral integrity. Caesar's wife and all that.'

'I understand, of course,' Clarke stutters, refraining from expressing the thought rushing through his head relating to kettles and black pots.

'Finally, Bob, this recent business at your home, the break-in. The commissioner has spoken to me about it and seems to be concerned it may have implications for national security. He is taking it quite seriously. Is there anything I should know?'

Jesus. This is worse than a fucking police station.

'Oh, nothing at all, Sir. I mean Gavin has to look at all the possibilities, but it seems to be nothing more than a routine burglary, an opportunist crime, according to the local guards.'

'Well, keep me informed,' says Lynagh looking up at the clock on the wall as it strikes three. 'Congratulations again. Our new Minister for Home Affairs. No better man. Send in O'Toole, will you?'

The conversation has lasted less than ten minutes, but Clarke feels, and looks, like he's been through the wringer. He could do with a strong whiskey to calm the nerves, but that would not look good for an incoming minister at this time of day. Back in his office he calls Eileen to tell her the good news and then Fenton, whom he arranges to meet in ten minutes in the Shelbourne. Over a pot of strong tea, Clarke relates the manner of his appointment and how he badly needs closure on this burglary business.

'I'll have to meet senior department officials and the commissioner in a day or two and I don't want this mess hanging around my neck. I need to know how the investigation is going and why Gavin mentioned it as a matter of national security. What are the Brits saying?' Clarke asks.

'They're in a state over this missing soldier and moaning about the failures of the police in Dundalk. They'd invade the place if they thought they'd get away with it. Of course, if they hadn't let this mad captain spend his nights singing rebel songs in the pubs of Crossmaglen he might be at home in bed by now. He's probably lying in a ditch with his brains blown out. As for the burglary, I asked Martin Crawley what he knew, but he couldn't find out anything beyond what was in the papers. He said the first they'd heard officially that it was your house was during a security briefing by Gavin last week,' Fenton explains. 'He seemed pretty uninterested and there were no comments, subtle or otherwise, about the missing documents, so I actually believe him.'

'What the fuck is Gavin telling them for? Garda matters are no business of theirs unless it's to do with the North. Gavin's a loose cannon, if you ask me,' Clarke says, pouring himself another cup. Fenton suggests that the best course of action is to await the results of the local police investigation and hope the affair just fizzles out.

'That's easy for you to say. It's not your private papers floating around out there. I need to find them, and fast.'

'Well, the latest from Inspector O'Malley is that a couple of people have been arrested, including the man who took photos at the fundraiser, but that there seems to be nothing to link them to the burglary and they have no other leads on the thief,' says Fenton.

'Fucking Keystone Cops,' Clarke says under his breath. 'So what's our next move?'

31
JOE

When I open the door, she can see I'm hardly fit to stand. My eyes are black and blue and my arms are bruised from top to bottom. She lets out a cry. I try to smile, let her know I'm fine, even if I'm not.

She lets me lean on her as I struggle back to the bed, limping. 'I can't believe those bastards did this to you,' she says, tears welling in her eyes.

'At least I'm alive and so are you,' I say gently as I touch her hair. We hold each other close for a long time. Both lost for words. Her heat fills my bruised and battered body. I try hard not to fall apart.

Eventually, I ask what happened to her. She tells me about being picked up and how she asked for Neilan, like I told her to. About the three interrogations she sat through, including one with detectives from Blackrock who wanted to know what she knew about Bob Clarke, his house and family. How she'd kept her mouth shut, just like Neilan said.

'Then, the day after I was picked up, about midday, the door of my cell opened and the groper was there. "Collect your stuff and fuck off," she says, so I did. As I was leaving there was one guy who stood and watched me intently the whole way down the street. It really rattled me. I went straight home to let Mam and Da know I was okay, to have a hot shower and wash off the stink of that place, and to get something decent to eat. Of course, Mam was all in a flap. A neighbour had seen me being taken away. I told her the guards had got it all wrong, that I had done nothing and they'd let me go without charging me. Da was all for marching down there to have it out with them, until I persuaded him to let it go. The whole time I was there all I could think about was you, wondering if you were okay, if they'd let you out yet.'

'I'm surprised you cared after the mess I've made.'

'It's not your fault,' she replies. 'I walked into this with my eyes open. I wanted to be involved. I'm as much to blame as you.'

'What did I do to deserve you?'

She gives me that radiant smile of hers and then says, 'Neilan told me they couldn't hold you for more than forty-eight hours without charging you, so as soon as I reckoned that time was up I hopped on a bus. I couldn't wait any longer to see you. If you hadn't been here, I don't know what I'd have done.'

'I'm glad you're here – I was worried sick.'

'The state of you and you were worried about me?' she laughs. 'When was the last time you ate?'

'Can't remember.'

She's brought eggs, ham, cheese, bread and milk and the newspaper with her and sets about making an omelette, while talking about anything not to do with our recent adventures.

'It's my granny's own recipe – three eggs, milk and a drop of water to make it fluffy. Hot pan and add in the ham and cheese filling. Perfect. Get that into you,' she says as she serves it with tea and fresh toast. 'Just what the doctor ordered.' Ravenous, I lash it down and lie back, tired and sore, on the bed.

My eyes are closed, the back is killing me. My mind is racing and sleep is impossible. She is here, beside me, this woman I love and failed to protect. I've been depressed since my rude eviction from the garda station, thrown out on the street in filthy clothes, scared out of my wits. I couldn't get away from the place quick enough, certain that I was being followed by thugs who were just ready to pick me up again and continue the brutal ritual of modern detention. My gaff is just a few streets across the bridge, but it felt like it took an hour to get here. My uninvited guests left the place in a shambles, with every box emptied, the contents of drawers strewn across the floors and the bookshelf cleared. My albums were scattered in all directions and the couch was overturned. That is bad enough, but the reason I'm haunted and want to weep is gently holding my hand and caressing my left arm and shoulder, which have turned from black and blue to a rusty brown colour.

No matter what she says, she's the one good thing in my life and I led her straight into the harsh arms of the law with my fucking madcap scheme. I've also ruined whatever chance I had of appearing strong and determined in her eyes. Instead, I'm lying here a physical and mental wreck as she wanders around repairing the damage in gentle and small ways, cleaning the kitchen, fixing the mess and then holding my hand with a tender touch. I can sense her, smell her and, when I get the chance, I caress her. I've let her down. I'm weak. I don't want her to see me like this, a paper tiger, all talk and bluster until the first sign of trouble. I want to tell her the truth about why they kicked the shit out of me, about my 'infamous' drug-dealing past, but I'm afraid it will drive her out of my life. And I can't lose the love I feel coming from this black-haired, greeny-blue-eyed beauty sitting on the bed as I drift off through the pain.

32

ANGIE

When he's sleeping soundly, I turn off the lamp and go into the kitchen, put on the kettle and the wireless on low. 'Madam George' from our favourite album is playing. I pick up the paper to read about Clarke's election victory and his future prospects as Home Affairs Minister. The leaders of the last government have retired in failure. To look at them smiling, though, you wouldn't think it.

'Those fuckers have gotten away with murder and Clarke's lot will be no better,' I say to myself.

I pick up the bits and pieces of Joe's life that are scattered across the sitting room and kitchen. His sacred record collection is lying dumped out of their sleeves and books are scattered across the floor. His torn poster of Che is lying in a heap. A hotbed of harmless subversion. A guitar with broken strings is still standing, as is a photo of him with a young woman and a child. His sister, Patricia, I suppose. I sit folding shirts and shorts and reading Neruda's love poems over a cup of tea.

I'm angry about the beaten wreck that sleeps next door, but not at him. Anyone with a passing knowledge of history, something that by the look of the books on the shelf he should have, would know that this 'great little country' is nothing but a con job on the poor. Emigration and poverty, dead bodies and broken limbs, Mam's bad eye and him lying on the bed next door, shaken to bits. I think about the priest and what he told me about the boy from the morgue. Danny Ryan. The sudden release I felt when he put a name to my recurring nightmare.

Joe's not like anyone I know, with his warm smile and funny grin, making me laugh over nothing, looking on the bright side and into my eyes like I'm someone special, the only one in the room, the only woman in the world. Me.

It's barely sunk in. I've another year in college, but I don't see the relevance of it all. We could just forget about all this bombing stuff and taking on the powers that be, and, if the guards let us, get out of this kip, go to London, hang out with Tony for a while, travel Europe. First we can go back to The Bistro, if we still have jobs, save enough money and then take the boat. I fix the cover on the couch, lie down and think about a new life, leaving home, college, finding myself.

'There's enough to be worrying about,' I say. There's one bright speck on the horizon. Joe Heney will be part of whatever happens next. He is smart and honest and wants to change the world for the better, but most of all he wants me, touches me every chance he gets, makes me tingle. Angie Whelan from East Wall is in love. I hear him turn in the bed, disturbing one of his painful joints and letting out a moan. I slip off my runners, slide in beside him and gently rub his arms, his legs, his neck, shoulders, his head. He sighs as his pain is eased. He slowly turns to lie on his back. The steady movement of my hands across his skin, the response of his body to my fingers wakes him from his sleep. He holds me close.

'Am I hurting you?' I ask.

'No, that's nice,' he says. 'I've missed you so much.'

I undress quickly and sit over him. He touches my breasts, my arms, my hair and lets me move him inside me, wet and warm. I sway to his thrust and come as he empties his pain and his love into me, unleashing a torrent of tears. I move off his chest for fear of hurting him and share the exhaustion, humiliation and terror that has visited us in recent days. And the deep pleasure of our love. We sleep till dawn.

***

I wake to the smell of coffee and burned toast. He's back on his feet again. I ask when he first learned to boil an egg.

'Why, can't you do it?'

'No. I mean, yes, I can boil an egg. I was just wondering if your mam taught you to cook.'

'Nope, I learned all by myself,' he says laughing.

'You never talk about your mam, your dad, your sister or your niece for that matter. Why is that?'

'There's not much to tell,' he says.

'You know a lot more about my family than I know about yours.'

'What do you want to know?'

'Everything.'

He doesn't hold back. He recounts his childhood in Crumlin, the brothers, Christian ones, beating the hell out of him at school, football, college and girls. He's had a few but nothing special, he says. He's godfather to Patricia's daughter. His only sister. In the photograph. The child's father is a fucking waster.

'A bit like myself,' he says, despondently.

'I'm sure you're a good brother and son,' I say.

I smile and kiss him gently on the cheek, grabbing my bag at the same time.

'I have to run.'

'There's more.'

'I've heard enough for one day.'

33

DUBLIN CITY CENTRE

'So Clarke still doesn't know who burgled his home?' asks Crawley.

'He doesn't know what to think. Worse still, the garda commissioner is banging on about it at every opportunity. He's trying to make it a matter of national security for some reason. He doesn't know anything about the missing Bermuda file,' Fenton replies.

'I thought as much, since sensitive bank documents were not mentioned by Mr Gavin during his briefing on the subject. If they turn up in the wrong place then it will be a matter of Bob Clarke's security, for sure. Security of tenure,' says Crawley. Fenton says nothing.

As they observe the comings and goings on Grafton Street from the high window of Bewley's, the two men envisage the possible outcome of such an appalling vista from their different perspectives. For Fenton it would mean the certain end of his career as a ministerial advisor, government spokesman and possible future senator and TD, or even senior diplomat. For Crawley, it would be the destruction of a carefully constructed relationship with a potential future Irish prime minister, whose career path, through careful manipulation, has been aligned to the trajectory of his government's plans to achieve the end of a terrorist campaign that is wreaking havoc across Northern Ireland and the mainland.

'The IRA is spreading its testicles across the whole of the province. That's what that loyalist chap said, isn't it?' Crawley sniggers. 'Another one of ours.'

'You mean McKeague? He doesn't seem like the brightest tool in the box. If his crowd weren't so busy butchering innocent Catholics we might have a better chance of reaching a settlement with the Provos. We're going to tell the IRA we'll release all their prisoners if they call off the campaign,' Fenton replies.

'That won't work,' says the Englishman. 'They got a whiff of victory with the secret talks a while back and they won't settle for half measures. That's why your man is our best hope. The people will take strong-arm tactics from your party that they wouldn't accept from the other lot, particularly from someone like Clarke with his bona fide republican background. The ambassador would like an early chat with Bob to plan our future co-operation. He's already met your leader but can't get a definite steer from him. Meanwhile, I can assure you that there is no question of any dirty tricks on our part. And I can't see the Americans or the Russians for that matter being up to anything of that nature either. It seems like a routine burglary to me.'

Fenton accepts there is logic to Crawley's argument. Bob Clarke is in a key position for the Brits and they have no reason to fracture any goodwill that exists. Besides, they know what's in the Caribbean papers, and it's almost certain they already have copies buried in a safe in Whitehall. Right now the issue of security co-operation is their priority, especially since the SAS man went missing.

***

The subject of the two men's conversation, who in his new role can no longer be seen lunching with British diplomats or those of any other variety, is finding that the job of Home Affairs Minister can consume the entire twenty-four hours of every day if he allows it to. Incessant meetings with cabinet colleagues, the security sub-committee, the garda and army chiefs. His ceremonial tasks largely appear to consist of welcoming new recruits and sticking medals on the boys in blue *for all their courageous work in defeating crime and subversion. He sometimes wonders why the rates of both seem to rise no matter how many new guards graduate or flashy trinkets he awards. But it's early days yet, he assures himself, with more hope than conviction.*

He settles into his duties with the consolation that it is only a matter of time before he moves on to more prestigious positions, with greater power and influence. His concern over the missing bank documents recedes as the investigation into the burglary runs into the ground. More important matters occupy his time and mind, including how to get rid of that young reporter from his social life, which is now inevitably more restricted and vulnerable to unwanted exposure. She is resisting any attempt to cut out their frequent liaisons altogether and he's certain she'll demand a promise to be kept in the loop for any big political stories as a concession for ending their affair quietly. If he lets her down too hard she could make life very difficult for him.

He has always been fond of warning his colleagues about the media: 'It's like having a fucking pet alligator. You feed it every day and then it chews the fucking arm off you.' Now he wishes he'd taken his own advice.

A bigger worry is what to do about the voracious demands by Crawley and his superiors in Dublin and London for early agreement on fresh anti-terror legislation which he is expected to draft and which will no doubt raise all sorts of hares about human rights abuses by the new government of supposedly republican ministers. It is one thing to let the gardaí do their thing in private, holding suspects and beating the crap out of them. It's quite another to stand up in the Dáil and propose seven-day detention orders, extradition on demand and cross-border forays by the British Army. Even if they do have the goods on his fucking offshore dealings, he is not going to give away every last vestige of freedom that his father and his revolutionary comrades fought for all those years ago. Not one Minister for Home Affairs was ever thanked for breaking the will of armed republicans, whether the people assented to it or not. It won't look good on his CV if he's the one to concede every British demand, no matter how many bombs are going off in Belfast.

Speaking of bombs, he also has to spend a lot of time reading up on files his predecessor left behind. All the unfinished and never-ending business of government and the enforcement of law and order in an unruly State. Among the documents to which he pays particular attention are those dealing with the unsolved crime that rocked the heart of Dublin and Monaghan in 1974. Sloppy investigation of mass murder, destruction of evidence, missing notes and records. Wrong intelligence, sinister forces, political myopia. The gardaí handing over the forensic and ballistic evidence to the British Army at Lisburn. A police and security failure of epic proportions. Even more outrageous is evidence of direct involvement by the Brits in the '74 bombs and the ones two years earlier which blew up Liberty Hall and killed two busmen in the city centre.

It all makes for very interesting reading and gives him the germ of an idea that might well take root and grow into a sturdy weapon which he can apply to good effect down the road. If only he can get to grips with that bollox Gavin, who always seems to be one step ahead of him when it comes to handling the state of emergency now threatening to engulf the country, North and South. The commissioner is no doubt keeping an eye on his domestic and other private affairs, and for any outcome to the investigation of the embarrassing, criminal intrusion of his home. Little or no progress has been made despite the 'top priority' label attached to it by Gavin. It should have been put to bed long ago.

34

DUBLIN CASTLE

When Inspector O'Malley addresses his special investigation unit, he is determined to accentuate the positive, even though he has nothing of any great significance to report regarding the first item on the agenda. He needs a breakthrough in the hunt to find the thief who broke into the house of the minister if only to satisfy the rantings of the commissioner. Despite the lack of evidence, suspects or leads, Gavin is convinced it is the tip of a very large iceberg that is about to engulf the nation in a storm of crisis proportions, with possible global implications if his theory about the Russians is given any credit.

From bitter experience, O'Malley knows that the commissioner is a great believer in conspiracy theories and when he isn't inventing one, he is sure to find another under the next stone he turns over. There is no shortage of suspects when it comes to undermining the legitimacy of the State and his long list includes everyone from free thinkers to freemasons and those in-between. If he wasn't a member of the Knights of St Columbanus, they would also be on the list. The object of his greatest ire is the left: socialist preachers in the press, Soviet sympathisers, anti-American and anti-British protesters who threaten the embassies of the country's friends, strikers, writers, rebels and all the campaigners against this, that and the other. If he had his way he would intern the lot of them and do a better job than the British did a few years back.

Gavin is wary of the new Fianna Fáil gang and is not convinced they are up to the job of defeating the IRA and the other groups of commies and subversives masquerading as defenders of the people.

He is also concerned that political interference in his job could reveal matters he thinks best to preserve from public scrutiny, in the interests of national security and the State itself. There are dark clouds emerging as the result of media reports concerning the activities of the Heavy Gang, of planted fingerprint evidence, of rising crime, details of which are dripping into the ears and onto the pages of pink liberal editors. For this reason, he is keeping a close eye on the investigation into the Clarke burglary, which he believes, for no obvious reason, has the potential to do for him and for Clarke what Chappaquiddick did for Ted Kennedy.

O'Malley keeps these thoughts to himself but tells his team that the commissioner is still convinced that it is no coincidence that the theft happened on the night of the fundraiser and that there must be a link between the two. The inspector informs his unit that he does not necessarily share Gavin's view but that any break-in at the home of a senior politician has to be taken seriously in the current climate of violence and subversion against the State. He does not reveal to his troops that what really annoys Gavin is that he was present at the party in The Bistro and is worried about what might come to light concerning his own behaviour on the night if this business is not brought to a close, and soon. If there are photos of the commissioner in a drunken condition, or any such compromised fashion, he wants them, no matter what it takes.

'In summary,' O'Malley says, after appraising the team of the progress made thus far, 'we have not identified the person or persons who broke into the home of Bob Clarke. We have no forensics to link any known criminals to the scene. We do know that someone out there has identifiable items of expensive jewellery that he will want to fence, but nothing has come to our attention so far. We also know that

the burglar is a skilled safe-cracker and there are not a huge number of those among the city's criminal fraternity. While I am not ruling out some obscure political motive, given the identity of the victim, despite the commissioner's concerns there is no reason to go down that particular avenue at present. The tests on the dog indicate that he died from a strong dose of rat poison placed in a large sirloin steak. It was not taken from the kitchen of the house but rather brought by the thief or thieves who clearly knew of the animal's presence and approximate weight.

'With regards to the photographs taken at The Bistro on the same night, we have made three arrests but none of the suspects has revealed the location of the prints or negatives. Only one of the three, Joe Heney, has a previous criminal conviction and known links to subversives. He and Angela Whelan share the same solicitor, Gerry Neilan, who has represented IRA men and women in the past. That may be just coincidence, as he is virtually a household name and is well known to be a bleeding-heart human rights type. This pair also work together in the restaurant. One or both of them is likely to have encouraged the photo-journalist Dunning to take the snaps on the evening. Although the full collection of these photos has not been found, we know from a contact sheet that was touted around the various newsrooms by Dunning that it includes pictures of politicians, wealthy donors, diplomats, including the British and American ambassadors, bishops and our own commissioner. There were several entertainers along with what are politely referred to as "party girls" in that circle.'

Some of the dozen or so officers fail to stifle a chuckle at this description and the image of Gavin half jarred and surrounded by a gaggle of smiling tarts.

'That's enough,' O'Malley barks, before continuing. 'The search of the homes of those arrested failed to reveal anything of significant interest, although it seems the Heney fellow has an interest in radical politics. As I mentioned he also has a record, having been convicted for possession of drugs, and is known to have associated with republicans and criminals some years back. All we know of significance about the girl is that her mother is a victim of the Dublin bombings, which might give her a reason to be involved with subversives, but we have no evidence of this. As for the photographer, he seems to pop up with his camera at every protest from the tree huggers to the abolitionists, of the death penalty that is. On Neilan's advice, the Bistro pair remained silent for most of their interrogations. It is unlikely much will be gained by pulling them in again. Unless there are further developments that require such a move. Okay, does anyone have any questions or suggestions?'

After a few less than helpful comments from some of those present, one of the younger detectives throws his hat in the ring.

'Chief, I have something that may or may not be useful,' says Detective Garda Ronan Meagher. 'The girl, Whelan – a while back I saw her at the Music Place, that dive in Dorset Street that criminal elements, potheads and subversives are known to frequent. I noticed her go in there some weeks ago. I recognised her when she was released from custody in Store Street last week. Not the normal spot for a nice girl from Trinity. The pub, I mean.'

'Thank you, Meagher. It's not much to go on, but follow up and see do we have any dirt birds of the safe-cracking variety hanging around the joint,' says O'Malley. 'And no one talks to the boys in Blackrock without talking to me first. Now, let's move on to other matters.'

35

JOE

Murphy is in his office when I walk in the door, apron under my arm.

'What the fuck? The cheek of you after the trouble you caused. Almost wrecking the business that we've built up here, blood sweat and tears, police knocking on the door, politicians bleating about their privacy, the fucking bishop worried about those photos. Whose idea was that anyway? I doubt if Angie thought it up on her own. There's a pair of you in it. And you've the brass neck to turn up —'

'I'm sorry, boss,' I say, before Murphy completes his litany of complaints. 'It's all a misunderstanding. I can explain. Neither me or Angie had anything to do with those photos. The guards blew the whole thing out of proportion. And sure look, nothing has happened. The Bistro is doing well and I need my job.'

'You must be fucking joking. I'm just about over the shock. And then you get dragged away the day my head chef is off, leaving me totally in the lurch, and now swan in here as if nothing happened? And you want to keep your fucking job. Jesus, are you mental?'

I'm prepared for this response and hold my tongue until Murphy has a chance to release all his pent-up anger.

'Mortified I am. One week the whole town is talking about how great we are, best venue in town. Next the police are crawling around the place searching for pictures of the country's entire cast of VIPs before they appear in the tabloids. And you're telling me it was just a misunderstanding. So what about the bruises over your eye? I suppose you slipped on a banana skin?' he wails.

Before he rattles on about my post-State-detention condition, I point out, in as mild a manner as I can, that the restaurant is as busy as ever, there's no shortage of politicians munching their way through the mid-morning and lunchtimes, and Murphy himself seems none the worse for wear. Besides, as I established during a consultation this morning in Liberty Hall, there is no basis for me getting the sack, and even less for Angie to lose her job. I didn't do anything in breach of my contract and there are employment laws, weak as they are, which protect workers. I deny all knowledge of Donal's plan to photograph the partygoers. I say that he has a habit of using a different name because he collects the dole. He could get cut off the social welfare if they find out he's doing odd jobs.

'I thought he was doing us a favour because you were stuck and needed an extra pair of hands,' I suggest, while at the same time fervently hoping that the guards failed to mention my murky past to Murphy. 'I didn't know that Dunning had a camera with him. He did it off his own bat, trying to make a name for himself. Anyway, the papers didn't publish so no one is any the wiser. The cops went over the top, but they let us go as soon as they realised it was nothing to do with us. My solicitor says there's no basis for any charge against us or for us getting sacked. In fact, we are owed an apology if anything for all the hassle,' I lie, with a straight face.

'A fucking apology. Maybe I should be on my fucking knees as well, thanking you for returning to work in one piece. I've a good mind to –'

Murphy is just getting into full flow when he is interrupted by Pierre, who barges in to ask whether he is expected to prep and serve the food as well as cook it given the shortage of staff in the kitchen. He throws his apron on the desk to Murphy's visible astonishment.

'I'm expected to do everything in this place. Cook, clean, prep, serve and for what, for peanuts. I'm going back to Paris where the chef is treated with some dignity and respect. I've had enough,' he declares.

Timing is everything and his well-rehearsed entrance from stage left is enough to convince the boss that The Bistro is about to go into meltdown just as the Friday lunch crowd is filling the tables outside. The implicit threat that I might take legal action against any ill-judged dismissal also seems to finally work its way to his brain.

He needs time to think this one out. First, he has to calm the chef down and check the roster, which to his unpleasant surprise is down two staff, one on the floor and another in the kitchen.

'Ever since this whole nasty episode she just hasn't been herself,' he mumbles, blaming his wife for the rostering error. He glares at me and says, 'I suppose you can help out in the kitchen seeing that you're here now. But I'm not happy one bit about this whole thing, the trouble you've gotten me into. In the meantime, just get back to work, both of you, and get in touch with that girlfriend of yours to see if she's free to come in this minute.'

We quickly disappear into the kitchen and resume normal duties as if the past few days had never happened. Though not before we share a wink and a smile to confirm the successful outcome of our pre-planned encounter with the completely outwitted boss. Angie is serving tables within the hour without a word from the boss. I brush off queries from other staff about my injuries with mention of a row in a pub that got out of hand.

We had to get our jobs back. We need the money. Over the last few days, Angie and I have been discussing our future and we've decided that we want to go abroad, to Europe, America maybe, if they let me in. She says she'll come with me, degree or no degree. Anywhere away from here. But first we've some unfinished business with Clarke, Fenton and his English friends.

As the busy summer afternoon trade comes to a close, Murphy calls us in to his office to reassert the authority he surrendered earlier and to try to find a way of restoring some harmony to his once relatively peaceful regime. He has clearly grappled all day with the dilemma of dealing with two staff members who, inadvertently or otherwise, almost destroyed his valued reputation and his even more precious business, without making matters worse.

A call to his solicitor has confirmed that technically we have not broken any law or provided sufficient justification for a dismissal. It seems that such a move could be challenged successfully in the Labour Court or some such monstrous forum for distressed employees. He has suddenly discovered to his horror that workers have certain rights when it comes to hiring and firing, too many in his view, and unless he wants a shower of commies marching up and down outside the door for weeks, maybe months, he has to back down while appearing also to retain control of his business.

Once he has cleared his planned course of action with his wife, who takes it surprisingly well, all things considered, he decides to be generous but stern with Angie and me. He admits that losing his commis chef at the height of the season would be disastrous and although we unleashed the unwanted attentions of the gardaí into his already complicated life, since we weren't actually charged, we mustn't have done anything unlawful. Innocent until proven otherwise and all that.

'However, if anything, and I mean *anything*, like this ever happens again, you are out the door, no ifs or buts. The trouble you and your mad photographer friend have caused me. The sheer indignity of it all, having a staff member dragged out of here like a war criminal. You're lucky there's been no negative publicity. No lost custom as far as I can see. But this is the last-chance saloon, so don't mess up again,' he says, before running out of clichés and before we break into fits of laughter in his presence.

'He's such a wanker,' says Pierre as the three of us settle over pints in the Palace, clinking glasses at the success of our double act and recounting what we feel we can about our clash with much more devious opponents than Murphy will ever be.

'It could be worse,' I say. 'Another boss would have told us to piss off. Most of them wouldn't think twice about giving us the sack. My way or the highway and forget about any money owed.'

'I think Paula put in a good word for us,' says Angie. 'She seems to like us.'

'She likes *you*,' laughs Pierre. 'Sure we all do.'

Paula even takes the blame for the mistake on the roster. She was sure she had a full complement of staff for Friday written on the board in the kitchen, which was, for some peculiar reason, no longer in its usual and permanent place and could not be checked.

She couldn't care less about the police or the politicians, whom she secretly despises for their constant abuse of powers and their general pretentiousness. She reserves particular contempt for 'that little prick Fenton'. So she told Angie anyway, after our dressing down from her husband.

Besides, she said, she's being spoken about as a possible choice for patron of a tourism initiative which the new government is about to announce, and Aidan is still in line for a place on the Trade Board 'or whatever it's called in Irish', so clearly they'd avoided any political fallout from the recent embarrassment.

Things could only get better for the ambitious owners of The Bistro. We raise another toast to Aidan and Paula Murphy, the supreme entrepreneurs.

Before the session ends, Donal joins us with his tale of abuse, which could have been worse. He was released within forty-eight hours with only minor bruises but a determined distrust of the forces of law and order. We all drink to that.

36
ANGIE

I'm just heading out when Father Bennett drops into the house to see Mam. As he leaves he asks me, out of Mam's earshot, when I'm going to collect the package I placed in his safekeeping, not that there is 'any rush or anything'.

'I'm sorry, Father, with all that's just gone on, I completely forgot about it. I'll drop around in the morning.'

'I thought that's what might have happened. Whenever you're ready is fine,' he says as he closes the door. He doesn't mention my arrest and I don't either.

I'm annoyed with myself for taking the priest for granted and leaving the photographs with him for so long. In truth, I've tried to plant them somewhere well at the back of my mind, along with Store Street and the strip-searcher. I vow to remedy the situation tonight when I meet Joe in the Music Place, the first time in weeks we're going to a session there. For obvious reasons.

The front of my mind is taken up with matters romantic. I've not been in love before and my every waking moment, it seems, is preoccupied with this man and our plans. Mam says I'm blooming and it doesn't take long for her to work out the source of my newfound happiness. Having made tentative and unproductive inquiries about the level of intimacy involved, she says she is delighted with the news and issues an open invitation to 'my young man' to come around for dinner. I don't mention the box of Durex Tony stuck inside the Joni Mitchell album he sent me last Christmas. 'Just in case you get lucky,' the note said. No flies on Tony, I say to myself.

Dad was more circumspect when he was informed by a more circuitous route of my new flame. A junior chef in a kitchen, a UCD dropout with no formal training in the culinary department or any other real-life experience.

'What sort of prospects does he have, with good jobs hard to come by and no proper apprenticeship?' he asks. It's among the questions he poses over the table at lunchtime as the radio pours out the latest and very sombre economic and unemployment figures as if to deliberately back up his concerns.

'But sure who cares what I think? I'm only your father, after all,' he mutters as he returns to his rounds.

'Don't mind him,' says Mam. 'He's not been himself this long time, God help him. He's forgotten what it's like, young love. It's been a tough time what with my eyes and everything. Sure we haven't been out together since the world blew apart.'

She's not the only one who's half blind. I've been so wrapped up in my own life that I hadn't even noticed. They used to go to the pictures once a month, walk the canal to Glasnevin or drive to Howth or Wicklow on Sundays. Now, I realise that, while they share the same bed, they essentially live apart. She won't let him help her and unconsciously is pushing him away. How helpless and lonely he must have felt these past few years. The bombs ruptured his life as much as hers. My heart breaks a little and though I can't fix everything, I try to make a small improvement. I make steak and fried potatoes for his tea and buy them a bottle of red wine. When he gets home the radio is off and Sinatra is crooning from the record player. Me and Mam are singing along. For the first time in years I watch the two of them together, almost relaxed. I leave them alone to enjoy each other's company.

Later, as I take that final glance at myself in the hall mirror before hitting the town, he turns up behind me to concede that he was wrong to pass judgement and that I deserve all the joy the world can bring. He slips me a tenner and says, 'I was wrong about the college thing as well. You've done us proud, love.' For the first time in years, he gives me a full, unrestrained hug. I almost skip down the street to catch the bus. I forget my talk of dropping out and travelling the world with Joe, for now.

He is at the bar talking to Heno when I walk in. The smile on his face when he sees me settles my nerves. I join some of his mates from the Palace who are here for the first Dublin appearance of Clannad, an Irish-singing trad music family from Donegal. We're gathered around a table of pints upstairs as the music is about to start when Joe sits down beside me, kisses me on the lips and slips his fingers through mine.

'Beautiful as ever,' he smiles. 'Just met Heno. All quiet on the western front.'

'The priest is asking when I'm going to collect the stuff I gave him. I'll have to do it soon,' I reply.

'We'll sort it tomorrow and get rid of this mess once and for all,' he smiles and pulls me tight as the music takes over.

We stumble out of the pub well after closing time and a night of magical sounds, and cross the road to the chipper.

37
THE DETENTION CENTRE

'That's the meat man,' says the bloke in the back to his companions. 'He was talking to Heno Moran at the bar tonight just before I rang you.'

'And he's with the pretty chick from Store Street,' says Detective Garda Meagher to his front-seat passenger.

The three are in an unmarked dark-blue Cortina thirty yards down the street from the Music Place. They're watching Joe and Angie leave the pub, both with a few jars on board by the look of them.

'Thanks, Richie. We'll look after you for that, now fuck off back to the sewer,' says the third man, Detective Garda Frank Joyce.

As they drive back to the station, Meagher and his partner consider this latest piece of the jigsaw and how their patience has paid off. Now there is at last a slight break in the investigation into the mysterious burglary of the house of the new Minister for Home Affairs a few weeks back.

'O'Malley will be pleased. It seems the young student and her commis chef are mixing in bad company,' Meagher says, looking at the black-and-white photo of Joe Heney stuck to the dashboard.

'Skullin' pints with Heno Moran, the notorious safe-cracker and general thug about town,' says Joyce. 'Not for long.'

When the front door crashes in two days later, Heno is in bed with his wife.

'Not even a fucking knock,' he says as he grabs his jocks and pants before the boys in blue push in the bedroom door and grab him. It's not the first time, so he knows the drill. Molly Moran screams and runs to the kids' bedroom as her man is pushed down the stairs and onto the living-room floor, his arms secured behind his back. She hears them kick the shite out of him and him shouting at the fucking pigs, telling them to leave him and his family alone, sure he's done nothing. As two hold him down, digging him in the ribs and asking about some fucking sparklers, the other three are going through every room, from top to bottom, out in the garden shed, scraping every box and bowl for whatever it is they want to find. But Heno Moran doesn't stash stolen goods in his house. Everyone knows that. An hour and a fruitless search later he is bundled into the back of a black van, his face bloodied, his arms and legs bruised and him still shouting and screaming at the fuckers.

'You think you're the tough guy, do you?' says the big brute who is doing most of the digging. 'We'll see about that, so,' as he sits on top of Heno before the doors of the paddy wagon close and his wife watches it boot down the street, hammer and tongs, taking him God knows where. By this time the neighbours are out on the road shouting at the cops, making a fuss and taking over Molly's kitchen to boil countless kettles and help her with the four wains, all of them in tears.

Heno's ordeal is only beginning. He's unceremoniously dumped out of the van onto a country road and told to go and do a piss behind the hedge. As he pulls his zip down he gets a massive blow to the back of his head and drops into the ditch. The brute and his mate kick his back, his sides, legs and arms, any piece of body they can find before dragging him back half conscious to the van and on down the road. He loses track of time, has no idea where he is and is barely able to see through the one eye that is not spattered with blood dripping from somewhere on his skull. He's used to beatings from the gardaí, but this one is fucking rough and it isn't about to end anytime soon, he thinks, as he shields his head from another blow and drifts off to a world without pain. When he wakes he's in a dark cell with a tiny ray of light breaking through the crack on the wall that passes for a window.

'Where the fuck am I?' he mumbles, before establishing that this isn't one of the cop shops he knows in Dublin, familiar as he is with the inside of most. His body hurts all over, his ribs are cracked and the bone in one elbow is sticking out from its proper place. The slightest movement on the wooden bed and stinking mattress causes excruciating pain.

'You are nowhere, Heno,' comes a voice from the corner of the room. 'And you are no one. Unless you tell me where the fucking jewels you stole from the house in Booterstown are gone, you will be a walking mental case when you get out of here – that's if you get out of here.'

'Who the fuck are you,' asks Heno, 'and what the fuck are you talking about?'

'DG Joyce, Special Branch. I've been sent down from Dublin to have a chat with you. What about the meat man, Heno? And what are you doing with a bag from that posh restaurant in the kitchen drawer? I didn't think you shopped on that side of town,' comes the voice.

'Don't know what you're talking about.'

'Fucking Joe fucking Heney, the meat man, I'm talking about. Did he give you the meat to poison the fucking dog? And for what? A couple of sparklers and a silver necklace. How much cash was there in the house? Who's your fence? Who was with you on the night? Do you know the Minister for Home Affairs is the victim of your crime? That's why you're dealing with us and not some local squad. We've taken over the job. That's why you're in this hell hole and not drinking fucking tea in Blackrock.'

'Fuck off, pig.'

Those are the last words uttered by Heno before he is lifted off the bed by two heavy bastards, one on each end of his limp carcass. Before he can register another round of obscenities, he's dragged up a set of stairs, into a long room with high, open windows. Outside he can see trees, no houses, no sign of human life or life of any kind.

'Did you rob the home of Bob Clarke in Cross Avenue, Booterstown, in June?' DG Joyce asks. 'Wrong answer and you're dead.'

'Fuck off, you mother-fucking pig bastard.'

Another severe beating around the head, arms and legs and Heno finds himself in the air halfway down between the second floor of the building and a garden surrounded by a spiked railing. As he descends he instinctively pulls his right arm across his head and face for protection. On landing, he screams like a wild animal and lapses into the unconscious.

For at least another day and night he lies in the cell with the crack in the wall, not knowing time or place. Every now and then a bowl of greasy soup is thrown on the floor with a plastic cup of water. He can't reach the cup or attempt the painful journey to the hole in the corner with the stink of piss and shit from the poor fuckers held here before him. He is covered in his own, mixed with blood and vomit.

He asks for a doctor and a brief but neither arrives. He is taken to a room where Joyce and the other fucker ask him questions he hardly hears or understands. On and on it goes for hours and hours, one day seeping into the next, one session into another, a leather belt across the back, a chair placed on his hands with a large bollox sitting on it. Pain travels until his whole body is joined up with cuts, sores and bruises into a complete and awful mess of agony. He knows his life is going to end in this fucking place. He won't see Molly or the kids

THE DETENTION CENTRE   239

again. They won't let him out for all the world to see the torture and pain they've inflicted.

How was he supposed to know that the gaff in Booterstown was a fucking minister's? For fucking Home Affairs of all people. That stupid fucking meat man and his documents. He should have told him the guy was a politician. If he watched the fucking news more often he might have sussed it. That's what it's all about, the fucking offshore banking stuff. He had read some of the stolen papers and was long enough around to know that this was some scam to hide money from the taxman and who knows who else. A government fucking minister. His only chance of survival is to say fuck all and pray. They can hold me for fucking days with these new laws, he thinks, if I live that long. He falls into a deep and disturbed sleep only to wake with a jolt every now and then gasping for breath and a drink of water. He dreams of dogs, the dogs of war, barking mad policemen, politicians on the TV, children in the bath, happy faces, Molly's tears, Redcoats and drums, big ugly fucking cops sitting on his broken hands.

When Detective Garda Ronan Meagher sees the state of Heno Moran in the dark cell of the garda station near Clonmel, the unsophisticated but brutal torture centre of the recently empowered and largely unaccountable Heavy Gang, he almost pukes.

'Orders from the top,' says Joyce with a smirk. 'No doctors, no briefs. Make him talk.'

'And whose orders would they be?'

'I told you, the very top.'

'To fuck him out the window and leave him for dead? Who gave you those kind of orders?' Meagher snaps.

'He wasn't pushed. He jumped,' comes the smart reply.

'And the window just happened to be open. Get him out of here before I fucking report you and your fucking gorillas.'

It rapidly dawns on Meagher that he has been excluded from his own investigation precisely because he hasn't the stomach for the new regime of torture instigated under Gavin's watch. O'Malley or Mullen waited until he was off duty to arrest the suspect he had identified in relation to the Booterstown burglary. It seems that things got out of hand and he's been sent down to this kip to clean up the mess. To make matters worse, the savage exercise is totally counter-productive as they haven't managed to get any information out of a prisoner who's now incapable of putting two words together after the merciless barbarism. And he is partly responsible for this inhuman state of affairs. Guardian of the peace, my arse.

After two consecutive and legally dubious forty-eight hour deten-tions, Moran is a babbling, brutalised wreck of a man, but he isn't broken and will no doubt return to his chosen trade a more bitter, angry and callous individual. These are the conclusions of the young detective garda as he assists with the removal of the suspect into the paddy wagon. There Moran is provided with the small comfort of a mattress and blanket for the three-hour, bumpy journey back to Dublin, and a large lemonade bottle full of water which he gulps in seconds before collapsing in a heap.

When he wakes he just about recognises the face on the man in a white coat.

'What happened, Heno? Who did this to you?' the young doctor asks gently.

'Where am I? Is that you, Doc? Are they gone?'

'Who, Heno. Is who gone?'

'The fucking pig bastards,' he can barely whisper.

'You're safe here. Someone dropped you off in a black van at the front door last night. You're in an awful state. You need to rest up.'

'Doc, tell the meat man they're coming for him. Tell him to get offside, the stupid bollox.'

'Who's the meat man?'

'The fucking chef with the bird you were chatting up last weekend. From East Wall.'

'Angie Whelan?'

'That's the one. The cops know all about him, but tell him they were only asking about the sparklers and the readies, not the paperwork.'

Dr Brian Hickey had seen a lot in his short few years in the Mater, but the injuries on this patient are like nothing he has witnessed before. A victim of what was patently a severe beating. His head is badly cut and bruised, at least four ribs on each side are cracked, his legs and arms are fractured, fibula and tibia, the bones in the fingers of both hands are shattered. Internal damage could be serious.

'Padre Pio would have been proud of the marks on his hands,' he tells the nurse as he cleans up after the brief consultation. 'Worse than a car crash. And it seems this is justice as administered by the defenders of our glorious State.'

'We've seen a few patients recently with injuries consistent with a fall from a height after spending a few days in garda custody. I've reported them to the hospital manager, but he just grunts and nothing happens,' she replies.

'He's afraid of his own shadow, that man. Someone will have to put a stop to this or it will be dead bodies showing up soon.'

As he ends his twenty-four-hour shift, he gives instructions that no one is to be permitted to visit Mr Moran, especially anyone from the police, and that the patient is to be fed and watered intravenously.

A heavy dose of morphine will also be required for at least two days for the pain, so he won't be in a position to make sense to anyone for a while, the young doctor calculates. He tells the senior nurse he will personally contact the man's family and assure them he is stable and in recovery.

Hickey goes straight to the Music Place to find out where Heno lives. Even though he has done nothing but administer to a sick man, the young medic feels a distinct pang of fear as he walks at a fast pace up Dorset Street from the hospital. He is concerned for Angie, the best-looking girl he knows, whom he first met beside the same bed where Heno Moran is now conked out. It doesn't take long to get word to Heno's wife as his best mate, Jimmy 'the Knacker' Dunne, is on the early drinking shift in the pub when he arrives.

'He's in a bad way, but he'll recover. Tell her not to visit for a couple of days as I have him sedated.'

'Fucking pigs,' says Dunne and downs his pint in seconds. 'Thanks, Doc,' he says as he heads out the pub door and into a yellow Toyota Hiace driven by his son.

38

ANGIE

I'm getting ready for work when the barman from the Music Place knocks on the door.

'What brings you here, Brian?' There's a worried look on his face. 'Is it Mam? Is she all right?' Mam's been out since early.

'No. I mean it's not about her. Can I come in? You need to warn your friend Joe – is that his name? – the chef guy, that the guards are on to him. I haven't a clue what it's about, but Heno Moran is lying in a bed in the Mater with almost every bone in his body broken. Thrown out an upstairs window, he claims. He told me to get a message to your bloke to get offside. That's all I know.'

Without a second thought or question, I pull on my coat and leg it towards the bus stop with the young doctor trailing behind. He insists on stopping a cab. If I'm quick enough I can catch Joe before he gets to The Bistro, if he's not been picked up already.

I haven't felt such fear since I had to look for Mam after the bombings. I'm trembling all over. The Doc is telling me everything will be okay, that it's probably just some terrible mix-up, whatever's going on. He hasn't a clue.

'It's no mistake, Brian. The guards think we're terrorists because we were trying to find out who bombed my mam and half the bleedin' city, and Joe did something really stupid. I have to find him before they throw him out a window too,' I whisper to him in the back seat of the taxi. He can hardly make out what I'm saying.

'The bombings. Is that what this is all about? Look, I have to go. But, if you need me I'll be on the wards every morning this week. Keep in touch,' he says as he jumps out of the taxi on Amiens Street and gives the man a fiver. 'Good luck.'

As we turn into Thomas Street I see Joe's familiar jacket in the distance as he heads towards the city centre. I ask the driver to pull up alongside. Joe jumps in, with a smile and a kiss on the cheek. The smile doesn't last for long, though, as I put my finger on his lips.

'Drop us off back at Trinity,' I say to the taxi driver.

Over a coffee in the Buttery, deserted in the summer holidays except for a few wandering tourists taking in the *Book of Kells*, I explain the visit from the doctor, Heno's distressed condition and his warning for Joe to get offside. Close to tears, I recount the doctor's description of the injuries inflicted on the small-time crook by the Heavy Gang. It's surely only a matter of time before we get another knock on the door and who knows what.

'We should leave, tonight, for London, before they do the same to you and me,' I say. He's quiet for a long time. The calm before the storm.

'They won't do it to you. I should have told you a long time ago, but I couldn't, Angie. I was afraid you'd walk away.'

'Tell me what?'

'The reason they clattered me so badly is because I've done time. The day of the bombing do you know where I was coming from? The 'Joy. I did a spell in jail. For hash dealing. I'm sorry. I was going to tell you in the house that day when you were asking about my folks but …'

'I'm sleeping with a convict. Oh my God,' I say. 'Joe "Manson"

Heney. The butcher from the southside. Rips the babies out of pregnant women. Joe Heney, do you really think I'd fall out of love because you did a spell in jail for hash dealing? And they think that gives them permission to beat you black and blue. Jesus,' I say holding his hand tight and looking into his sad blue eyes.

'I thought you'd leave me for not telling you the truth. I'm fucking thick.' He recounts his Dutch adventure and his time in the nick, reading books, football in the yard and learning to cook. How his cellmate, Seamus Russell, helped him do his time, giving him a short-wave radio, books and lessons in Irish political history. It turned out his fellow captive was organising the famous Hallow'een helicopter escape of IRA prisoners in 1973 while he was inside.

The mention of Russell by the senior officers in the Bridewell has given Joe an idea. Risky as it may be in our current circumstances, he thinks the republican might be able to help us find out more than we know about the bombings, and even a route out of the tangled mess we find ourselves in.

'He's sure to know stuff that we don't and might give us a good steer. We don't have much choice. We need all the help we can get,' Joe says. It seems likely that Heno revealed little or nothing to his inquisitors or he would have been charged instead of being left almost lifeless at the doors of the Mater by persons unknown.

Both of us are expected in The Bistro sometime soon and if we don't turn up, or at least provide a seriously adequate explanation for our absence, our jobs are on the line. It's evident that Joe is a suspect in the burglary, an accomplice of some sort, even if he has a cast-iron alibi for the evening, which can be provided by any number of those attending the party fundraiser. The cops are looking for jewels and cash, according to Heno's brief and confusing account to the doctor, with no mention of sensitive documents. In which case, there is nothing to link Joe to the crime they are investigating other than his association with a known safe-cracker and the coincidence of the two events happening on the same night. I calm down as he takes my hand.

'Let's talk to Neilan first. He's the most important friend we have right now,' says Joe.

'First we'd better ring in sick,' I say.

I call Pierre from the public phone in the arched entrance to the college and report in with food poisoning, knowing that it is the one complaint sure to frighten the life out of Murphy and guarantee his instruction not to come near the place until we are fully recovered. Then Joe calls Neilan, who invites us to his office, pronto. I tell him about the visit from the doctor, the warning to Joe from Heno and the state of him in the Mater. The solicitor advises that we are unlikely to be charged with any offence in connection with the illicit photographic exercise in The Bistro, but is quite disturbed to hear of the brutal assault on 'Mr Moran', as he calls him. It is not the first time the activities of this garda Heavy Gang have been brought to his notice and it represents a significant shift in the direction of a police state in his view, or, at the very least, a growing disregard for the basic human rights of citizens. He doesn't ask whether we know of any reason Moran might be a suspect in the burglary of the minister's home and how we might feature in the investigation of that crime. Perhaps he's afraid of the answer.

'The guards clearly believe there's a relationship between the fundraiser and the burglary, are aware of your acquaintance with Mr Moran and have reason to suspect he is the safe-cracker from that night,' the solicitor says. 'From what I've heard the garda commissioner is quite agitated about this whole business because he was at the party. There were also a lot of other very senior and influential people in The Bistro that night who might not want it known that they are funders or supporters of the party, or want their names kept out of this for other reasons. That might explain why the guards are trying to track down all the photos of the night on the ostensible grounds of "protecting State security". Unless you are incriminated in relation to the burglary, I see no reason for them to arrest you again. If you have any other information that would help to explain why this affair has raised such a head of steam you can, of course, tell me in full confidence at any time. In the meantime, go about your normal lives and try to keep out of trouble.'

39

GOVERNMENT BUILDINGS

Bob Clarke is having a bad day when the commissioner walks into his office. He was out late the night before, trying to gently wean Evelyn Fagan off their relationship, had far too much to drink and ended up impotently trying to fuck her in a room in Jury's hotel. His great plan for a soft landing to their affair went off the runway. She insisted, correctly, that he had expressed his undying love for her only a few weeks ago and promised that it was only a matter of time before he and his wife were to separate, that they hadn't slept together for years and were only keeping up the appearance of a stable marriage for the sake of their almost grown-up children.

'Then everything changed because you're now a fucking minister,' she said. 'Or were you lying through your fucking flashy white teeth?'

His efforts to calm her down with copious glasses of white wine and then double vodkas had the opposite effect. Instead of his notion of heading home after he broke the bad news, he had to book a room to stop her screaming obscenities at him in full view of the bemused patrons of the hotel bar. She collapsed in a heap after her frantic efforts to get him to screw the fuck out of her 'to show that you love only me'. Afterwards, she unleashed a tirade of abuse which included a none-too-subtle warning that he would live to regret the day he dumped her. He believed her, even if she was pissed at the time. When he slipped out of the bed in the early hours the thought crossed his mind that he should pour another gallon of vodka into her, a can of petrol over her and set her alight, but it was only a thought. Instead, he went for a strong pot of tea in the Coffee Dock and headed to the office.

Ned Gavin isn't in a much better mood when he takes a seat across the desk from the minister. His team has failed to progress with their investigation into the burglary at Clarke's home, even though they identified and arrested a key suspect. Unfortunately, four days in detention was insufficient time to secure a confession. There was some evidence at his home of a link to The Bistro, which, he stated, the minister might recall was the venue for the function on the same night as the break-in, but it is very tenuous and there were no stolen goods in his possession.

'What does tenuous mean, Ned?' Clarke inquires in his softest voice. Anything more demanding or authoritative might reveal his deeper fears over the possible outcome to this whole, messy business.

'Well it's not much, just some packaging from the restaurant that we believe may have contained meat products of the type used to poison your dog. It seems the young chef we detained some weeks ago might have been providing the thief's family with meat which the suspect, a well-known safe-cracker, dosed with rat poison before giving it to your unfortunate animal.'

'That's it? Nothing else? No confession, no fingerprints? What about the jewels and the cash?'

'An extensive search of his house failed to uncover anything else of material or evidential value. He observed his absolute right to silence during questioning and despite extensive probing by an experienced team of detectives during a number of interrogations, he did not provide us with any useful information.'

'What an anal gobshite,' Clarke thinks. 'Can he not speak plain fucking English?'

Out loud he asks, 'How did you identify him as a suspect or is it just one of your famous hunches because he robbed a few safes before?'

'Some intelligent police work and the co-operation of one of our network of informers in the criminal community. We discovered that the chef and his girlfriend, whom, as you know, we detained some time ago, frequent the same drinking establishment and indeed were seen in the company of the suspect in recent days.'

'And have you brought them back in to ask what they might know about this man and whether they helped him steal my property?'

'We are discussing that prospect and are seeking advice from the Chief State Solicitor as to the propriety of detaining the couple again and in the certain knowledge that they will, again, observe their right to silence on the advice of their solicitor, Gerard Neilan,' the commissioner replies.

'So where does that leave us?' the exasperated Clarke asks.

'Not very much more advanced in the investigation, I'm afraid. We also have to consider the prospect that some of the material which we suspect the young man has in his possession might reach the public domain if we make a provocative move in relation to him or his girlfriend.'

'What material?'

'The photographs from the event in The Bistro where you and the Taoiseach, of course, were present, along with a lot of other influential people, as you know.'

'Including yourself, if memory serves me right,' says Clarke.

'Of course.'

Clarke wonders if Gavin is more concerned with the thought of photos of himself gargling pints and chatting up 'the entertainment' emerging in the fucking press than anything else. Or perhaps he is up to something. Maybe he knows about the bank documents but is holding on to that particular nugget to use as ammunition in a later battle.

'Is there anything else I need to know about this sordid business before we move on to other matters?'

'Not that I can think of. But I will keep you informed of developments, Minister.'

After some careful circling around other awkward topics such as media reports of the excessive use of emergency powers and prolonged detention orders, and a discussion on recent forays across the border by British Army undercover squads, Clarke raises a subject which has been exercising his mind for some time.

'This report on the '74 bombings,' he says as he raises the folder from his desk. 'Ned, what can you tell me about the role of the British in the atrocities? Could it possibly be true that the Brits, I mean agents of British intelligence, were involved with the loyalist gang that devastated the city centre and hundreds of our citizens? This file from your people and army intelligence appears to point in that direction. It seems our army intel people are convinced that plastic explosive was used that could only have come from British Army stocks. They don't believe the loyalists could have pulled this operation off on their own. I mean the last government never mentioned this appalling prospect. A major foreign power bombing a friendly neighbouring state, or at least colluding in that awful business, is that what we are looking at here?'

'As you know, Minister, I was not commissioner at the time, although I was part of the investigation.'

'Which was wrapped up after just three months. Were you happy with that?'

'Well, there were known suspects, loyalists whose arrest we sought. Unfortunately, we did not receive the co-operation we might have from the RUC, or the British for that matter, but relations are much *better now, as you know. The most important thing is to build on that so we can rid this country, the whole country, of the terrorist networks.'*

'That may be so, but I'm asking whether it was known by the previous administration and yourself that agents of the British State may have been involved in the attacks in Dublin and Monaghan three years ago and what was done about it? Specifically, why was the ballistic and forensic evidence handed over to the British Army in Lisburn where we know their spooks hang out? Were you involved in that? Who closed down the investigation so soon?'

'As I've said, Minister, I was not in overall command. We did not receive the co-operation we would have liked from the other side. I can assure you that representations seeking their full co-operation and access to all relevant information were made at the highest level, although with the turmoil in British politics, and the disagreements and tensions between the various security agencies, it is not clear whether they got to the bottom of exactly who knew what, when and where, Sir.'

'It's not too long ago that some of your own crowd were selling information to the Brits. I wonder how many other sleepers you still have in the ranks? The place is crawling with spies if you ask me and some of them with thick Irish accents. I take it you are not compromised in that regard?'

'Absolutely not, Minister. We did have a problem a few years back, but I think I can confidently say that our internal security today is much better equipped to weed out any bad elements who may have got too close to their British counterparts, particularly along the border. We share a common enemy, and breakdowns and disputes on intelligence matters and over-zealous officers acting under their own steam only disrupt our discipline and communications.'

'I'm sure they do, but I'm not one bit happy about the contents of this file and I believe it is something we should pursue. I certainly will when I meet with the ambassador and his people. Thank you, Ned. I'll see you next week, same time, same place.'

'Very well, Minister. Give my regards to your good wife.'

'The fucking sneaky bastard. He knows about last night in Jury's already,' Clarke thinks, as Gavin leaves the room. He looks again at the file marked confidential and stamped 'March 1975' in thick red ink. A year-long investigation into the bombings and nothing to show for it. In fact nothing much happened after the garda inquiry was stood down after just three months. Yet it took three senior officers another nine months to write a report that fails to uncover anything that could lead to identifying the perpetrators, let alone a conviction. However, there's enough in it to make life uncomfortable for a few people.

Clarke places the dossier in a locked drawer. A smoking gun, he thinks, which might come in handy in his dealings with Gavin and the Brits. It's risky, but he's marked the card of the garda commissioner not to fuck with him. He could see he touched a raw nerve when he brought up the bombing investigation, or lack of it.

He has a lot to learn about the complex workings of the force which has been placed under his political control. Control, that's a joke. He doesn't know the half of it.

40

NORTHSIDE

Word about Heno Moran's plight spreads like wildfire across the northside. As it travels along the bush telegraph from the Music Place to the Rivermount bar in west Finglas and back to the flats in Dominick Street, the scale of the assault by the filth on the man and the story of his abduction to some secret torture centre in the sticks gain serious legs.

Although his condition does not require exaggeration, with X-rays showing multiple broken bones, by the time the news reaches the traders on Moore Street 'the poor divil' has had his right eye torn out of its socket and 'his balls are hanging off him'.

Heno's friends, many of them, like him, former inmates of the perverse industrial school and prison system, discuss revenge for the brutal treatment of their partner in crime. The debate is largely confined to the rougher bars of the inner city and outer suburbs.

Taking one or two cops out would teach them a lesson, argue some of the younger Turks with access to a range of weaponry, including assault rifles and pistols used in the now frequent bank heists in and around the capital. Burning down a cop shop or two is another proposed solution. Wiser counsel advises that the State is adequately equipped to deal with any such criminal uprising given that it is grappling with one of the world's most lethal guerrilla armies. But they are also determined that the matter will not be let rest and that Heno will be avenged.

These informal and not-so-secret underworld consultations inevitably come to the notice of gardaí of all ranks, including the ordinary boys in blue on the street. They've been experiencing a heightened hostility from people of all ages, men, women and kids, in some of the poorer slums. Graffiti begins to appear in the inner-city blocks with unflattering suggestions of what should be done to them, some of it borrowed directly from American gangster movies, the rest home-grown.

'Pigs will die' is scrawled on some walls, 'Pigs will fly – from the top window' on others. 'Heno's Army will beat the cops' is plastered over hoardings around Croke Park and Sheriff Street. The street artists reckon that even culchie guards will get the reference to Dublin's Gaelic football supporters – Heffo's Army.

This disturbing news from the street reaches the upper echelons of the force in the Phoenix Park and there are rumblings of discontent from experienced officers. Some fear that the uncontrolled activities of the Heavy Gang are bringing the force into disrepute and threatening to damage relations built up over years and decades which help to identify problems and their makers before they happen and to solve crimes quickly when they do. The last thing they need is for riots to break out over the treatment of one thug who may have deserved some heat but not the beating doled out in a remote torture chamber by a bunch of fucking sadists.

Among the most displeased is DG Meagher, who confronts his colleagues and his superiors at the weekly meeting of the investigation team.

'There is no chance of pinning anything on the one suspect we have for the burglary at Clarke's house. We were that close to getting Moran behind bars and you fucked it with this obsession of beating the shit out of anyone who comes your way. The fucker couldn't even speak after four days, never mind make a confession,'

Meagher argues, directing his remarks to the top table and his eyes to Joyce.

'The streets are ready to explode. It's one thing beating the shit out of the Provos, but brutalising a man with only the skimpiest evidence against him is something else,' agrees Mullen in an unexpected criticism of Joyce and his gang of heavies. Joyce is unrepentant. After all, it was his idea to bring the informer, Richie Duggan, to the Music Place where they got the breakthrough that led to Moran and the meat man in the first place. It cost him fifty quid from his informer fund, but it was worth every penny. Meagher may be smart, but he's not ruthless enough to get results, he thinks to himself. They may have been partners in the investigation at one point, but that doesn't make them friends. Besides, they are in competition for promotion.

'We can deal with it,' says Joyce, who is not about to apologise to anyone for carrying out instructions from his boss. He had an assurance that no less an authority than Commissioner Gavin had passed down the orders from on high. 'There are a lot of windbags out there threatening us with hell and high water. We'll give them something else to think about.'

Within hours, new graffiti appears on the walls of the Dominick Street flats.

'Duggy is a Rat.'

It doesn't take long for Jimmy Dunne and his crew to work that one out. The hunt is on for the man who grassed up Heno Moran and every one of his soldiers is on the prowl.

***

When Father Rory opens the door he is taken slightly aback but composes himself to invite Angie in for a cup of tea.

'So you've come to collect your stuff, Angie.'

'Yes, Father, and to apologise for the delay in taking it back off you. I hope it hasn't caused too much –'

'Angie, I am always pleased to help a friend. In this life we should reward those who do good by others around them and I have seen how you have cared for your mother. If you are ever in any difficulty you can always come to me, even if it's not for Mass or confession,' he laughs.

'Thanks Father, Rory. I won't forget your kindness to my mam. She'd be lost without you and her prayers.'

'She finally seems to be getting back to her old self after all that trauma. But tell me, Angie, how are you getting on? I have been hearing things ... as you can imagine in this small community there is little that goes on without some little birdie finding out. And the plain-clothes police presence outside your house was hard to miss. Is this connected to the material you gave me? You don't have to tell me anything you don't want to. I'm only asking out of concern for you,' the priest says.

'They seem to have eased off in the past while. I'm not the terrorist they think I am but there is a connection with the photos I gave you. As I said to you before, Father, we've discovered that elements of the British government had some role in the bombings that blinded my ma. Bob Clarke knows they were involved because they told him. Then his house was robbed and bank documents were stolen which prove he got a large sum of money for some reason. Now he's the minister and he's being almost blackmailed because the British know he's hidden the money offshore. There's photos of some of them in the envelope I gave you. The guards are looking for the photos. They arrested our friend, Donal, who took the photos during an election fundraiser in

The Bistro. I'm not sure what else is left to tell you, but it's all getting out of hand and a man was thrown out of the window of a police station last week and he's lying with his arms and legs broken in the Mater in the same bed as Mam was in. I'm scared. They beat up my boyfriend Joe as well and I don't know what will happen next.'

She resists the urge to weep into the cup of tea the priest has put before her on the table. Whether out of instinctive trust of the man in front of her, or because she can no longer hold it all in, she unburdens herself of the extraordinary knowledge which she has been carrying around for the past few years: what she and Joe found on the red napkin, how they made a tape of British agents talking to the politician who is now a government minister. How the Englishman referred to the British role in the Dublin bombings. How they were involved in the taking of photos of the rich and famous, and the theft of the financial documents. She tells him they think they have enough to bring the evidence to the attention of a public sick to death of the cover-ups, lies and deceit committed in their names by people they elect. As she talks, he flicks through the photos, a Who's Who of the elite who keep the wheels of commerce and corruption turning in this town. And the representatives of the two powerful nations that see themselves as the policemen of the world.

By the time she has recounted her story, the priest is determined to help in any way he can, not just with her immediate predicament but with the wider issues at stake, including the answer to the burning question of the day. Who was actually responsible for the bombings of May 1974? He tells her that he has already heard concerns from other parishioners that raise troubling questions about the attacks, who carried them out, how and why. If they can help bring the guilty parties to justice, then he believes that is God's work.

It was not so long ago that Father Bennett witnessed the elimination of a democratically elected president and his replacement by a brutal dictatorship, which turned its guns on the best of the people first, and then the rest. Angie's story brings the trauma of Allende's overthrow in Chile back to him. A couple of years ago he shook the hand of the late, lamented president's widow, Hortense, when she visited Dublin and the political refugees from her country. It's still fresh in his mind. He has helped people before, good people accused of bad things, and his instincts have rarely been wrong.

'You have these sensitive documents and tape which may in fact be your best protection against these people in authority who are upset with you. If you wish, I can keep them safely until the time comes when they should be made public, although not by you of course. Where there's a will there's a way. We'll have to be careful, but I don't expect the police will come rampaging through this place anytime soon. However, I can't guarantee your safety when all of this comes out.'

Angie does not know what to say, but her heart tells her that Father Bennett will not let her down and might just provide the support that she and Joe badly need in their feeble battle with a far greater power.

'All I can promise is that I will help you try to get to the bottom of what went on and what is still going on, if only to reassure those so deeply affected. That is my pastoral duty, Angela,' he says. 'I have been thinking about some sort of event to commemorate those who were killed and maimed, and for their relatives. And to find answers to their legitimate questions and their quest for truth and justice. This may give me the excuse I need to look into things. Perhaps we can work on this together.'

'Whatever I can do, Rory. I want to know who bombed my mam and why.'

'Very well, Angie. You're a courageous young girl trying to do the right thing. Leave it with me for a few days and we'll decide what best to do next.'

41

GRANBY LANE

Richie Duggan is hugging the walls and lanes as he sneaks through the flats, a woollen cap covering his remaining strands of hair. His name is scrawled on every street, around every corner, as he makes his way to the dole office on Gardiner Street. The kids are shouting 'Duggy the Rat' before they leg it offside and out of reach.

'I'll wring your fucking necks when I get me hands on you,' he shouts to the wind that is left in their wake. 'I'll tell your das on you …'

Ever since he identified Heno and the meat man to the Branch men outside the Music Place, his life has been hell. He knows his card is marked. The writing on the walls has told him as much. He hasn't been in his flat, or on the streets, since he first heard that his name was being taken in vain as the tout who grassed up Heno Moran, but he has no choice other than to move on a Tuesday morning if he is to collect the brew.

On his return journey past Seán McDermott Street, up Temple Street and down the alleys off Dorset Street, he considers his chances of getting to London and maybe Spain in a few weeks. Then a yellow Toyota Hiace pulls up. Jimmy Dunne's gang. Before he knows it he is lying in the back with his head covered, a smell of horseshit from under the balaclava placed backways on his head, pissing himself in fear.

In the lane beside the sausage factory on Granby Row he is fucked out the sliding door of the Hiace.

'You'll be on the breakfast table with the rashers tomorrow, you rat,' says a voice before he hears a crate of bottles landing beside him on the road. 'Keep an eye out for the pigs, you, the ones with two legs.'

'Who did you tell, you fucking grass?' comes the distinctive voice of the Dunner as an empty bottle is smashed on his head. 'Whose fucking pockets are you in? Name the bastards.' Another bottle rains down, then another on his head and arms. With every question comes the pain of glass on bone, every bone.

'Meagher and Joyce,' he wails as the hands covering his face are hit, his fingers smashed and cut.

'Who else did you grass up you fucking stoolie bastard?'

Five bottles later he has listed a string of conmen doing time for a litany of smaller or greater offences.

'Pull down his jocks,' another voice says, one of the higher achieving graduates of the Daingean school of abuse and anal rape.

'The next one's up your arse. How much did they give you for Heno? You scumbag. Where's the loot?'

'Please, don't. It's in me ma's gaff. In the hot press.'

With that, the spike of glass on the last bottle in the crate slices through his rectum like a searing hot poker. Richie Duggan passes out and away. Before they leave they empty his pockets of the dole money.

'To cover expenses and a few pints,' says the Dunner.

Richie the Rat is found the next morning, a filthy broken, bloody mess and another screaming headline for the Herald.

'IRA torture victim dies on city street.'

DG Joyce neglected to calculate the unforeseen consequences of his bright idea to plaster 'Duggy the Rat' on the wall opposite the Black Church and around the north inner-city flats. It was intended to deflect attention from the beating of Heno Moran and to channel the anger of his criminal friends in a different direction. Now the consequences are beginning to add up very quickly. Blaming the IRA for the latest violent incident on the streets might play well initially, but before long his not-so-subtle ruse will be rumbled, especially if Meagher has anything to do with it.

'That fucker is on the warpath over that precious fucking Trinity student and her friend,' he thinks as he lays down the newspaper with the story he has fed to its willing crime hack. A good beating would sort them out in no time and he'd have those fucking photos that O'Malley and Gavin have told him in no uncertain terms to recover by 'any means necessary'. And a dead tout isn't much of a price to pay unless of course Duggan put Joyce's name in the pot before he was snuffed out by Moran's thugs.

'Who knows where that could lead?' he says to himself, as he folds the paper and ponders his next move.

The first thing is to get the local guards in Store Street to pull in some suspects for the murder of Duggan, to keep the serious crime squad happy. Heno Moran can't be touched again, but some of his mates are bound to blurt out their murderous secrets eventually. All things come to those who wait. And in this case he is in no hurry to establish the full cause of the brutal death of Richie Duggan, another casualty in the war to protect civilised society and democracy as we know it.

42

ANGIE

When I tell Joe about my unexpected confessional moment with the priest he's surprised but not shocked. 'After what's happened over the past while, the stress of it was bound to get to you,' he says.

'Father Bennett may be the break we need, if you are sure you can trust him,' he says after listening to my account of the meeting with the priest. He agrees to collect the goods from Pierre and to meet me early under the college arch on Sunday to hand them over. He throws me a kiss as I leave the kitchen of The Bistro.

Mam is pleasantly surprised to hear me offer to escort her to eleven o'clock Mass, although not so pleased to hear my declared reason for going. She likes the young priest, but the idea of arranging some sort of remembrance for the victims of the bombings resurrects carefully buried memories of her anguish from those awful days over three years ago. She often prays for the victims, those not as fortunate as herself, who died or lost loved ones, and even for the men who carried out that wicked deed. But to have her neighbours and friends and all those across the city who suffered forced to revisit those horrible times does not strike her as the most comforting or Christian thing the generous curate could do.

Eventually, after much pleading on my part, she concedes, 'I suppose it won't do us any harm to listen to him.' She lets me take her arm for the five-minute stroll to the church. Once we arrive, I let her go inside to take her usual pew. When I see the Black Widow also go inside, I run around to her shop to retrieve the package that I left in my hiding place earlier this morning.

'Where were you? The Mass is about to start,' Mam whispers when I take my seat beside her.

'I met a girl outside from school,' I lie.

We absorb the sermon, delivered from the raised pulpit half-way through the Mass to mark the Feast of Saint Peter. After-wards, Father Bennett invites all those interested or concerned to join a new group being set up to remember those who died in the 1974 bombings and to assist the injured and bereaved.

'Those who cannot heal may be comforted and those who lost their loved ones, consoled,' he says. After listening to the priest for a few minutes, Mam whispers that a memorial service for the victims is not such a bad idea. 'After all, a few prayers never hurt anyone.'

For me, it is a secondary and longer-term element to the two-pronged plan hatched by the good Father. The first part involves me depositing a brown envelope marked 'parish dues' into the solid wooden box inside the front door for collection by the priest as soon as Mass is over. All the pieces of the unsolved puzzle are now in the hands of the curate. Bank documents, tape, photos and the napkin which Joe was sensible enough to keep. The plan is to release everything, including the crucial references to those responsible for the bombs, to the press. Anonymously. The bank documents which are referred to on the tape suggest that some British authority figures have compromised the new Minister for Home Affairs and show that he holds a very large, and undeclared, cash deposit offshore. The photos of the fundraiser include people recorded on tape cavorting with the great and the good in various states of inebriation. Adding them all together amounts to a potentially significant media story so early in the days of the new Irish government.

When I get to Joe's place that evening, I find a note.

'Hi love, having a pint with a friend down in Fallon's in the Coombe. Come join us and we'll grab some food after,' it says. When I get there, Joe is in the snug, engrossed in discussion with a man a few years older than him.

'This is Seamus Russell,' he says as the bearded stranger stands to shake my hand.

'Hello. Joe's told me a bit about you,' I say.

'Not all bad, I hope. Can I get you a drink?' he asks with a friendly smile.

'Sure, a pint of Guinness, thanks.' I'm hoping he doesn't notice that I'm a little nervous about sitting in a public house with a notorious IRA man. Joe does.

'Don't worry, Angie,' he says taking my hand as his ex-cellmate goes to the bar. 'I've told him what's been going on. He's sound and he's offered to give us a hand with our little campaign.'

Joe has given him the gist of our misadventures, from the napkin to the secret tape recording, the photos of the fundraiser, the retrieval of the bank documents and our pursuit by the forces of law and order.

Joe explains that Seamus is a member of Sinn Féin and the party has been gathering information about the attacks, including about some of the main suspects in the loyalist community in Armagh and Belfast.

'He has some ideas that can help get the story out,' he says. Seamus has offered to meet with Father Bennett and work out some way to expose the truth, if I will ask and the priest is willing.

Seamus asks about my mother, discusses the priest's plan for a remembrance committee, finishes his drink and gets up to leave.

'It's not a good idea to be seen together. From now on we should meet somewhere more private,' he says before walking out.

'What do you think?' asks Joe.

'It can't do any harm to have someone who knows what he's talking about,' I say.

***

Three days later we are sitting in a room in the back of the Black Widow's shop a few doors down from the church in East Wall. Mrs Flanagan has already poured tea for me, Joe and the priest when Seamus arrives with another man. It was Father Bennett's suggestion that we meet here rather than in the Presbytery.

'Nora obliges me on occasion as there are some parishioners who would rather not be seen going in and out of my house,' he explains. 'I'm not sure the bishop would take too kindly to me hosting your republican friends.'

'You're always welcome here, Father,' the widow says as she closes the door behind her. Once she's gone, Seamus shakes the priest's hand and introduces himself and his serious-looking friend from Belfast, whom he calls Kevin. 'We appreciate your meeting us,' he says.

'Well, I promised Angie that I would assist her and Joe. They need and deserve all the help they can get in their effort to find out who bombed Dublin and injured so many, including her brave mother,' Father Rory responds. 'That does not mean that I support the appalling things done by some of your people. There is no excuse for such blood to be spilled, no matter what the provocation. Sure the British and loyalists have a lot to answer for but there must be another way out of this.'

'I don't disagree, Father,' says Seamus. 'Sinn Féin is trying to find a political alternative. I wouldn't be too optimistic though. But you can't believe all you read in the papers about us. Including the lies they've told about the recent death of Richie Duggan. Republicans didn't do that and I've a fair idea his death is not unrelated to what we're here to talk about. It's another reason why Joe and Angie here could do with some help. The people who bombed Dublin are as ruthless as they come. Kevin can explain what we know about May '74.'

'All the evidence points to British agents inside or working with the loyalist groups,' the man from Belfast says. 'The UVF and UDA have done plenty of bombings before, including in the South, but this one was different, at least the Dublin ones were. Better co-ordinated, military precision, high-quality plastic explosives the loyalists hadn't used previously. Sightings of known loyalist killers and British Army personnel on the streets of Dublin, a mysterious van on the docks, a known loyalist supporter and police informer in the hotel on the quays.

'Seamus tells me you have a taped conversation between Bob Clarke and some English officials, suggesting why and by whom the Dublin bombing was carried out and threatening to expose his offshore dealings. All pointing in one direction: the dirty tricks brigade, British intelligence,' he continues.

Kevin hands out some photos of loyalist and other suspects seen in Dublin on the day of the bombs. 'The RUC showed these mugshots to arrested republicans in Belfast and Armagh in the weeks after the attacks. We have spent the past few years tracking as many of them down as we can. We will be waiting a long time for those who know to tell us the real story.'

When Joe looks at a photo of a blond-haired man in his forties he lets out a gasp. 'That's the guy I saw in Parnell Street. He parked the green Hillman there about twenty minutes before it blew up,' he says. Another piece of the jigsaw.

The Belfast man then pulls out another set of photos. Older, grainier.

'These are shots of a British Army SAS unit in Aden over a decade ago. Frank Kitson's boys. Do you recognise anyone?'

This time Angie reacts first.

'Jesus, sorry Father, but that's Alan Richards in the middle. A younger version but definitely him.'

'And there's Mr Hillman standing beside him,' says Joe.

'Mr Hillman is Roger Hanbury, originally from Belfast. Came back from Aden and served in the North as a British Army officer with the UDR. A known loyalist killer. Based in Lisburn when the forensics from the bombs were delivered by the gardaí. His mate, Alan Richards, moved up the ranks of the intelligence service in London. Now you have him on the tape inferring that the British were involved in the Dublin bombs and he is known to be an associate of one of the leading suspects. We're trying to get proof that others with a similar pedigree were involved as well, including a serving British diplomat in Dublin,' says Seamus.

It doesn't take too long to agree that we have enough to bring the story to the media, and the sooner the better.

AUTUMN 1977

43

GOVERNMENT BUILDINGS

Bob Clarke is getting it from all sides. Dead bodies on the streets of Dublin, beatings in garda custody, the SAS killing IRA men south of the border and vice versa, the republicans bombing the bejasus out of London, the commissioner pressing for more powers, and loud complaints from Downing Street about the Irish bringing a case against Her Majesty's government over the torture of innocents in her jails. And things aren't much better on the domestic front, with his wife still nagging him about his late-night disappearances and the rumours, floating among the chattering classes and the filthy rags that repeat them, over his extramarital activities. He can't work out whether it's the Taoiseach's people spinning against him, that bastard in Finance, or the opposition using the information they gleaned in government about their political enemies.

At the end of the day, however, he knows that the most likely source, including barely disguised media references to his now dissolved relationship with the spurned Evelyn Fagan, is almost certainly the biggest fucker of them all, Edward Gavin. He also knows that whatever Gavin knows, the Brits are bound to know soon after. It's obvious they're being well fed from the higher ranks of the police about anything and everything to do with the intricate world of Irish political life, including the most salacious details concerning the personal affairs of its leading lights. He's sure that's how they found out about him and Evelyn in the first place.

And now he has to meet the British ambassador. He has managed to avoid direct and formal contact with the embassy for a couple of months as he gets acquainted with his ministerial brief and the daily toll of emergencies that seems to beset his ministry above and beyond any other. Among his other concerns is the fact that the file that went missing in the mysterious and unsolved theft of his home over three months ago has not turned up, even though the investigation into the burglary has yielded more twists and turns than the road from Inagh to Ennis, including one dead body and another just about hanging on to life.

Gavin has assured him that it is only a matter of time before a file of evidence on the safe-cracker brought in for questioning is prepared for the Director of Public Prosecutions. The dead tout was apparently the victim of some internal, drug-fuelled, gang rivalry unconnected with the burglary investigation, the commissioner insists. Clarke is no closer to knowing what happened to his bank documents and is now in the invidious, and uncomfortable, position of having to request the assistance of his British friends if he is to obtain a necessary copy of the stamped papers in order to guarantee the safety of his undisclosed and undeclared offshore investments.

He puts on his ministerial face when a knock on the door interrupts his thoughts and his guests are ushered in.

'It's wonderful to see you, Ambassador. I trust you and your good wife are well,' he says.

'Excellent. Marjorie spent a lot of time in Somerset with her parents over the summer. The children love it there in the school holidays. And I don't mind the break either. Allows me to explore the wonders of your beautiful countryside and people, of course,' the diplomat smiles.

'We have the nicest-looking women in the world, wouldn't you agree, Ambassador?' laughs Clarke, instantly regretting his remark.

'I didn't quite mean it like that but, yes, that is another attractive feature.'

Martin Crawley extends his hand, which Clarke shakes with less enthusiasm. They are joined by Myles Fenton, who takes a chair close to the window.

A moment later, there's another knock on the door. The minister's private secretary announces the arrival of another member of the visiting delegation, straight from the airport. Clarke almost spills the coffee he is about to drink from the china cup when Alan Richards walks in, all hail fellow well met.

'Long time no see, Bob. It's great to see you. What a plush office you have. Quite a change from the shadow cabinet facilities, what?' says the newcomer.

'Alan, I wasn't expecting you. Martin, you never told me Alan would be joining us,' the minister says to Crawley.

'Oh, it was a last-minute suggestion from Whitehall. Alan has a bit of business in Dublin and we thought it might be good for him to catch up with old acquaintances, including yourself and the ambassador, of course.'

'Yes, we toiled together in the Queen's foreign service, many moons ago,' says the ambassador to Richards as they shake hands.

'Well, down to business so,' says Clarke.

After some early exchanges over pressing issues such as border security and the ongoing IRA and loyalist campaigns, they agree to park further discussion on the subject until a follow-up meeting involving senior garda, RUC and army personnel later in the week. Clarke's pending meeting with his counterpart, the Secretary of State for Northern Ireland, is raised and the ambassador brings up the subject of the promised counter-terror emergency laws. In particular, the British demands for tough new measures for detention of suspects, a plan for the extradition of republican suspects on demand to the North and England, and more flexibility in the movements of armed security personnel in pursuit of gunmen across the border. Time to call a spade a spade, Clarke reckons.

'This wish list is not an easy one to deliver, gentlemen. As you know our courts are rather jealous of their independence and do not look kindly on legislative changes that infringe on our long-held constitutional freedoms, such as the presumption of innocence. They are likely to knock down any suggestion of sending people to another jurisdiction on the basis of someone's suspicion alone. The cross-border activities of your undercover soldiers have already caused us some problems and we are getting anxious reports from areas where we have enjoyed solid political support for decades over the operation of what is now being called a shoot-to-kill policy by the SAS.'

After some diplomatic meandering by the ambassador and sporadic replies from the minister between top-ups of the almost cold coffee, the hard man in the room sits forward in his leather chair and asserts the authority he almost certainly enjoys over his compliant colleagues.

'We are not here to negotiate these issues, Robert,' Richards interrupts, with his familiar ability to drop the niceties and get to the rotten core of the particular quandary at hand. 'I notice you have taken the precaution, wise I may add, to exclude your civil servants from this meeting, presumably because you may have anticipated what may arise during our discussion, including some very uncomfortable truths. I suspect you are somewhere between the proverbial rock and a hard place.'

Ignoring protocol and the ambassador's preference for a polite exchange with the new minister, he continues in his irritating drone.

'*After all, we are aware of your recent difficulties, what with details of your offshore activities now floating about somewhere and possibly about to seep into the media at any moment following the unfortunate episode at your house. We are also conscious of the number of other, let's say, domestic difficulties you have encountered in recent months including the very upsetting, and rather public, contretemps with your young journalist. We are concerned that these may have the effect of distracting you from the urgent tasks facing you, indeed all of us, on the security front.*'

Clarke decides that attack is the best form of defence. He plays the only card he has in an effort to force a retreat from the inevitable and in a bid to restore some of the respect he thinks he deserves as a minister of government of a sovereign nation.

'*Before we go into the comparatively trivial issues you have raised, Alan, there is a matter I would like to discuss. Have a look at this,*' he says as he dramatically reveals the March 1975 file with the word '*Confidential*' stamped in big red letters on the cover and the understated title '*Events in Dublin and Monaghan – 17 May, 1974*'.

'*To save time, Ambassador, I would look at the conclusions on page 43. The one that refers to a suspicion, indeed almost conclusive evidence, that agents of the British security apparatus, specifically military and other intelligence agencies, colluded with the bombers in the biggest single atrocity of the Troubles so far. Gentleman, this is not the sort of behaviour we expect from our closest and supposedly friendly neighbour. So far, of course, this report has remained strictly confidential, but if any of it were ever to come to the attention of the general public, well then, who knows what the consequences might be. There's plenty of meat in this file for the media hounds from here to Timbuktu.*'

A look of ice-cold anger flashes across the face of Alan Richards as the ambassador leans over the file with an expression that appears to reflect genuine concern and amazement. Silence descends as he absorbs the contents of the ten points on the final page of the report. He recognises immediately that the material could detrimentally alter the complexion of Anglo-Irish relations for years to come if any of it were to get into wider circulation. It requires the tact for which he is well known and has resulted in the appointment to this most difficult of diplomatic postings, worse than Aden and those bewildering Arabs, in his view.

'This is of the utmost seriousness,' he says. 'I'm sure that all of your concerns in this regard can be allayed. Unfortunately, I am only new in this position and have little or no knowledge about this matter, other than, of course, being shocked and appalled at the bombings. While there is always a sensitivity about such security matters, I can promise you I will seek to obtain answers to your questions from the highest level in Whitehall. And you can be reassured, Bob, that we don't intend to pry into your private business in any way. I trust our mutual friendship can be maintained, notwithstanding the inevitable tensions we each have to endure in our respective roles.'

'That sounds like we are both singing from the same hymn sheet, Ambassador,' says Clarke as he puts the smoking gun back in the holster, sits back and smiles.

'By the way, Alan,' he says, as the British delegation prepares to leave the room with business concluded, if not resolved. 'About those missing financial documents you raised. I need those original files for my records, if you don't mind. Perhaps you could ensure that Myles gets them as soon as possible. All copies. Or we could pick them up in London during our visit next month.'

***

Evelyn Fagan is sipping a plastic cup of bad coffee at her desk in the offices of Independent Newspapers on Abbey Street when the runner drops a package on her desk. As she spills out the contents one photo immediately catches her attention. Among the revellers at some highbrow party or function is none other than her recent bedmate Bob Clarke. She knows from his expression that he has a good few drinks on board and that he is unaware that his photo is being taken. She knows this from long experience of the politician, who somehow manages to adopt his 'statesman' look at the drop of a hat, or the click of a camera to be more precise. On this occasion, his beaming red face is focused on the not-so-well-covered cleavage of a woman not his wife, and his eyes are asking for more. On closer inspection, she's the fat bitch who does the food reviews for her newspaper, no less.

'The lying, sneaky, fucking bastard,' she says out loud. Half the newsroom looks around. They are well used to cursing in the office but not often from the lips of the boss's favourite reporter. Her good looks and ruthless sense of purpose in pursuit of a story have won her the dubious title of the 'blonde ambition'.

'That bastard,' she thinks, when she calms down. 'Screwing his way through every bird in town and leading me up the garden path. Well what goes around comes around,' she says to herself as she examines, composure regained, the contact sheet of photos and other documents before her. She has heard of the controversy surrounding the secretly taken photos at the party fundraiser and can now see why there was a desperate and, until now, successful effort to ensure they are never published. The most powerful men in the town gathered in various states of drunkenness, a full glass in one hand, a woman's waist, arm or arse in the other, in most cases not the one they had married. The bishop, the garda commissioner, the British and US ambassadors, and

a host of the city's finest on the tear, not a care in the world as they dine and drink their way to oblivion for the good of the party and the country.

'These would look good on the gossip pages,' she muses as she opens a separate envelope to find a cassette tape marked 'Bob Clarke and his British friends. October 1976, The Bistro, Dublin'. Finally, she unseals a third which reveals a document headed 'Bank of Bermuda (London) Ltd. Annual Financial Statement. Robert S. Clarke Esquire. September 1976'. The account was opened some two years earlier, in 1974.

'What the fuck?' she says again as she pores over the figures in the concise five-page document setting out the details of an account held in the name of her estranged boyfriend and amounting to, if she is reading it correctly, the princely sum of £112,000 including interest.

She pulls the tape recorder from her desk, inserts the tape and sits back with a pair of headphones. She senses she is on to something big, potentially journalistic rocket fuel of explosive proportions provided by an anonymous source. There is no name, no return address, no stamp on any of the envelopes or papers to indicate their progeny. Even her name has been printed in bold capitals so the handwriting can't be identified. It almost certainly has come from someone, not unlike herself, with reasons to detest, even hate Bob Clarke and who wants to bring him down with a crash. She presses the play button and gets a rush of excitement mixed with loathing as she hears his voice on tape. He's with his lap dog and ubiquitous slimeball, Myles Fenton, and two well-spoken Englishmen.

When it ends some seventy minutes later, she lets out another stream of expletives before gathering up the sensitive materials, replacing them in their wrapping and heading for the door.

'I'll be in the pub, if you need me,' she tells the news editor. He is well accustomed to the unique and unusual customs and habits of his chief political reporter and knows well not to question why.

As she sits over a gin and tonic, watching the six o'clock news, Evelyn Fagan knows that what she has just learned can make or break her career and Clarke's. It is far more significant in the wider scheme of things than her falling out with one of the country's most powerful politicians. This is not just a dramatic political story but possibly a scandal of far greater proportions than any she has come across and is unlikely to see again. If it is true that the British authorities had foreknowledge of the Dublin bombings, then it suggests collusion with paramilitary killers at the highest level. Worse than that, it looks like British security forces helped organise and participated in what were sophisticated military attacks, even though they have since suggested that a bunch of loyalists from Belfast and Armagh carried these out. And it turns out that our Minister for Home Affairs has been told as much and has yet to inform the public, not to mind the families of those who died and all the people injured. On top of that, it's well known that the gardaí handed over crucial forensic evidence to the British Army personnel involved and closed down the investigation after three months.

It's so big that she doesn't know what to do with it. It will take more than one G&T to decide. The first task is to verify, if possible, its contents, although the photos and the tape stand on their own irrefutable grounds, while the financial paperwork appears credible unless someone went to the trouble of forging it in order to further damage Clarke. Such a deceit would be easily uncovered and would also undermine the evidence on the tape. She wonders who could have collected such information and where.

And then she recalls the drink-sodden politician complaining to her about how his home had been burgled on the same night as a party fundraiser and then for some reason pleading with her not to run a story on the whole debacle. She hadn't really understood what his problem with people finding out was. She only ran a short piece about the robbery when the guards had confirmed it to the media. She agreed to leave out details of the victim. But if these documents were part of what was taken, it is suddenly very clear why Clarke wanted the whole thing swept under the carpet. He must be terrified of the bank details getting out. Well, he'll soon find out the true meaning of hell hath no fury, if she has anything to do with it.

It's time to find out what her friends in Garda HQ know about that burglary, she decides. She also calculates that it is best, for the time being, not to share the story from the anonymous source with her boss, for fear that it might frighten the life out of him. If they'll suppress damaging but relatively harmless photos of a party fundraiser, the paper's owners will surely want to bury this and her, if necessary. But a good story never refuses ink. All she has to do is prove it.

44
JOE

I'm not too surprised when I hear that the attractive woman occupying a table laid out for two at the back of The Bistro wants me to join her. She learns my name by the simple method of asking the waitress about the guy who makes the lovely Greek salad with the feta cheese. It can't be had anywhere else in town and is a talking point for all her friends, she says. The waitress tells me there's a fine thing looking for me, and winks. When I walk through the door from the kitchen, she already has her notebook and pen at the ready, and I realise this can only be the journalist the priest warned Angie to expect.

'Keep an eye out for one particular member of that honourable profession,' he told her. 'If she's as good as they say, I have no doubt she'll track you down.'

She was sent the tape, documents and photos, not just because of her reputation, but because it's common knowledge that she and Clarke had a fling but have recently had an acrimonious falling out. She is unlikely to be dissuaded from chasing a story that will do him real damage by virtue of any friendship or his political influence. Indeed, she's told anyone who'll listen that she hates the cheating bastard. She's said it more than once before an audience of conscientious drinkers in the Oval Bar beside the offices of the newspaper. It does not take long for this snippet of political gossip to reach the ears of the wide variety of people who take an interest in these things. The dogs on the street know that Clarke was bonking the reporter from the

Indo who has been singing his praises for years and building a career, for both of them, with the help of sensitive documents leaked from the highest levels of the civil service. All designed to damage the Blueshirts and ensure her name is at the top of many of the newspaper's best political scoops.

'I'm Evelyn Fagan from the *Independent*. And you're Joe Heney, I believe,' she says with a smile as I wipe my hand on my apron before shaking hers.

'I am. What can I do for you?' I smile back.

'I'd like to show you some documents and a tape that have come into my possession. I think you might be able to help me verify their authenticity. If I'm not mistaken you might have helped to generate them, or some of them at least.'

'What makes you think that?'

'A little bird in blue tells me that you got yourself arrested over some of these documents. Don't play coy with me, Mr Heney, I know you had something to do with the photos at least.'

'Okay, okay,' I reply. 'But not here and not now. I'm not even finished my shift. Maybe later.'

'Of course. Would tomorrow suit? The Gresham at two maybe?'

'No problem,' I say as the next piece of the plan prepared by the priest falls into place like a well-chosen move on a chess board.

Angie is watching from the front of The Bistro as I chat with the blonde reporter. I go easy on the flirting. I can feel her stare.

'This is all off the record, isn't it? I don't want my name splashed all over the *Indo*,' I say.

'Joe, I can promise that you won't be identified in any report I do. It's strictly confidential,' says Fagan.

'I'll talk to you if it helps to get the truth out about the bombings and corruption that's going on. I'll be there tomorrow,' I promise.

When we meet the next day I confirm to the reporter that I organised the informal photo shoot on the night of the fundraiser and that I had also overheard an earlier conversation involving Fenton and Martin Crawley. I tell her this led me to the rather outrageous and probably ill-considered plan to tape their subsequent conversation at the next opportunity when Clarke and the other Englishman were present. I deny knowing anything about the financial documents she has in her possession but say that, to my admittedly untrained mind at least, they seem to substantiate some of the contents on the tape. I am also certain, and surprised, I say, that the cassette she has is not the one I inserted into the recorder that day and that the contact sheet is a copy of the original compiled by the photographer.

'I don't know who sent you the tape and documents but they didn't come from me. The tape you have is not the one I made.'

'Someone else has got their hands on this material. Now who could that be?' she wonders aloud as we sit in a quiet corner of Toddy's bar in the Gresham.

'One man who's got something to do with the whole thing has gone to an early grave, I'm told,' I say.

'What do you mean?'

'The bloke who was battered to death beside the sausage factory a few weeks ago. I heard that his death has something to do with a burglary at Clarke's house on the night of the do in

The Bistro. That's why they brought me in. They both happened on the same night and the cops added two and two and got five, as usual.'

'And who killed him?'

'That's the thing. Nobody knows, but the Heavy Gang beat up another bloke very badly and he "fell out" the top window of a cop shop down the country. Seems to be an occupational hazard for suspects these days.'

'How did you hear about the dead man and his connection to all this?' she asks.

'Go to any pub around the Dominick Street flats and you'll hear all about the poor fucker. Richie Duggan. They say he was a tout. He's to be buried in the next day or two. There's also a lot of talk about the guy who was beaten up. He's not long out of the Mater by all accounts. The whole thing stinks. The truth about the bombs in May '74 has been suppressed. The tape suggests official British involvement and Clarke being told about it. And the British guy, Richards, has Clarke compromised over his offshore accounts. I'd love to know where that bastard gets that sort of money.'

'So would I and I've every intention of finding that out, Joe.'

45

NORTH INNER CITY

At the end of the chat, Fagan doesn't know much more than she did at the beginning, but at least she has some new leads to follow. She thanks Joe for his help and says she'll be in touch. First, she needs to talk to her editor about the tape, the bank documents, the dead informer and the man falling out the window of a police station. A lot of questions and very few answers.

'You're telling me that Bob Clarke and the British embassy are somehow involved in covering up the greatest atrocity this city, this country has ever witnessed. He wasn't even in government at the time. You must be out of your mind, girl,' is the angry response of her normally calm editor.

'He's covering up what he knows because the Brits have sensitive information on him about his offshore bank account. It turns out that British agents helped the loyalists with the bombings and that he has discussed it with them. There's a tape of his conversation and a document showing a Bermuda account in his name with a lot of cash in it.'

'Who made the tape?'

'I can't reveal my source, but I have a copy. On it, Clarke talks to two senior British officials about the bombs and how they were organised. They say that they have embarrassing information about his finances as if they are going to blackmail him. It's crazy stuff.'

'I suppose you'd know that voice anywhere, wouldn't you? How do I know this isn't part of some crazy personal vendetta? I mean who goes around making secret tapes of politicians in Ireland? What

do you mean you can't reveal your source? Who do you think you are, Bob fucking Woodward?'

'There's already one man dead because of this. A police informer wrapped up in the whole thing, and another guy who seems to have been involved claims he was thrown out the top window of a police station.'

'This is going a bit far now, Evelyn. No matter how much you dislike the man, Clarke is not the sort of bloke to have offshore accounts or order the assassination of touts. Someone is winding you up.'

'Here's the tape and the bank documents. There are also some rather embarrassing photos of the great and the good. Some of them feature in the story, including Clarke, the garda commissioner and a guy from the British embassy. I'm not making this up, Harry, much as I hate the bastard.'

'Okay, let's have a listen,' says the newspaper man, now genuinely intrigued at his top reporter's latest scoop, even if it never makes it to ink on a page.

By the time he has finished, Harry Molloy is a worried man. If even half this story is true he is going to land in the shit. If he doesn't let her pursue it he could be accused later of sitting on the biggest splash of the year if the Press gets its hands on it. But if he does, he's in danger of running up against his conservative owner, who doesn't want stories about corrupt politicians, dodgy cops or British dirty tricks across his front pages when the State is facing a threat to its very existence from 'those murdering IRA bastards'. To make matters worse he buried the photos of the fundraiser when they were first offered to him weeks ago, on instructions from the top. Now he might have to revisit that decision and risk the ire of his boss once again. It's a no-win situation.

He decides not to rush into anything but agrees to let her follow up her leads. First, ask the gardaí about the dead man, then some questions to Clarke, directly, and not through the Government Press Office, and then maybe a feature on the stalled garda investigation into the bombings with some input from British sources. Find out what happened to the last government's inquiry and report into the bombs.

'This is not going to break quickly. We need to follow up the different parts separately and carefully before anyone knows what we're after. Check out that bank in Bermuda. And no, you're not going to get a holiday in the sun out of this. Keep this between us. Not a word to anyone.'

'Absolutely, boss.' The smile on her face says it all. She's not going to let this one go.

'Jesus, I need a drink,' Molloy says.

***

It takes almost a week for the broken body of Richie Duggan to be released from the morgue. Not that too many people are worried. Bernie Duggan goes to Mass every day seeking some reason from God for the bitter end to her only son's life. She takes solace from the local priest and her best friend, Rosie, who is never one to question the motives of the Almighty – He knows best and theirs is not to reason why.

'These crosses are sent for us to bear,' she says time and again, 'and only the good Lord knows why.'

Sitting in the living room with the open coffin and her brain fried from a day of neighbours mumbling prayers for the dead, countless decades of the rosary and incalculable cups of tea, Bernie Duggan turns to her dead child and says: 'Richie love, from the day you were born you had that lovely smile, but the trouble you've brought into this house! I've never had a day's rest since you were a chiseller. Robbin' and stealin' your way across the town, bringing shame on your father, God rest him, and me. What happened to you, Richard, and your beautiful smiley face?'

She hasn't paid much attention to the stories going around, but she knows that no one deserved the beating her son suffered down the back alley. All she wants now is to give him a decent send-off.

'Whoever did it will have to answer to the Lord on the last day. That's one sure thing,' says Rosie, for the hundredth time.

Among the slow stream of visitors this evening comes Jimmy Dunne with his mate, caps in hand, to pay their respects to the bereaved mother. The big man walks out of the kitchen with a fresh mug of tea and stands beside the open wooden box that holds the battered remains of a useless tramp and stoolie, a description he keeps to himself. He blesses himself over the coffin and gives the corpse a cold look.

'I'm sorry for your troubles, Mrs Duggan,' he says as he shakes one hand and places an envelope in the other. The paper is still warm from the bottom of her hot press. Then he gives her a small box wrapped in fancy paper.

'Richie asked me to give this to you if anything happened to him. He said he was keeping it for your birthday. He wasn't all bad, ma'am. The cops should never have left him like that after beating his brains out. Lying all night on the road. This'll help you with the funeral,' he says. Before she has time to thank him or to open the package, the Dunner is blessing himself with holy water and out the door.

'Nice fella,' she says to Rosie. 'Tinker or not he's from a good family. If it wasn't for the gargle, my waster of a son, God be good to him, could have been like that. Showing some respect for people. But Richie's gone now, may he rest in peace.'

'There's some bad bastards in those blue uniforms all right. Culchies the lot of them,' says Rosie only half listening. She's bursting to know what's in the little box left by Duggy for his ma.

'For my birthday,' Bernie snorts. 'If you believe that you'll believe anything.' Inside the box is a beaded necklace the likes of which she has only seen in the window of McDowells by the Pillar.

'Would you credit this?' she says as she slides the pearls around her neck and fastens the back.

'Jesus, Bernie, he left the best till last, the bold Richie did.'

'There must be fifty quid in this,' says Bernie, as she looks inside the envelope – more money than she's seen in folded notes since she pawned her father's original copy of the Proclamation. 'That'll surely pay for the send-off and a few drinks after.'

As the coffin is carried on its final journey from Dominick Street church to Glasnevin the next morning, all the talk in the flats is of Bernie's gorgeous necklace, left to her by her poor creature of a son who died at the hands of the Heavy Gang in the lane behind the sausage factory. Discreetly observing the ceremonies, DG Meagher cannot help but notice the lavish jewellery bedecking the grieving mother, who is surprisingly chirpy as she takes the sorrowful greetings from the handful of mourners who have bothered to witness Richie Duggan's final hours above the ground. Also watching from a distance is Evelyn Fagan and a young photographer keen to get a shot of the sparkling pearls dripping from the neck of the tragic widow who has just lost her only son.

***

'*The shower of bastards,*' *says Gavin when the unexpected appearance of the necklace matching the very expensive earrings worn by Eileen Clarke to the party fundraiser is reported to him that very afternoon. The front-page photo the next morning of the beaded Bernie Duggan by her son's coffin only compounds his anger. His press office has already received calls from that bitch in the* Independent *about some rumour that Duggan was somehow involved in the theft and was left for dead by the Guards who went a bit too far in their efforts to get a confession out of him, just as they had with Heno Moran.*

She has already spoken to Moran, who is claiming he was wrongly accused of involvement in the theft and whose body still bears testimony to the time he spent in the custody of some of Gavin's finest. She also inquired about the fundraiser in The Bistro and whether any other guests who were present suffered a similar intrusion of their homes on the night in question. Gavin knows that Fagan has fallen out with Clarke, but she is putting her hands very close to the flames with her pathetic little exercise in vengeance.

'*It's safe to presume that she has all the photos and it won't be long before they decide to publish the fucking lot, now they have the bit between their teeth,*' *he thinks, with consequences he is not prepared to tolerate.*

And the last thing he needs is the papers sniffing around the important work of his elite squad, who are leading the fight against terror and subversion, one hand already tied behind their backs.

'*We need to charge someone with Duggy's murder. Anyone and soon,*' *he barks to the team.*

He will also ask the minister to issue a strong denial that the police force is engaged in the abuse of people's rights in custody. If anything, his men are hamstrung by all the bureaucratic red tape and other nonsense they have to endure just to arrest and detain suspects, never mind getting the evidence they need to press charges. He could do with some of the Prevention of Terrorism powers his colleagues on the mainland enjoy. 'That would end it all soon enough,' he says to himself, as he wonders how the fuck he is going to get the jewels off that brasser and return them to their rightful owner without a hell of a row. Clarke, for one, will want to know how they ended up around Bernie Duggan's neck and her prancing around like the Queen Mother in the north inner city. That is if he hasn't already choked on his cornflakes from the sight of his wife's precious gems all over the morning newspaper.

46

ANGIE

Only a handful of the bereaved and injured turn up for the first meeting of the 'Remembrance Committee' announced by Father Bennett to his parishioners at Sunday Mass two weeks ago. In a room in the credit union, which Da helped to set up, the priest outlines his hopes that in time they will try to connect with many more of those affected by the awful tragedy. Myself, Mam and Da are in the front row. Joe and Donal are hugging the wall at the back.

Across the city, Father Bennett says, there are families grieving over their loss. In Monaghan town and in other parts of the country. Grieving parents in France and Italy. The absence of any event or occasion to honour the memory of the dead more than three years on is a matter of concern that they must address, however small their number.

'And,' he adds, 'the failure of the authorities to identify those responsible for the wicked deed that day in May is another matter we must deal with given the persistent rumours about who was behind the attacks.

'This committee is not about seeking retribution,' he cautions, 'although those who lost loved ones or suffered terrible injuries are entitled to justice. It's about finding closure and an answer to the question so many have asked. Why did my innocent mam, dad, brother, sister or the unborn baby in the womb, die such horrific deaths as they went about their business in town that day? It's about healing, not revenge.'

He then invites some of those present to recount, however difficult it may be, their recollections of that fatal day. When it comes to Mam's turn, she takes my hand and for the first time ever, to me anyway, recites in detail how her trip, just before the close of business that day, to buy me a pair of shoes for the debs, ended up on a bed in the Mater and an almost total loss of sight. Like all the shoppers on Talbot Street, she heard a loud and thunderous blast as she entered O'Neill's shoe shop. The noise came from a few streets away.

'At first I thought, there's a bomb gone off, but then I thought, ah no, it must be thunder. Then I pulled the door open and I went to step down into the shop. As I lifted my foot, there was a big flash – there was a window on my right – there was a big flash up in the sky and as I looked up the bomb exploded and I was caught in a kind of a whirlwind or something. But I didn't realise that it was a bomb. And I thought this thing that was going through my body, these vibrations, was an electrical shock. But the place shook and shook and shook. Shelves and ceilings and everything collapsed. So eventually everything stopped falling, the ground stopped shaking and everything settled. I could hear somebody moaning very weakly. And I was saying to them, "Where are you?" I was telling them to moan louder so I could find them. So I was going around scrabbling on my hands and knees, looking for this person ... "Look, I'll try and get help for us." It was then I realised I couldn't see. I remember saying, "Jesus Christ, don't tell me I can't see, ah please don't let me be blind." And, at that moment, now, maybe it was the dust rising, I don't know, but all of a sudden, sight started to come from the ground up, back into one eye. And I could see where I was going now. But what was O'Neill's shoe shop now looked like a demolition site. I was just looking out into the street, it was empty … the silence in the street … and the dust … you could touch the silence. Everything was grey, *everything* – people were lying on the street, people were grey – everything was grey – grey and bloody. And I remember standing where the window was in O'Neill's, and looking at Guiney's window across the road. There was a car blown into it. And there was a fireman. I knew he was a fireman because he had the moulded feather down the back of his hat. He had a body in his arms, and I thought they must be taking the mannequins out in case they get broken. It never occurred to me that these were living people five minutes before. I just *thought* he was taking the mannequins out, because … you were always brought up to mind things … and not be destroying them, not *break* things, so – in *my* mind – these mannequins were so important that they had to be taken out of the window! I was carried to the hotel down the road and I remember this doctor shouting at one of the workers in the hotel to get sheets. And when she arrived with the sheets, he's standing in front of me and he's tearing up this big long sheet and he's bandaging up my head. We were told to get on a bus, a red one from Busáras. There was a bus strike you know, but the drivers got them running when they heard the bombs. I was taken to the Mater, then the Eye and Ear. For days and weeks.

'And when we spoke at home, we called it "the accident" – I never said it was a bomb, it was my accident. As if I'd tripped over a shoe in the shop or something.'

The tears are falling from my ma, and from my da sitting next to her, holding her other hand. She looks at me and then around the room. Everyone is flowing.

'Sorry,' she says. 'I've never told anyone that before. It's funny what you remember. My accident. As if I'd fallen over a shoe.'

She laughs. We all laugh. I can feel the weight lifting from her brows, her hunched shoulders, her body, her tortured mind. She talks of her first weeks at home when both eyes were covered.

'I was blind as a bat, dropping dishes and bumping into things. I burned my hand pouring water from the kettle because I missed the teapot. I felt so stupid that I didn't tell anybody. I kept asking to open the curtains, to clean the windows because I couldn't see out. But sure my eyes were covered with the bandages. I was a walking eejit, blathering on. I hated Barney seeing me like that, helpless like a child, not able to cook or clean. You must have been driven mad looking at me, love. If it wasn't for this girl beside me and her patience I wouldn't be here today. I'd be floating in the river.'

She talked of recovery, of finding her place at home again, of cooking, of finally being able to get back to her knitting and sewing. And the headaches, the fright when she hears a loud noise, the fear of another bang when she walks down the street. She doesn't go to town anymore.

When she finishes, others tell their stories. Some, like me, tell the story of searching for loved, and lost, ones. A few talk of those they know among the injured and dead, and of the peculiar silence that seems to prevail over the people of the city when it comes to discussing those ghastly and gruesome events. One man describes how a neighbour from Portland Row was killed in the first blast in Parnell Street. He said that a porter in the Posts and Telegraphs building just down the street from his house saw what he called a suspicious-looking van parked outside the door, which was driven away just after the bombs went off. The porter helped the police find the man and the van, which had a British Army uniform in it, near the Holyhead ferry on the docks.

A local taxi man comes forward to describe the hijacking of his cab to the Dublin mountains the night before the bombs.

'I never read about that in the papers,' I say, scribbling notes of the proceedings in my capacity as self-appointed secretary of the Remembrance Committee.

'You never saw these either,' says Donal pulling out black and white photos from a large brown envelope. He shows his shots from that day in Talbot Street to those who want to see them. For the first time, I see the shattered windows of O'Neill's, the bodyless head, the legs and the scattered shoes. All shrouded in a grey mist, just as my mam described. I don't show her the images and just stop myself from breaking down.

'We got through a lot today. I'm sure we'll have to ask many more questions of people in authority if we are to get to the bottom of all this,' says Father Bennett as he brings the meeting to a close, some two hours after it starts, with a decade of the rosary for all of those who lost their lives or their dearest.

As we put on our coats and head for the door, the priest approaches from the back of the room with a young man I hadn't noticed earlier. He has a patch over his right eye, the side of his face is badly scarred and he walks with a limp. His left eye looks straight at me. I nearly faint on the spot.

'This is Danny,' says the priest. 'The man I spoke to you about, Angie, who was –'

'I know, Father. Danny Ryan. You were blown up at the filling station on Parnell Street,' I just about manage to say.

He puts his hand out as the tears start. Now my mam is comforting me.

'What's wrong, love? What's the matter?' she says.

'Your daughter found me alive in the morgue,' says Danny. 'I remember your face. You called someone to help me. I came here to thank you.'

'Thank you, Danny, but you saved yourself,' I say as I hold on to his hand.

'I want to help you find out who did it,' Danny says.

My tears dry up and I smile in the face of his courage. 'Well, we need all the help we can get.'

Joe, who was sitting at the back of the room, puts his arm around my shoulder and I take my mam's hand. My mind is reeling but my body feels light.

The meeting is the beginning of a journey of discovery for me. I start to divide my time between Joe's warm and tender company, and the intensifying search for the truth behind the bombings, for which he is also by my side. We walk the canal or watch the Brent geese over Dollymount Strand, or on occasion jump on the Nifty Fifty and track the Wicklow hills with rucksacks and curious cows outside our tent. On other days when we're not working in The Bistro we sit together in the National Library, ploughing through old newspapers, trying to fit the pieces of the real-life murder mystery together. At night we explore each other between the sheets of Joe's familiar bed. We are open with each other about everything.

Now that I know about his past, Joe is much more relaxed talking about himself. He tells me more about his time in the clink, his introduction to the political classics, to music and sounds from around the world through his short-wave radio, the chopper landing in the yard to pick up the IRA men, the euphoria in the jail that afternoon and the misery every other day inside. He talks about everything, every emotion, every thought, but mostly about how much he loves me and everything about me. I get to meet his parents, his sister and her child, born to the sound of breaking glass.

My remembrance work brings me to other places and people damaged by the bombings, including a trip to Monaghan to meet some of the survivors and the families of the deceased in the town close to the border. Not quite the trip Joe and I were planning on taking a few months back, but he comes anyway.

In the course of my diligent recording of testimony from the mainly working-class people across the city affected, I uncover some new and revealing facts. Mam and I meet the man who saw the white van parked outside the Post and Telegraphs building on the day of the bombing. He was suspicious of the English reg, and the way it was left there empty most of the day before a well-dressed man returned from the city centre and drove away towards the docks just minutes after the bombs went off. He brought the gardaí to the ferry port where they found the man, with his army uniform in the back. When the guards asked him about this, he said he was in the British Territorial Army and was going on manoeuvres the next day in England. The Special Branch arrived while he was explaining this to the gardaí. That's the last anyone heard of him. The witness said he had a visit from some detectives the next day, but no one took up his offer to make a statement. He heard later from a friend who worked in the docks that the soldier also had a weapon in his possession.

He must have had a good excuse, the man said, because he was
on the ferry to England that night.

47

DUBLIN 2

Evelyn Fagan is not stalling. The story is. Clarke is giving her the runaround. She tries to doorstep him, hanging around Government Buildings in the hope of hitting him with a few questions. Nothing personal, she has to remind herself, just some pertinent queries about the burglary at his home, the killing of Richie Duggan, the progress of the investigation into the Dublin bombs and, of course, the little matter of his intimate discussions with the smooth-talking Englishmen and the bank account in the sun.

The Bank of Bermuda, she discovers from a nerdy financial reporter, is a holding bank for offshore assets used by the wealthy of several countries to keep their money out of reach of the Revenue and penal income-tax rates. A lot of Irish businesspeople have such accounts, it seems, and this particular bank offers the additional benefit that you can withdraw cash from its London branch without incurring bank charges or alerting the taxman.

The question she wants to put to the bastard Clarke is how he has managed to accumulate the tidy sum of over one hundred grand when he always moaned, at least to her, about his wife's profligacy and the hardship of living on a politician's puny salary. She knows he is keeping out of her way, but he can't hide forever and the moment will come when he is forced to deal with her one way or the other. In the meantime, she has run a series of articles on the bombings to remind readers of the scale of the attacks in the city just a few short years ago, accompanied by testimonials gathered by a group of people headed by a young priest from East Wall.

She attends public meetings in the inner city, Artane, Coolock and as far into the southside as Sallynoggin, where the families of the dead, along with many of the scarred and wounded, turn up to recount their stories. Over a few months, the Remembrance Committee, as it is called, has brought hundreds of people together who are beginning to ask many awkward questions about the events of that day and their tragic aftermath, two in particular: who were the bombers and why did the police close down their investigation after less than three months?

She can't get a straight answer to either, despite numerous and persistent questions to the garda press office and the Department of Justice. If anything, she is being treated as a bit of a troublemaker for her bothersome insistence on pursuing this story, while the presence of unmarked garda cars outside the public meetings she attends suggests that the Christian exercise of bearing witness to suffering is viewed with some suspicion by the authorities.

Her break finally comes when she is assigned to cover the launch of a new book on the history of the Garda Síochána written by the sycophantic security correspondent of her own newspaper, who has criticised her more than once for her apparent obsession with the bombings and the irrelevant death of one of the lowlifes in the city's criminal food chain. His contacts in the gardaí, which she has to admit are better than most and close to the top at that, have suggested that she is barking up the wrong tree and is being misled by known subversive elements clinging to the edges of the priest's campaign in order to advance their own evil cause.

It does not surprise her one bit that the book is an uncritical hagiography of the force, full of fascinating insights into the undoubted bravery of many of its members over the decades since independence. There's not a single line or word to reflect the deep unease in public *life about the uncontrolled behaviour of some of its units, not least the Heavy Gang. The recent scandal over the illegal planting of finger-prints by investigators to get convictions of suspected terrorists does not even warrant a mention and it's also unlikely to feature in the minister's speech tonight in the grand surrounds of the Shelbourne Hotel, just around the corner from Bob Clarke's office.*

From the back of the room, she listens to Clarke's twenty-minute eulogy on the gardaí and his effusive praise of the 'hugely talented author' of 'this extremely valuable and historic work' who somehow manages to fit six decades of 'valour and commitment, sacrifice and endurance in the face of periodic and unrelenting violence from those determined to undermine our State and democracy itself' into the 300-page volume.

Clarke is feeling pleased with himself. Commissioner Gavin is the first to shake his hand in front of the row of cameras beneath the stage, while the room is buzzing with gardaí and politicians falling over each other to fork out £10 for a signed hardback. As he turns to take a much-needed glass of red from a moving and rapidly depleting tray, he finds himself unexpectedly eyeballing the tiresome bitch who has been leaving messages for him to call her for weeks on end.

'Well, Robert,' she smiles, 'you haven't lost your way with words. I must say I didn't realise you were such a devoted fan of the boys in blue. It's not so long since you were calling them Blueshirt bastards or was it O'Duffy's fascists? I can't quite remember.'

Evelyn is speaking loudly in an intentional ploy to get him to move her away to a place out of earshot and the prying eyes of Gavin and his men. They are all too aware of the minister's lukewarm, occasionally even hostile, relationship with the force when in opposition.

'How are you, Ev? Before you say anything I do apologise for

*not getting back to you sooner. As you can appreciate the demands
of office –'*

'Cut the shit, Bob. I want to know what the fuck is going on.
Who robbed your house? Why did the cops beat up one suspect and
throw him out the top window of their torture chamber? Who
killed Richie Duggan? What's going on with the Dublin bombings
investigation? And what the fuck are you doing with money in the
Bank of Bermuda?'

'Jesus, Evelyn, where is all this coming from? I mean we've been
friends a long time. Maybe we should arrange to meet up in more
appropriate circumstances –'

'Are you fucking joking? Friends my arse,' she spits, raising her
pitch an octave for dramatic effect and for the curious minds and
quietened mouths around them.

As his driver and bodyguard approach to deal with the unruly and
intrusive young woman, Clarke waves them away, grabs her by the
arm and leads her through the crowd, smiling as he goes to those facing
the disappointment of not being able to bend the ear of the minister or
get his scrawl on their new literary purchase. Edward Gavin is not
among them, but he is annoyed at the manner in which this irritating
reporter has managed to hijack the main guest of the evening and
somewhat astonished at the speed of the minister's exit. He is well
aware of Clarke's entanglement with the ambitious blonde before he
entered government but has heard nothing since that suggests any
revival of their sordid affair. On the contrary, he is reliably informed
by the men he has carefully placed to mind the politician that he is
well rid of her and has been refusing to take her calls over several
weeks. Now, by the look on Clarke's face as he hastily scuttles out of
the room, she's calling the shots again.

As they sit in the back snug of Foley's bar, a pint of stout and a G&T before them, he asks her in as innocent and soft a tone as he can manage what this Bermuda thing is all about.

'There must be some mistake. I mean the Bank of Bermuda. Who ever heard —?'

'Listen, Bob. I won't take any bullshit. I would have published this weeks ago except you refuse to answer my calls and that creep Fenton keeps brushing me off with crap about your busy schedule. Now listen carefully before you open your mouth. I have a copy of a tape where you are discussing a hidden offshore account with some Brits. I have a copy of documents in your name setting out the details of the amount held in the Royal Bank of Bermuda. So the first and simple question is where the fuck did you get a hundred grand to stash in the Caribbean? A hundred and twelve to be precise. Think carefully before you answer.'

'Where the fuck did you get that stuff? If this is the proceeds of the robbery of my home, then you could be in serious trouble. What tape, what Brits are you talking about?'

'So the bank documents were taken from your safe at home. That's a start. Now we are getting somewhere. The tape was made in one of your favourite joints, The Bistro, a few months back and there are some intriguing and disturbing references to the '74 bombings. It seems that your friends in the embassy or Whitehall or wherever know a lot more about them than they have ever admitted, in public anyway.'

'I don't know what you are talking about. I have been doing my own investigation into the attacks, but there's nothing to indicate any complicity of that nature if that is what you are suggesting.'

'I said think before you speak, you prick. Did you and Fenton meet two Englishmen in The Bistro at any time over the past year?'

'I meet people all the time. That's to say I could have but who on earth would bother to tape our conversation? And even if someone did, that's illegal surely ... You couldn't possibly use material obtained in such a fashion. Anyway with a few drinks on board I can, as you know, talk any old shite that comes into my head.'

'Tell me about the Heavy Gang, the man who fell out the window of a garda station, the rat kicked to death near Parnell Square, his mother wearing your wife's best necklace. Tell me about all that, Bob.'

'Are you trying to destroy my career over the stupid fling we had? I mean, I'm very fond of you, Evelyn, and if I wasn't in such a prominent role there might be a way –'

'I don't give a fuck about our stupid fling, but if you want me to start on that scéal you might be here all night. You fucked me, then dumped me, simple as that, you lying bastard. But that's over. I'm interested in the biggest political story of my career, which is much more important to me than yours,' she says. 'I want answers and soon. I can get you a copy of the tape and the documents if that will help jolt your poor memory. I will give you forty-eight hours to reply, in full, to all of my queries. If you don't respond I will publish and be damned. And don't even think about interfering with the paper. My boss is four square behind me on this one. I'll be in touch tomorrow. You'd be wise to take my calls from now on. Thanks for the drink. I'm sure you'll pick up the tab.'

The tab is a lot longer by the time Clarke falls out of Foley's well after closing time, his head reeling with the effects of porter and strong whiskey and the weight of pending conclusions from the information imparted by his former squeeze.

'Someone is out to get me. But who? The Brits, Gavin, the fucker in Finance?'

To put it mildly, she is about to fuck him again, but not in a good way. Unless he can find an escape route.

***

At their weekly conference in Dublin Castle, Inspector O'Malley and his team are assessing all the evidential material relevant to a number of incidents and crimes, including the unsolved burglary at the home of the minister.

They also have to deal with the constant badgering of the woman from the Independent whose unanswered questions are causing concern at the highest level of the force, sitting as they are on the desk of the commissioner himself. The latest instructions are for arrests or at least some concrete action that can be reported as progress and a good enough reason not to reveal 'sensitive details pertaining to an ongoing investigation' to the media.

That very morning Gavin was called in by the minister for an update on a series of interrelated issues and it appears that the conversation was not as civil as might be expected. In the unfriendly exchange it emerged that the journalist apparently has information, including sensitive documents taken from Clarke's safe, which he previously failed to mention to the gardaí, despite the unit having spent months looking into the theft at his home. It also transpired that the journalist has a tape with some inflammatory information on it, although Clarke refused to divulge any significant details. Instead, he demanded that the guards get their act together and that someone is punished for these breaches of his privacy, preferably in a way that will totally discredit their actions and any information related to them that may get out.

O'Malley addresses the troops.

'It seems the Indo has new material they are going to publish which may cause something of a political storm. There may be an effort to destabilise the government with false information concocted by the same group of conspirators who secretly took photos in The Bistro on the night of the party fundraiser. The commissioner is very concerned about this and does not want to see those photos appearing in the newspapers along with some other stuff that could damage diplomatic relations. The other thing is that this young Whelan woman is popping up all over the city stirring up people affected by the bombings and in open association with known members of the Provisional IRA. This business of dragging up the past, including our inability to find those responsible for that atrocious attack on our capital city, is in danger of getting out of control. According to the commissioner, there is now a discernible link between Whelan's activities, the IRA and the brazen theft at the minister's home. If his suspicions are anywhere near correct, there is an immediate threat to the State. The reporter has already been rehashing the stories of the bomb victims in the paper, which is only stoking up anger against us and the government. Orders from the top are to stop it. Now.'

48

JOE

I'm lying awake with Angie next to me. A naked rounded breast is peeping from under the sheet, long black hair draped across two pillows, mouth half open as if waiting to speak, breathing steady. Who sent this perfect creature to me? Why and for how long? I've never loved like this before. I press her stomach, her thigh, my hand between her legs. She turns to me, wakes to my touch, feels her way to my need. Eyes of bright turquoise meet mine.

Loud banging on the front door halts our lovemaking. I jump out of bed and grab my jocks and shirt. Open the front door to an invasion of four big animals going straight for the bedroom. A man who calls himself Meagher shows me a piece of paper. Mentions the words warrant and Angela Whelan.

The gun stuck to her head as she tries to pull on her T-shirt and jeans says it all. They're not here for me. As two push her out the door, Meagher and the other invader root through the bag of college notes Angie left lying on the kitchen table. Plates, records, books, cupboards and shelves are banged and smashed as they rifle through the three small rooms. Nothing is sacred or safe.

I follow the first two out and call to Angie as she is crammed into the back seat of a cop car between two large and sweaty bodies.

'I love you. I'll find you. I'll call Neilan. Don't worry. We'll get you out.'

The car screeches off, lights and siren blazing. The other two leave with Angie's bag and some other bits and pieces they have found.

'I see you haven't given up the hash, Joe,' says a sneering Meagher. He sticks the ash-covered roach under my nose. 'Best be careful with the funny stuff. You can get done for that.'

'Fuck you,' says I, finding courage somewhere, before they disappear in a second, unmarked car. I'm fucking scared. I will call to Neilan. It's only seven in the morning. Angie is gone and there's no knowing what they will do to her. I try to put stuff back where it should go. I have a cup of tea, wash and leave the house. My mind is spinning. Every second car looks like the Branch. It's the early morning rush hour and I'm due in work at 9 a.m. I catch Gerard Neilan as he arrives at his office soon after eight.

'Early starter,' I say.

'Need to be with clients like you,' he laughs.

'They took Angie away this morning.'

'Damn. Come inside.'

Over a cup of tea we discuss the options. They can hold her for forty-eight hours and hope she'll confess to something, or else they've already decided to charge her. She could be dragged to court any time. Neilan makes a few calls but can't get any information on her whereabouts.

'Is there anything I should know, Joe?'

'Like what?'

'Well last time you didn't tell me of your little holiday in Mountjoy, your taste in drugs or the trip to Amsterdam. I see Angie has been busy recently.'

'She's been helping a priest with the campaign for the victims of the bombings.'

'She's been making a name for herself all right. Human rights activist the *Indo* calls her. The police don't like that. And there are strong rumours of a political scandal about to break arising from the fundraiser you secretly photographed and the break-in at Clarke's house. Someone's drip-feeding the papers. It wouldn't be you by any chance?'

I tell him everything. Why not? He's my solicitor, pledged to confidentiality, and there's no one else to turn to. The more he knows the better. The tape we leaked to Fagan, the photos, the bank papers, the whole lot. The meetings with the relatives, the IRA, Heno Moran and how the police set up the bloody execution of Duggy the Rat. The man who blew up Parnell Street and his friend Richards from Aden. SAS men.

'Holy Moses, Joe. I knew you were up to something but this takes the biscuit. And you think you can take on the system all on your own? Brave but foolish. I'm going to look for Angie. I'll start with the Bridewell. Do you want a lift into town?'

He lets me off near The Bistro with a promise to call me when he has news. I thank him, again. Since our rude awakening this morning, my worst fears have been realised. Angie's been taken God knows where and I'm to blame. Now I've got to face the boss and pretend life is normal.

'So you've decided to turn up, have you?' says a sarky Murphy as I walk in five minutes late.

'And nice to see you too, Aidan,' I say. 'Angie is not feeling the best though. Might need a few days.'

'Maybe if the pair of you left out the late nights and the beer you might be able to do your jobs. I can only pay people who actually turn up for work,' he says.

'And fuck you, too,' I whisper as I grab my apron. Pierre smiles and hums 'Money, Money, Money'. Abba should be banned.

49

ANGIE

'You won't get it so easy this time, Miss Whelan,' says the one on my left while the other one sticks the butt of his gun into my ribs. When we reach the unknown destination I'm pushed roughly from the car, through the back door of a building somewhere in the south inner city and into a room, where I'm confronted by two bean gardaí, one taller and wider than the other. The bigger woman tells me to strip.

'Take your fucking clothes off, you bitch,' are the exact words as the other puts her gloved hands up and down my body, between my boobs, inside my arse and vagina.

'Are you enjoying that?' I say, my eyes welling up.

'Not as much as this,' screams the bigger one as she lashes a closed fist into my kidney. 'You fucking scumbag terrorist.'

Within minutes, and with my clothes back on, I'm sitting on a plastic chair in a bare room facing two male interrogators. On the table are photos of me taken in various locations over recent weeks and months and in the company of different men and women, some of whom I recognise, others I don't.

'You're spending a lot of time with some murdering bastards,' says the rib poker. 'I hear you've joined up for the war effort, you stupid bitch. Do you think we don't know what you're up to? Helping the victims my arse. Helping to make victims is more fucking like it.'

'I want to see my solicitor,' I say and repeat this mantra after every question. And there are plenty of those. About the tape,

Clarke, the Englishmen, the jewels, the meat that killed the dog, the photos, time and again the photos, and the stuff taken from the minister's safe.

'Things could go easy for you, Angie, if you just tell us what we want to know. I'm Detective Garda Ronan Meagher and you are in Sundrive station, Crumlin. If you co-operate with my colleague and I, you will be out of here in no time. Now if –'

Before he can finish his sentence, his angry mate interrupts. 'Where did you get the fucking tape? Who is on it and what are they saying? Who has the full set of the famous photos? What are you doing associating with known IRA men? What do you know about sensitive documents taken from Bob Clarke's house? Do you know that you are facing serious charges under the Offences against the State Act, including the spreading of sedition, ten years at least, membership of an illegal organisation, five minimum, possession of materials likely to undermine the security of the State? Robbing the minister's home is the least of your worries.'

'That's why I would like to see my solicitor,' I insist. I've heard Sundrive Road garda station is notorious for the beatings doled out by the Heavy Gang to subversives, criminals and innocents who just get in their way, and I can hear some poor man getting the treatment in some nearby cell. Or maybe they're just trying to frighten me with sounds. Trying to make me talk.

I'm not going to ignore the advice drummed into me by Joe and all the other 'political experts' I've met on my journey of discovery. Keep my mouth shut until the brief shows up. Silence brings its own reward.

During a break in the one-sided shouting session, I sit

alone in a filthy cell and think. Evelyn Fagan has been sitting on the story for weeks now and must have put questions to the government and the guards in the course of her efforts to land a scoop. Otherwise, how would they know about them? The bank documents are enough to destroy Clarke and yet the cops in this room don't seem to know what is in them. They're asking me. I'm not going to make them any wiser. And there can be no hard proof that the steak that killed the dog came from The Bistro. If there was, they would have locked up Joe a long time ago.

As I listen to the cops barking on over several interview sessions, it is clear that a deep sense of panic is pervading the establishment and that our campaign for justice for the forgotten victims of the '74 bombings is at least making some people pay attention.

When Neilan arrives eight hours after my arrest, and after a fruitless search of most of the city's police stations, it quickly becomes clear that I'm not leaving this place anytime soon.

'They are threatening to charge you with several breaches of the Offences against the State Act, including IRA membership, illegal possession of official documents, the unlawful interception of conversations in breach of the Wireless and Phones legislation, unlawful association with subversives, and aggravated burglary. I didn't realise, Angie, that you are such a threat to democracy and civilisation as we know it,' says Neilan.

'From what I can gather they are not happy that we are lifting the stones of their investigation into the bombings and finding more questions than answers. Did you know they closed the inquiry down after three months, they never followed up on several suspects, lost files and forensics, they didn't take statements from key witnesses and they've covered up the role of the British security services in the whole operation?' I reply.

'That's enough Angie, unless you want to make matters worse,' says Neilan, pointing at the walls and his ears at the same time. 'I would advise you to continue exercising your right to remain silent and I will maintain contact with Detective Garda Meagher in order to ensure that I'm available if and when they bring you before a judge. If there is anything you can tell me that could be of assistance in your defence, please write it down on this piece of paper, and quickly.'

Grabbing his pen, I write just five words: *Father Bennett, East Wall church.*

'He'll tell you everything you need to know. He has the tapes, bank docs, everything,' I say quietly.

The brief closes his case and bangs on the locked door of the interview room. 'Joe asked me to tell you to stay strong and that he loves you very much,' he says with a friendly smile as he disappears into the free world. I'm taken from the interview room to continue my indefinite detention.

I break down in tears when the steel door of the stinking cell is closed tight. I know I'm here for the night, at least, and want a shoulder to cry on. Joe's shoulder. Eventually I drift off. Some hours later my fitful slumber is disturbed by someone roughly shaking my arm.

'Get up, you slut, and put this on,' says the garda as he throws a stained, light jumper at me. Next thing I'm on the street listening to the bells of the church in Crumlin. I've no money for the bus. I won't need it. Meagher and his boys appear from nowhere. They grab their favourite arm again.

'I'm charging you under the provisions of the Offences of the State Act with membership of an illegal organisation. Anything you say may be taken down and used in evidence against you. Do you understand?'

I've no idea why they'd release me from their custody only to rearrest and charge me, but before I can ask I'm back in the blue car with the sirens blaring and across the Liffey like a shot. At Green Street we pull up outside the Specials. Judges, no jury, special criminal court.

'I've the word of a chief superintendent, as required under the Act, to confirm that the defendant is a member of an illegal and proscribed organisation, to wit the IRA,' I hear the wigged-up prosecuting lawyer say to the almost empty room and the three elder lemons on the raised bench.

'The gardaí and the Director of Public Prosecutions are very concerned that this and other serious offences with which the defendant may be charged should get an early hearing of the court, your lords.'

'And has the defendant or her counsel anything to say on the matter?' booms the judge in the middle of the three while looking in my direction.

'Em, she does not appear to have anyone representing her at this time, m'lud,' says the prosecutor.

'Are we expected to proceed to trial without any defence counsel? That would be most unusual,' says the fat beak on the left.

After some further verbal jousting, which goes well over my head and involves some technical discussion about my rights under such-and-such an Act, I'm told that I'm to be removed to the cells underneath the courtroom and held there until the case resumes later, by which time it is hoped that my solicitor or other legal representative will be present.

They don't ask for my opinion.

In the meantime, I'm to be fed and watered, as it looks like I'm about to wither away and could probably do with a warm cup of tea. At least that is what the only pleasant person I meet has to say. A local woman in charge of what passes for a kitchen in this hellhole, she sees me stumbling under heavy escort to my cell.

'Here love, get this drop of tea into you. I don't know what this place is coming to, dragging young ones in with barely a stitch on them,' she says, stroking my unwashed hair.

Some two hours later, I'm dragged back upstairs and into a room where I find Joe, Neilan and a man with a wig, who introduces himself as my senior counsel, waiting for me. I collapse into Joe's arms. When I recover, Neilan confirms that the police want me convicted for various crimes under the Offences against the State Act.

'But I've material here from your good friend the priest that may upset their plans,' he says, patting a thick folder on the table.

After a hurried but substantial consultation with the wigged brief, I'm brought by a garda into the now bustling and busy court where I see several friendly faces, including Father Rory, Danny and my da. I return his weak attempt at a smile. The old man is terrified for me. I feel guilty for putting him through all this. I hope Mam's all right. It's strange to see so many familiar people in the same place at the one time given that I've spent almost thirty hours in solitude other than when I was being barracked and abused by hostile and angry Branch men.

Given the numbers in the packed courtroom I'm surprised to learn that I'm the only person being arraigned this morning and the only case to be heard. I notice Evelyn Fagan has taken up position close to the judge's bench. She smiles over at me. I hear words of encouragement and support cast in my direction by people I don't know before the main and middle beak bangs his wooden mallet and calls for silence.

Following fresh, and lengthy, submissions by the prosecutor, he repeats the same charges he made earlier this morning but amplifies his case by reference to a litany of alleged offences I've apparently perpetrated, including 'burglary of a politician's home, theft of sensitive financial and State documents as well as jewellery and cash, illegally taping a privileged conversation between the same politician and members of the duly accredited diplomatic staff of a friendly and foreign embassy, and membership of a proscribed organisation, senior members of which have been seen and photographed in the company of the accused, who is clearly involved in sinister activities that threaten the very existence of the State and our fragile democracy.'

The words of the wigged wonder seem to establish a pretty robust case against me, even though I don't recognise myself from the character he portrays. Neither, I'm sure, does anyone who knows me. It's clear when my own barrister gets to his feet that he's thinking the very same thing.

'This young woman, your worships, is a student in the University of Dublin, Trinity College, with which you are no doubt familiar. She is from an upstanding and respected family, none of whom, including herself, has ever found themselves on the wrong side of the law. Her father is present in the courtroom to support that contention. Her only crimes, if they can be described as such, are her heroic and selfless efforts to help those upon whom pain was inflicted by the terrible bombings in this city some three and a half years ago, including her unfortunate mother whose eyesight was terribly damaged following the Talbot Street attack.

'As for the claim that she might have been involved in a burglary at the home of our current Minister for Home Affairs, it is simply ludicrous and the gardaí and my learned friend know this to be so. For a start, she was nowhere near the politician's home that night and can be plainly seen in photographs, which I will now pass to your lordships, showing her at work in a prominent city restaurant that very evening and indeed serving none other than the same politician at the very time gardaí believe his home in Booterstown was being burgled by persons unknown.

'Further, I must object to the manner in which the prosecution is trying to cast aspersions on my client's character by using photos secretly taken by agents of the State. I submit that these are intended to promote an absolutely false assertion that she has more than an indirect link to others in the photographs. Indeed, I will call several witnesses who can prove that while my client may have attended some meetings where persons of interest in garda investigations also turned up, she had no way of knowing of their connection to subversive organisations. I will also show that the prosecution case is influenced by an entirely different and disingenuous proposition, which is that my client, because of her overt political activities in raising justifiable concerns at the inadequate and indeed ham-fisted manner in which the 1974 bombings have been investigated, is now being pursued in some sort of misdirected vendetta by the garda authorities. And that the politician who features at the centre of this strange concoction of conspiracies has himself a case to answer with regard to certain matters that may well require him, minister of government or not, to attend at this court as a material witness. I will not, your honours, go into the detail of these matters lest they appear on the front page of tomorrow's newspaper when the appropriate forum for their examination is by this court.

'Finally, I would like to state unequivocally that my client has never been or ever intends to be a member of a proscribed organisation as specified by the Act but will not deny that her work in highlighting the appalling treatment of those who suffered in the callous attacks in Dublin and Monaghan in May 1974 may well have brought her into close contact, unbeknownst to herself, with alleged subversives of various hues. I will call witnesses, including from the religious and academic communities, who will testify that Angela Whelan is an intelligent and courageous young woman who is helping to heal the wounds endured by countless numbers of people whose lives and those of their loved ones were shattered on that day when our capital city was traumatised by the real enemies of the State.'

When he mentions the newspaper the six eyes on the bench turn to Fagan. She returns a glance that invites them to fully assess the consequences of any statements they might make in full knowledge that everything from this packed but juryless court will be reported without fear or favour. As my lawyer delivers his final flourish, the gallery erupts with cheers and the middle beak is forced to bang his gavel and call for order in the court. I'm almost cheering myself.

The three judges are in a quandary as the clock strikes 12.30 p.m. They've been given documents and tapes and cannot adjudicate on a membership charge without hearing witnesses, including the chief superintendent, whose word they will have to take as gospel if they are to go for a full trial. More contentious, however, is the implication that the defence is about to widen the case to embrace issues of intense political interest and to call on a minister, and possibly the garda commissioner, to explain themselves. They have no choice but to adjourn to study the material handed over and the submissions made by both sides. Besides, their stomachs are rumbling.

As soon as they indicate their preferred course of action, the prosecutor is on his feet warning his lordships that he expects 'the defendant' to remain in custody while their private deliberations continue. An irritated defence counsel objects to the unlawful detention of his client, who has after all been charged before the court and is entitled to apply for bail.

'One cannot use the court as some sort of holding centre for accused people, particularly innocent people who are the victim, as is my client, of a pattern of bungling and incompetence as displayed by the garda authorities in the several cases associated with these charges, including the burglary of the politician's home where my client could not have been present. Although it does not pertain directly to the charges against her, the wider context of this case involves the beating of people in garda stations, the murder of an alleged accomplice in the robbery in broad daylight, the theft of jewellery and cash, the poisoning of a dog and other bizarre features.

'What I will show is that the tape recording and other

documents which you are about to study carry in themselves justification for some of the behaviour which has brought her before this court and that her campaign for the truth surrounding the bombings is also a factor in the animus directed at her from senior levels of the political and policing regime in this country. I request that my client be released, on station bail if necessary, for the duration of this short adjournment.'

'Granted. She is to be back before this court at 2 p.m. sharp,' says the main beak after a brief consultation with his colleagues. It seems that they are disconcerted at the way this extraordinary hearing is progressing and the political and security implications in the defence lawyer's words of warning. They also know that their well-rounded necks are on the line if the newspapers report even a portion of the allegations aired in court this morning. Judging by the demeanour of the attractive young journalist, the only presence in the press gallery, she is satisfied she has a strong and exclusive story. There also seems to be an unusually disproportionate number in the public gallery intent on causing a disturbance. The head judge calls for the tipstaff to lead him and his two colleagues from the court and away from this unruly mob. Over lunch they will consider the evidence and plan a way forward.

Before we leave, Neilan has a word with me. 'You need to know, Angie, that in a normal court with a jury you'd walk away from this. But in the Specials nowadays it's only when you do a deal and plead guilty that you get a suspended sentence. And that's not on offer today. We can fight it but chances are we'll lose in this court. You could be locked up for a long time trying to prove your innocence. So you may need to consider all your options. And that may involve getting the hell out of here.'

The temporary relief I had been feeling at being let out on bail quickly disappears.

All hell breaks loose as I find my way to Joe and Da blocked by a phalanx of plain-clothed and uniformed gardaí. With Neilan and the barrister at my side I try to force my way through as the crowd on the balcony shouts abuse at the cops. My counsel warns the leading garda obstructers that they are in breach of a court ruling by preventing my exit from the court and will be the subject of an immediate complaint, in judge's chambers if necessary. The cops back off.

'Don't let her out of your sight,' are the last words I hear from DG Meagher as I struggle to find Joe's hand in the crowded corridor of the courthouse. I can't. I'm whisked away in the bustling, boisterous melee. When I turn in the crush another figure with long dark hair like mine and a similar build is standing next to me. Wearing identical clothes to mine and a red woollen hat.

'Jesus, Terry. What happened to your lovely red hair?' I say.

'Shut the fuck up, Angie,' comes the hissed reply.

With that, the red hat is pulled over my own head and I'm dragged out the half-open door between bodies of people blocking the entrance and, more importantly, the exit of the now excited and bemused forces of law and order. They can't move for the crowd heaving in their direction rather than leaving the building. A snapper with two cameras around his neck is pushed aside. It's Donal. I'm put on the back of a motorbike. Someone straps a dark helmet over my new headgear. I look back and see several guards surround and grab the girl with the long black hair, causing a stream of expletives from Terry, before we boot down to Capel Street and the quays. Waving from the pub door across the road is Houdini Russell.

Behind, in the distance, I hear the wail of sirens as the Honda Benly 125 screams along beside the river, ignoring lights, cars and pedestrians en route. When we reach the new bridge we can see a posse of blue cars and flashing lights some way back. Crossing the bridge the biker waves to a man on a platform high above us. There's a tall boat in the river below. As we reach the other side the man on the platform pulls the lever that raises the bridge to allow boats to pass through. The goons are forced to come to a sudden halt as the bridge rises and their prey disappears in a trail of smoke towards Ringsend. I'm gone.

'Here you go,' says my rider when we finally reach our destination overlooking the bay at Dun Laoghaire. I get off the back as he removes his helmet and gloves, and I recognise him instantly. Steelie. He walks with a slight limp as he leads me up the steps to a large yellow door.

'Tell Joe I said hello,' he says.

'Thanks for helping us out, Steelie.'

'Well, I owe him a favour from a while back.'

'Joe told me all about you and the funny stuff in the pottery.'

'Listen, I have to go. I need to get rid of this yoke. Shame really, it's some fucking machine,' he says, taking my helmet back.

The door opens to the smiling face of Pierre. And another man.

'This is my friend, Patrick. He's an artist, my very best and secret love,' says the chef.

'Welcome to my home, Angie. Any friend of Pierre's …' says Patrick.

Steelie waves before he puts back on his helmet, revs up and heads for the Wicklow hills to dump the stolen bike.

I gratefully accept the offer of a stiff drink, some food and the latest news on the radio.

'For such a small little thing you've left a big trail of chaos in your wake,' laughs Pierre.

After a warm bath I crawl into the comfortable bed I've been offered. I'm shattered, though it's early yet. I sleep through the evening and night.

When I finally emerge the following morning, the early edition is on the dining-room table along with juice, pancakes and jam, and a boiled egg. Above the fold and a photo of my head covered by a red hat are the words: 'Where is Angie?'

50

GOVERNMENT BUILDINGS

Bob Clarke sits at his desk amid the ruins of his shattered and short-lived ministerial career. Across the front page, his former girlfriend details the remarkable flight of the young woman from the Special Criminal Court and the extraordinary and complex tale of the Minister for Home Affairs, his offshore bank account, long extracts from the taped conversation with the Englishmen and the obtuse references to the real perpetrators of the greatest atrocity of the Troubles. The story is continued across two inside pages peppered with Donal Dunning's photos of the party fundraiser in The Bistro, where the rich elite gathered to pay homage to the new wave of political leaders just waiting to take their place in the sun. There is Clarke rubbing shoulders with bishops and builders, bankers and big farmers, and there he is with the man from the British embassy whispering in his ear in a corner. Gavin, well over the limit, is also there with his hand firmly planted on the arse of a young bimbo in one photo and, in a later shot, on the expansive breasts of another. Meanwhile, the report that accompanies the photos states that while the chief of police was out enjoying himself, thieves were rifling through the Booterstown home of Clarke. It's all there in black and white, including Dunning's previously unpublished and shocking photos of the Talbot Street bombing used to illustrate that aspect of the story.

The supposedly secret donors to the party, and their partners on the night, are pictured in various states of inebriation in the newspaper scoop of the year which, no doubt, has the people of the city and the country scratching their heads in disbelief and wonder.

Fagan has even managed to include a photo of Clarke's wife wearing her best pearl earrings alongside the photo of the bereaved Mrs Duggan with a matching necklace, and a gruesome description of her son's bloody murder. The street execution, the story suggests, is connected to the burglary of the minister's house, while another suspect in the robbery investigation mysteriously fell through the top window of a garda station in Tipperary during interrogation. Fagan discloses for the first time that among the items stolen was a file detailing the unexplained lodgements in the Bank of Bermuda of a total of £112,000 in the name of Robert Clarke. A copy of the scribbled notes on The Bistro napkin is reproduced alongside the bank document, ragged out on the page for maximum effect.

Fortunately, the paper editorialises, it has been able to exclusively reveal this explosive story, including the contents of the tape and the bank documents, after they came into the possession of its leading political reporter and following an intensive investigation she has doggedly pursued for several months. The minister has declined to provide an explanation for the offshore funds and is now facing the court of public opinion and a thorough consideration of his options, it pompously continues. Meanwhile, the garda commissioner has been exposed as a bit of a party animal, while his force is subjected to more serious allegations of mistreatment of suspects in custody, the abuse of the emergency powers it has been given over recent years and its failure to hold anyone responsible for the 1974 atrocities which sent thirty-three people and an unborn child to early graves.

'Now,' the leader writer says, 'if the tape in the possession of the newspaper proves to be any reflection of the truth, there is at the very least a strong suspicion that elements of the British State, a supposedly friendly neighbour, colluded in some way with those who carried out the attacks in order to influence Irish security policy. Worse still, this newspaper has received confirmation that a leading loyalist and UDR member, Roger Hanbury, a former member of the British Army who fought with the SAS in Aden, has been identified as the driver of the green car which blew up in Parnell Street, killing several people, including a couple and their children, and wounding dozens more. We understand this man has never been arrested or interviewed by the gardaí. Why not? That he relocated to England a year after the attack. Why and to where? We have also learned that another individual, whom we cannot name for legal reasons, who served with Hanbury in Aden with the SAS and is now a senior official in the British intelligence service, is implicated in this evolving debacle. Further, there is a suggestion that a diplomat based in the British embassy in Dublin is another veteran of that elite army unit.'

'The extraordinary suggestion that British agents, possibly reaching to the highest levels of the administration, are implicated in the atrocity in our capital city, and the failure of the police investigation, shut down just three months after the bombings, are deeply disturbing. The gardaí have not arrested even one of the many suspects identified in witness statements, which is enough to raise public concern over the willingness of the State itself to confront the increasingly powerful enemies of democracy,' the editorial thunders. It calls for the immediate resignation of the minister and the garda chief responsible for this latest, embarrassing episode. Not to mention 'the humiliating spectacle at the courts when a young woman, apparently guilty of only wanting to discover the truth of what happened on that fateful day when her mother's eye was almost torn from her head, made a dramatic escape on the back of a motor bike under the noses of the elite Special Branch.'

'That bitch from The Bistro,' Clarke says as Fenton walks in the door.

'Speak of the devil,' says the advisor. 'Have a look at this. Paula Murphy gave it to me this morning.'

He slides a large brown envelope across the minister's desk.

'Not more shit,' says Clarke, as he pulls out a photo with his red mug, dishevelled hair and octopus hands all over the infamous Angie Whelan revealed in glorious Technicolor.

'The fucking whore. I'll find her and I'll fuck her right and proper … We'll make her life so fucking miserable …'

'No, we won't,' says Fenton. 'We lay off her or this photo of you will appear in every rag from here to Honolulu. And if anything happens to the bitch, Paula Murphy's going to screw me completely. "Leave Angie alone or I'll send your wife the bill for my abortion." Those were her exact words. We're in this heap of manure together.'

Clarke looks like he's been hit by lightning. Shock and horror.

He's already made up his mind that if he doesn't jump he will surely be pushed in quick time. His only chance is to limit the damage done to his now almost utterly worthless reputation, but he has no idea how that can be achieved. He needs a credible explanation for the offshore monies and some excuse for the unguarded comments attributed to him in the illegally taped conversation with the English bastards. He is about to call his leader, who is no doubt uncomfortably digesting the first major scandal to hit the new government over his porridge.

'We have to pull on the green jersey,' says Fenton.

'What the fuck does that mean?' Clarke asks.

'Blame the Brits for trying to influence your policy direction and force you to bring in extradition, cross-border raids by the SAS, shooting suspects on sight and even threatening to unleash the dogs of war in our capital city, if they haven't done so already. That smooth talker says as much on the tape, if you remember?'

'And what about the fucking account in Bermuda?'

'Well, let's just say that you are aware of it but that you didn't open it. It was set up by solicitors acting for your family trust, inheritance money or something from your late father's estate. We'll get some paperwork to back up the story. That's what solicitors are for and we have plenty of them in the party. You haven't touched the money. The Brits found out about it because the bank was set up as part of a global intelligence operation directed at tracking the movement of monies, including illicit funds, and the people hiding them. In your case, it is simply parked there while you establish a trust for your family which can make a legitimate inheritance more tax-efficient. Anyway, it is not uncommon for Irish businesspeople to avail of revenue alleviation measures particularly with the escalating levels of taxation brought in by the previous government. Perfectly legitimate.'

'Who the fuck is going to believe all that? And where would my late father, God rest him, get that kind of money?' asks Clarke.

'That's not the point. You think anyone here wants to place a focus on the offshore lodgements made by half of the cabinet, past and present, and every director of every major business in this city, along with most of the people in The Bistro that night? Where do you think their money goes? I can guarantee you the Revenue does not get its greedy paws on it,' Fenton counters.

'Play the green card. So I admit to being put under pressure by this English spy to turn against my own people?' says the incredulous Clarke.

'Not only that, but you are to set up an inquiry into the bombings after reading of the allegations of collusion between agents of the British and loyalist killers in the files you inherited from the last crowd of incompetents. Although you were given certain details of that collusion during an informal meeting in the famous bistro you frequent, it could not be confirmed without a comprehensive investigation by the proposed inquiry. You are deeply dissatisfied with the failures of the gardaí in respect of its wholly inadequate investigation. You might go so far as to say that there is evidence that members of the force were feeding sensitive security information to the British only a few years ago. And that you believe that officers at senior rank may have been compromised. In other words, you are the victim of dirty tricks after months of trying to get to the bottom of a conspiracy that goes to the very heart of our democracy. You could of course offer your resignation if it would help to stabilise the government at this difficult time, but that would only play into the hands of those who are seeking to cover up the serious crime inflicted on the people of Dublin and Monaghan just a few short years ago.'

'Okay, I'll talk to the boss. Meanwhile, you get Gavin on the phone and tell him to be in here at 2 p.m. sharp. That bollox has it coming to him.'

To his surprise, the party leader is looking for a way out of the latest crisis rather than Clarke's head on a plate. It does not suit him, he says, to lose a senior cabinet member so soon into his first term of office even if the convoluted explanations he has given are less than solid or convincing. One thing is certain, however, and that is his absolute resistance to anyone looking into the offshore activities of the country's leading business figures, who also happen to be the main supporters of the party and played no small role in smoothing his rise to the top. They are also his guarantee of a soft landing when his political career inevitably ends and where a directorship or two could provide some small comfort in retirement. Opening a can of worms that could bring down some of the beef, banking and construction barons would be suicidal for the economy, the party and, more importantly, for him.

What goes unsaid is that the Minister for Home Affairs is not the only beneficiary of the secret windfall attached to the unwritten terms of a deal, which he, as party leader, personally brokered, for the disposal of the country's largest mineral asset to the world's biggest and most corrupt oil major. It was to be deposited in two tranches, one year before and exactly one year after the controversial decision by the new government to sell this large piece of family silver at a knockdown price. The first instalment was delivered. From the Bank of Nova Scotia to the Royal Bank of Bermuda. The rest will follow when the sale is complete. A total fee of half a million quid to be divided between five parties, Clarke and himself included. His hapless minister thinks he's the sole winner in this particular arrangement, and the boss is not about to inform him otherwise. Besides, the final payment will come after new, more flexible legislation on oil and gas terms is enacted, which does not require Clarke and his bungling. They just need to get him out of the hole he has dug for himself.

'A way has to be found to shore up your position, Robert, and if dancing the anti-Brit routine, at least in public, can do the trick, then so be it,' the Taoiseach says. 'By tomorrow the story of the missing human rights activist or whatever she is, the Bermuda accounts and the tapes will be history, if Fenton and the other handlers do their job.'

The first thing he and Clarke agree to do is to summon the British ambassador to raise deep concerns over the alleged role of agencies of his government in the 1974 blasts. Given that the Indo has flagged the unlikely coincidence that chargé d'affaires *Martin Crawley, Alan Richards* and a bombing suspect all go back to a British hit squad in *Aden*, a request for the diplomat's immediate recall by London would not be out of the question.

'Some heads have to roll,' says the boss.

The new inquiry into the failed garda investigation of the appalling attacks will be headed by a retired High Court judge and a compensation fund is to be set up for the survivors.

In late afternoon, the final editions of the Herald and Press lead with the sudden resignation of Garda Commissioner *Edward Gavin*, who, it is reported, has stepped down over the lapses in the force in recent times. The newspapers report in detail how, according to informed government sources, he had not admitted his full role in the original investigation into the bombings, including the disappearance of garda files containing statements and other vital documents and information, the transfer of relevant forensic and ballistic material to the British Army in Lisburn and the failure to preserve a necessary chain of evidence. His inability to apprehend the robbers who stole from the minister's home or to find young *Angie Whelan*, who dramatically escaped during the lunch break at the Specials and is now something of a folk hero for her civil rights work, is also cited. There is an oblique reference, quoting an unnamed government source, to the commissioner's inappropriate, undisclosed meetings with senior British security personnel at Garda HQ and subsequent unauthorised border operations. Then there were his frequent trips to London for Chatham House rule meetings and briefings from MI5, which, the same sources said, the Minister for Home Affairs raised during their final, brief chat, before Gavin announced, in a one-line statement, that he was taking an early bath.

By the following day the government is basking in the glory it has earned from facing down the old enemy and refusing to capitulate to the incessant clamour from London for ever tougher security measures against the IRA and all the other republican, communist and anarchist subversives who threaten the existing order. A quiet call from the Taoiseach's office to the owners of the main newspaper groups ensures that the investigation into the Bank of Bermuda or any other such havens availed of by the elite, including themselves, comes to a halt. The government announces its intention to examine how the Irish tax system can be improved to ensure that people like Clarke, who come into sudden wealth from inheritance or otherwise, might maintain their funds at home without fear of impoverishment by the Revenue.

The Minister for Home Affairs emerges on the steps of government buildings for the Six O'Clock News, with half a dozen cabinet colleagues in tow, to denounce the British authorities for their suspected, if unproven, complicity with known loyalist thugs in the bombings and to postpone any further high-level security meetings until certain questions he has in that regard are answered. The prospect of making a complaint to the European Court and the United Nations over the arrogant and extra-jurisdictional interference in the affairs of a friendly neighbour is flagged. Five minutes later he is on the phone to assure London that the storm will shortly blow over and that all will return to normal once the dust settles. The British minister agrees to go along with the deceit and to recall their chargé d'affaires, Crawley, from Dublin. He agrees to consider a request for access to all relevant files held by the authorities in London concerning the 1974 attacks.

'But I'm fucked if the Paddies are getting any of our files, at least none of any real significance,' the man from MI5, listening to the call, says to himself. Alan Richards will bite his tongue, for now.

***

Resting his pint and his elbow on the counter, Bob Clarke is the toast of the Dáil bar. Backbenchers from all sides congratulate him on his courage in the face of adversity and the duplicitous John Bull, and for the pride he has instilled across the land. His future is secure. As for his past, he's made sure that he is no longer on the bad side of the woman whose scorn came so close to destroying all he has achieved. Evelyn Fagan, it is reported the next day, has been appointed with immediate effect as government press secretary to replace Myles Fenton, who has been named as the likely new ambassador to the United Kingdom, in a bid, says the Minister for Foreign Affairs, 'to restore harmony to relations between our two great countries'.

Meanwhile, The Bistro is doing a roaring trade on the back of all the publicity surrounding the nefarious activities of some of its better-known customers. As well as the bulging revenues, the owners are particularly pleased to unveil a new Patrick Donnelly painting with its cynical and colourful portrayal of the modern parliament and its occupants. It is loosely based on the cover of the Beatles' Sergeant Pepper album, but is much more irreverent, and it now looks down on the heads of the hungry and curious.

Joe Heney is a minor celebrity and willingly poses for photos when asked by the crowds who flock to the eating house in the hope that some of the glitter of fame might land on them. Donal is getting steady work now that his original shots of the bombing in Talbot Street and the fundraiser in The Bistro have been spread across the media. In the evenings, Joe shares a few pints with the lads in the Palace, keeps *up with the thriving music scene in the city, plays guitar and writes songs. He keeps his nose out of politics and has few visitors to his flat, except the two heavies in the blue car who pass every morning in the hope of catching sight of the elusive Angie Whelan. She hasn't been seen or heard of since the so-called 'Battle of Green Street courthouse'. Her face was all over the news for weeks and the search for the 'missing activist', 'suspected terrorist' or 'possibly armed and dangerous escapee' depending on which rag you believe, continues.*

SPRING 1978

51

ANGIE

Over three months, I move from one house to the next, no questions asked or answered, making new friends among the most ordinary and generous of people. My few years in college did not teach me as much about my own country and its various ways, characters and codes as my months on the run, where everybody knows who I am but nobody says. Warm hearts and hearths, the chat and the music in kitchens and pubs, the pipes in Clare, fiddles in Roscommon, the blues in west Cork, a convent in Connemara, people and places, farmers and fishermen, solicitors and suits, shopkeepers and customers who haven't a bean to their name but are rich in their souls.

I left the artist's house in the city with nothing but the shirt on my back, dyed and cropped hair, and Paddy Donnelly's old trenchcoat. I'm told by the man who delivers me to my first safe house not to contact Joe, Mam, Da or anyone else. Otherwise, I'll be sure to get another early morning knock on the door.

Eventually I get a message from Joe, scribbled on a couple of cigarette papers stuck together and in tiny handwriting. Wonder who he learned that from. It comes wrapped in plastic from a cigarette packet and Sellotape.

'Love you, can't say how sorry I am for all this mess. Am well. Keep the spirits up. Your proud folks in good form, missing you, send their love. Well done. See you soon. Told to keep it short and sweet. Advise to keep the head down for another while yet. Thinking of you always. Love Joe.'

At the remaining words the tears fall, at first in drops, then in floods. I feel a pain in my gut. I remember the words I read in his book of Neruda poems.

No one else will travel through the shadows with me,
Only you, evergreen, ever sun, ever moon.

The drops save me the bother of shredding the message, as it disintegrates in my hand.

I try to become part of the lives of those who shelter me, their children, their friends, their pets, but much of the time the loneliness gets to me. I often think of walking in the door of a cop shop, ignoring the advice of Neilan, among others, not to throw myself at the uncertain mercy of the justice system.

Not now, not yet.

I lie awake all night in a schoolteacher's house on the edge of a cliff in Erris, north-west Mayo. A wild sea is bashing the rocks. Heavy rain and wind howl over the bleak bog with all its secrets. I'm desperate, sad, alone. I miss my mam and my beautiful, long, black hair. I shed more tears for her as I clasp the red woolly hat close to my face. Again, I read the carefully embroidered inscription that must have taken her hours to weave under the back fold with a steady hand and the guidance of her damaged eyes.

For my brave little angel, love Mam.

A week-old newspaper that comes with the note outlines the shock in political and legal circles at a report by Amnesty International about the routine abuse of suspects in garda stations.

Twenty-eight cases of ill-treatment were examined between April 1976 and May 1977. Several of them, believed innocent, have been convicted of serious offences and are serving long sentences – among them the men accused of robbing the train at Sallins. That explains the advice to stay on the run. But I'm desperate, sad and alone. I want Joe to come and get me, soon.

Ten long days and nights later, a welcome knock raps the door.

***

The plane from Dublin, chartered for the inaugural pilgrimage organised by the Friends of the Elderly and Infirm, touches down at Lourdes airport in the warm afternoon of a Sunday in early spring. I wait as the other passengers alight and watch as some priests and nuns emerge from the terminal pushing empty wheelchairs.

As my feet touch tarmac, a friendly looking face approaches. 'Sister Christina, I believe,' says a beaming Father Bennett.

'That's me,' I say.

The gendarme at passport control waves me through with a cursory glance.

The loaded wheelchairs carry the most infirm to their hotels around the shrine, including some of those seriously injured by the Dublin bombs. At least I have tried to find out some truth behind their suffering. I breathe in the clean and free French air.

'Welcome to Lourdes. That car will take you to Joe,' says the priest.

It's been four almost unbearable months. How do I look? Where is he?

An hour later we stop in a small town. Joe is waiting outside a small hotel in the square. Old people and children are enjoying the afternoon sun. We hold each other tight for a long time. It's like I only left him yesterday. He tells me he loves me.

'I know. I've missed you so much,' I say, pulling him closer. 'Don't leave me alone again.'

I lose the habit when I fall onto the cool sheets of the bed in the Hotel de Ville. Into his tender arms. We make hungry, warm love.

'The job's not done,' I say afterwards.

'No,' he says.

We fall into a deep, lovers' sleep.

ACKNOWLEDGEMENTS

This novel was inspired by the shocking and tragic events on 17 May 1974 when three car bombs rocked the centre of Dublin, while another exploded in Monaghan town, taking the lives of thirty-three people and an unborn child.

The two central characters in this fictional story meet in the aftermath of the explosions, which have affected their lives in different ways. While the story references actual events and people from the period, this tale is entirely a work of imagination.

There are many people who suffered greatly as the result of the attacks on that day, including those who died, were injured or lost loved ones. The survivors and bereaved families have searched to find the truth about those who carried out the bombings and their motives. In particular, 'Justice for the Forgotten', which was formed by survivors and bereaved relatives in 1996, has assisted these efforts and gathered hugely valuable information about some of those who orchestrated and engineered the atrocities. The co-ordinator of the campaign, Margaret Urwin, deserves particular mention for her commitment in this regard. Two of those seriously injured in the Dublin bombings, Bernie McNally and Derek Byrne, also gave invaluable help with the research for this book.

As a student, I witnessed the aftermath of the bombing along with many thousands of others in Dublin that day, and assisted with the injured on South Leinster Street. Subsequently, as a journalist, I researched and reported on the story over the ensuing decades.

However, the efforts to establish the truth have been frustrated by the refusal of authorities in Britain, and to a lesser extent in Ireland, to release files and other material which could help in that search. As a writer, I have sought to imagine, in a totally fictional way, how such deeds are carried out.

This book could not have been published without the support and encouragement of Mary Feehan and Deirdre Roberts of Mercier Press and members of its staff, including editors Wendy Logue and Noel O'Regan, and cover designer Alice Coleman. I am hugely grateful for their insight and patience. Thanks also to proofreader, Monica Strina.

My loving partner, Mary Tracey, to whom this work is dedicated, did much to inspire and improve the text during its evolution.

I am also thankful to my wonderful children, Oisín, Saoirse, Caomhán, Síomha and Liadh, astute observers, for their support, encouragement and love.

My grandchildren, Alannah, Rían and Fiadh, arrived while this book was being written and have brought much joy to our lives.

I am also enormously thankful for those who made useful observations and comments on earlier drafts, although I bear sole responsibility for the final outcome.

ALSO AVAILABLE FROM MERCIER PRESS

978 1 78117 607 8

'This funny, conversational and often very moving debut deals with the Big Questions while keeping tight focus on one life. A seriously impressive first novel, full of truth, heart and hope.'
Joseph O'Connor

On punch. That's all it took. One minute Chris is having a smoke, the next minute he's dead.

And there's not much about being dead that he likes. He's stuck in the middle place, able to watch those he loved – to know what they are feeling and thinking – but unable to communicate, to help them with their grief.

He's also watching the man who killed him, determined to figure out how to take his revenge.

978 1 78117 567 5

'*The First Sunday in September* really is quite an achievement. The stories are vibrant and authentic, brimming with intensity and desire. I enjoyed it immensely.' – *Donal Ryan*

It's the day of the All-Ireland Hurling Final. A hungover Clareman goes to Dublin, having bet the last of his money on his county to win. A woman attends the final, wondering when to tell her partner that she's pregnant. A retired player watches from the stands, his gaze repeatedly falling on the Cork captain, whom he and his wife gave up for adoption years earlier. Clare's star forward struggles under the weight of expectation. Cork's talisman waits for the sliotar to fall from the sky, aware that his destiny is already set.

With an unforgettable cast of characters, *The First Sunday in September* announces an exciting new voice in Irish fiction.

www.mercierpress.ie

ALSO AVAILABLE FROM MERCIER PRESS

978 1 78117 686 3

'Full of Irish nostalgia. Hilarious, charming and a little bit bonkers – I loved it!' – *Jennifer Zamparelli*, 2FM

Colin Saint James hates his older brother, Freddie. A true psychopath, Freddie has been hell-bent on destroying Colin's happiness since before he was born! So when the heats for the last ever Housewife of the Year competition are announced, Colin sees his chance to finally get one up on his brother. The only problem is he needs a wife.

Luckily, he lives next door to Azra, who happens to be single and anxious to get a ring on her finger. Unluckily, Azra is a Turkish concubine, and she and Colin don't exactly see eye-to-eye over her nocturnal activities. Will Colin be able to park his reservations about his X-rated neighbour if it gives him the chance to emerge triumphant over Freddie for once in his life?